"If you're looking for a laugh-out-loud, can't-put-it-down, quick read, you won't be disappointed."

—*Hardcover Therapy*

"I give *Tangled* . . . Five Spectacular, Swoony, Fun, Laugh-Out-Loud Stars!"

—*A Bookish Escape*

"I seriously enjoyed this book; any erotic romance that you can laugh out loud while reading and then be turned on in the next paragraph is an exhilarating book to read."

—*Schmexy Girl Book Blog*

"A perfect romantic comedy told through the eyes of a very cocky and sexy man."

—Literati Book Reviews

"So, not only is it funny, it's deliciously hot too! The sex scenes are great. Laced with humor and Drew's honest, frank way of thinking, they're just another stroke of genius that make this book such a must-read."

—*Smitten's Book Blog*

ALSO BY EMMA CHASE

THE LEGAL BRIEFS SERIES

Overruled

THE TANGLED SERIES

"It's a Wonderful Tangled Christmas Carol" in
Baby, It's Cold Outside

Tied

Tamed

Twisted

Tangled

Emma Chase, the *New York Times* and *USA Today* bestselling author who created the "hot, hilarious, and passionate" (Katy Evans) novels in the *Tangled* series, turns her award-winning talents to the erotic escapades of lawyers in love, lust, and compromising positions . . . the Legal Briefs series!

Raves for Emma Chase and her sexy bestsellers

Overruled

"Chase has proven, once again, that she creates heroes who are grounded, successful and lovable . . . There are funny, appealing characters introduced, and watching their love lives unfold is fun." —*RT Book Reviews*

"*Overruled* is even more proof as to why I have come to look forward to every single book Emma Chase releases." —*Harlequin Junkies*

"*Overruled* was sexy, fun, and a good read." —*Fiction Vixen*

"If you haven't read any of [Emma Chase's] books, it's time you gave her a go. She's an incredibly talented and fun voice in contemporary romance. —*Smitten With Reading*

Tied

One of PopSugar's Best Books for Women 2014

"Sublimely irreverent, massively sexy, and so frigging perfect, readers will be bursting with giddy smiles. This, praise Emma, is the ending we all wanted."

—Christina Lauren, *New York Times* bestselling author of *Beautiful Secret*

Tamed

One of PopSugar's Best Books for Women 2014

"Witty, endearing, laugh-out-loud funny. Emma Chase doesn't disappoint." —K. Bromberg, bestselling author of *Driven*

Twisted

"A great escape."

—Katy Evans, *New York Times* bestselling author of *Real* and *Ripped*

"A delicious treat . . . funny, witty, and very sexy." —*The Book Bellas*

"I laughed. I cried. I yelled. I wanted to stop reading, but I couldn't. . . . Emma Chase really knows how to evoke emotion from her readers!"

—*Harlequin Junkie*

"Emma Chase grabbed me from page one and put me through the wringer." —*Caffeinated Book Reviewer*

"A yummy read . . . interesting, intense, sexy, and challenging."

—*Literary Cravings*

"Is emotional whiplash considered a sickness? I am more in love with this series than I was before, my heart just took a severe beating along the way." —*The Geekery Book Review*

Emma Chase was chosen as the Debut Goodreads Author in the Goodreads Choice Awards for 2013 for her sensational novel

Tangled

Also a Goodreads Best Book of 2013!

"Well-written, clever, and charming." —*Maryse's Book Blog*

"Total stop, drop, and roll reading. . . . Oh, and the sex . . . completely and utterly scandalicious." —*Scandalicious*

"Addictively entertaining. If you're looking for a witty, laugh-out-loud insight into the male psyche, look no further: it's *Tangled*."

—*Miss Ivy's Book Nook*

SUSTAINED

EMMA CHASE

GALLERY BOOKS

New York London Toronto Sydney New Delhi

G

Gallery Books
An Imprint of Simon & Schuster, Inc.
1230 Avenue of the Americas
New York, NY 10020

First Gallery Books trade paperback edition August 2015

For information about special discounts for bulk purchases, please contact Simon & Schuster Special Sales at 1-866-506-1949 or business@simonandschuster.com

The Simon & Schuster Speakers Bureau can bring authors to your live event. For more information or to book an event contact the Simon & Schuster Speakers Bureau at 1-866-248-3049 or visit our website at www.simonspeakers.com.

Manufactured in the United States of America

10 9 8 7 6 5 4 3 2 1

Library of Congress Cataloging-in-Publication Data

Chase, Emma
Sustained / Emma Chase — First Gallery Books trade paperback edition.
pages ; cm. — (The legal briefs series ; 2)
PS3603.H37934S87 2015
813'.6—dc23 2015012565

ISBN 978-1-5011-0207-3
ISBN 978-1-5011-0208-0 (ebook)

For the heroes.

The champions.

For those who do what is brave and honorable and right.

You're the reason we believe in happy endings.

Acknowledgments

I was never a gymnast, but I've always enjoyed watching the sport. The way the athletes fly through the air, the gravity-defying control, the way they make it look so easy. All the routines are amazing to see—but every once in a while, there's one that really stands out.

It's solid. Clean. No wobbling, no quick adjustments, no almost-falls. And in these practically-perfect-in-every-way routines, the gymnast always—always—sticks the landing.

That's how it felt to complete *Sustained*. Like two feet planted firmly on the ground. Confident. Sure.

Landing stuck.

Finishing a book doesn't always feel this way. I've loved all my books, no question, but there's frequently the worry that readers won't love it. Is the plot too much of a stretch? Was it sexy enough, funny enough? Is the voice consistent? Will they be disappointed? Will they want to castrate my leading man (that tends to be a big one for me ;))?

After edits and revisions, more edits and more revisions, these worries quiet down—at least until release day. But right from the beginning, *Sustained* felt different. There's a depth and poignancy to Jake and Chelsea that pulls so hard on the heartstrings and yet is also so fun. Their passion, their hopes and fears, sadness and joy was an extraordinary thing to experience—I couldn't remember being more excited to share a story with my readers.

Anyone who knows me can tell you I'm generally not an overly confident person. In fact, I'm a little concerned right now that my opening thoughts sound kinda braggy (Drew Evans shakes his head at me). And I genuinely don't mean it that way. I guess what I'm trying to say is, to me, *Sustained* feels special. The kind of story that leaves you with a high, that you'll think about happily, long after The End.

And more than anything, I hope it feels special to all of you too.

Now, writers alone do not make great books, and I couldn't have gotten this one to the place it is without the most awesome team of people around me.

To my agent, Amy Tannenbaum of the Jane Rotrosen Agency—thank you for every word of advice, every phone call, and every email (even on the weekends, people). "Awesome" doesn't even begin to cover it!

To my editor, Micki Nuding—working with you is everything I'd dreamed of when I imagined being a professional author. I continue to be amazed by how perfectly you understand my characters. There's a wonderful security in knowing you'll catch any missteps and shape my stories into the best they can possibly be. Thank you for helping me to reach deeper and stretch those writing wings!

I'm endlessly grateful for my publicists—Nina Bocci of Bocci PR and Kristin Dwyer (my moon and stars) of Simon & Schuster—for believing in me, for saying just what I need to hear when I need to hear it, and for working tirelessly to bring my stories to the masses. You rock!

To author Katy Evans—I love you! Our chats mean the world to me, thank you for being there, for sharing your thoughts and for letting me know I'm not the only one :) .

To Christina Lauren, Alice Clayton, and all my author friends—

your support, encouragement and laughter are an amazing gift that I cherish every day.

All my thanks to my assistant, Juliet Fowler, for reminding me when I forget (frequently) and for flawlessly doing everything that needs doing, so I can actually write! I'd be lost without you!

Much gratitude to Molly O'Brien, for all that you do to make sure everything doesn't fall apart while I'm locked in my office with my characters! xoxo

To the wonderfully talented Simone Renou of In My Dreams Design and Hang Le of By Hang Le Graphic Design, for your beautiful and steamy graphics!

Thanks to my daughter for helping me decipher and come up with current teen-speak—there's no way I'm cool enough to have done it alone.

Thanks to Fener Deonarine, for helping me get those complicated Washington, DC, legal details right.

I'm so grateful to everyone at Gallery Books, including Marla Daniels, Sarah Leiberman, Liz Psaltis, Paul O'Halloran, the art department for those beautiful covers, and my amazing publishers Jennifer Bergstrom and Louise Burke.

To the fantastic bloggers who take the time to read and write so many fun and honest reviews—thank you for getting behind this new series and for all you do to let readers know these stories are coming!

To my readers—gah—there aren't enough words to express how grateful I am for every single one of you. It's a joy to chat with you on Twitter and FB, to giggle with you at signings, to talk stories and book boyfriends—thank you so much for your enthusiasm and beautiful energy!

To my parents, brother and sister, and entire family—thank you for your patience and love and constant pride in my work. And to my amazing husband and two beautiful children—you are my inspiration, my everything.

Prologue

I don't use an alarm clock. I'm one of those people with an internal timepiece that wakes me up at the same time every morning, regardless of how tired I am or how late I was up the night before. I was *that* kid—you mothers know the type I mean. The kind who makes you beg for just a few more minutes of rest before you eventually lay down the law that no one's allowed out of bed before the sun shows up.

Which explains why, even though it's Sunday, my eyelids crack open at five a.m. sharp. I stretch out the sore stiffness in my complaining muscles, caused by lack of sleep . . . and from the strenuous workout after we got home from the bar.

I kick back the covers and climb out of bed, still naked, and walk past the head of soft blond hair that peeks out from under the blankets, to the bathroom. After a satisfying piss, I brush the foul residue from my teeth and splash cold water on my face, slicking back my unruly black hair. With a groan, I crack my neck and stretch my arms.

I'm getting too old for this shit.

But then I remember the finer details of the evening's second act. The thrill of a new hookup, the verbal gamesmanship—saying just the right thing in just the right way. The sweaty foreplay, the hot, tight fucking, the long legs over my shoulders . . . and I grin.

There's no such thing as too old.

I walk to my closet for a T-shirt and sweatpants, then silently head out to the kitchen. I press the button on the ready coffeemaker—forget dogs; a good coffeemaker is man's real best friend. While it brews, I switch on the small flat-screen perched on the counter; the early-morning anchors drone on about the latest world horrors, sports stats, and weather.

Stanton, my roommate from law school, moved out last year to live with Sofia—a fellow attorney at my firm. Stanton's a hell of a guy, Sofia's a kick-ass woman, and though they started out as banging buddies only, I could see them going domesticated from a mile away. Having the apartment to myself has been fantastic. Not that Stanton was a slob, but he's a former frat boy. I'm an organized guy; I like things a certain way—*my* way. Routine. Discipline. *Neat* and *easy* are words to live by. My mother always said I'd make a great military man, if it wasn't for the authority factor. The only orders I follow are my own.

Steam wafts from my cup of black coffee as I step out onto the balcony, sipping it slowly, while the silent DC street comes alive around me.

The anchor's nasal voice seeps out from the open balcony door. *"I-495 was closed yesterday for several hours due to a collision that claimed the life of noted environmental lobbyist Robert McQuaid and his wife. The cause of the deadly crash is still under investigation. In other local news . . ."*

Delicate arms wrap around my waist from behind as small hands fold together over my abs. A soft cheek presses against my back. "Come back to bed," she whines sweetly. "It's sooo early."

Sorry, Cinderella, but the clock struck twelve. The coach has turned back into a pumpkin and it's time to collect your glass slipper. I never pretended to be Prince Charming.

Some women can handle a nameless one-night stand or a casual hookup. But honestly, most can't. As long as they understand sex is the only thing I have to offer, the only thing I want in return, I'm up for a repeat. The minute their eyes get that soft, sentimental—or worse—wounded look, I'm out. I don't have time for games, don't have any interest in talking about "where this could go."

I twist out of the blonde's arms. She follows as I walk back into the kitchen and put my empty cup in the sink. "I'm going for a run. There's coffee in the pot and cab money on the front table. You don't need to be here when I get back."

Plump lips—that were delightfully stretched around my cock last night—now form an unhappy pout. "You don't have to be an asshole."

I shrug. "I don't *have* to be . . . it's just easier that way."

I slip into my running shoes and walk out the front door.

1

Four weeks later

"They treated me like a common criminal! It was humiliating."

Milton Cooper Carrington Bradley. Heir to a renowned international luxury hotel empire . . . and a perpetual client of mine. Chronological age? Twenty. Mental age? Four.

"Stupid peasants didn't know who they were dealing with! I told them I'd have their jobs."

Yes—his name is actually Milton Bradley. Obviously his parents are dipshits.

"Especially the head stewardess—she was a rude bitch. You play racquetball with the president of that airline, don't you, Dad? I want her gone."

And this particular apple sure stuck close to the tree.

I lean back in my chair as he continues to whine to his father about the unfair rules of the flight crew and all he wants done in retribution. I'm a criminal defense attorney at Adams & Williamson—one of an elite group of rising stars at this firm. But this is the year that counts. It's time to pull away from the pack—to demonstrate to the partners that I'm one of their own. The stud in the stable. The best.

Unlike my coworkers, who also happen to be my closest friends,

I'm not hindered by time suckers like family, girlfriends, marriage, and kids—the ultimate third rail for any career-driven adult. My lack of outside distractions makes proving my commitment to the firm, displaying my skill, just a little bit easier. I like my job. Wouldn't say I love it—but I'm really fucking good at it. It's interesting. Challenging. Keeps me on my toes. Because criminal defense isn't about defending the weak or protecting the innocent—it's a game. Taking the hand you're dealt, the facts of the case, and spinning them to your advantage. Outsmarting, outmaneuvering the prosecution. Winning when all the odds say you can't.

The downside?

I have to spend my time with fucknuts like Milton Bradley.

He slips a cigarette out from his pocket and lights it with a flick of his Zippo. He jerks his head, flopping his thin blond hair back off his forehead as he releases a cloud of toxic smoke from his nostrils. Like an impotent dragon who doesn't know how to blow fire.

"You can't smoke in here."

"Who says?" he replies with a challenge in his eyes.

Moving smoothly, I'm out of my chair and in front of him, looming like a black cloud ready to thunder. I'm aware of my size—six five, two hundred and twenty-five pounds of rock-solid muscle—and the effect it has on people. I'm pretty goddamn intimidating, even when I'm not trying to be. But at the moment?

I'm trying.

"*I* say." My voice is low—menacingly quiet.

When you mean what you say and say exactly what you mean, there's rarely a need to raise your voice. Yelling is a sign of desperation, an indication that you're out of options, with nothing behind your back but volume.

I hold out a styrofoam cup with a bit of cold coffee left on the bottom. Without a word of complaint, Milton drops his cigarette into the liquid. It goes out with a hiss, leaving an unpleasant odor in its wake.

Most of my clients are wealthy, some not so much. But they all find their way to my office door because of similar personality traits. They're cheats, con men, those who think they're above the rules the rest of us have to follow, general lowlifes, their violent nature concealed by a smiling face. Criminal defense really isn't so different from proctology. In both fields, it's one asshole after another. This line of work isn't for the faint of heart—you have to have a strong stomach. And my stomach is steel.

"How do we make this go away, Jake?" the elder Bradley asks from his chair beside his son. His eyes, nearly as black as his suit, regard me with an acceptable level of respect. Because he understands what his progeny doesn't: that while I may work for him, he needs me more than I will ever need him.

I walk back behind my desk and look over the arrest report in front of me.

"The witnesses said your behavior was erratic—threatening."

"They're lying. Envious slime," Milton sneers.

"The stewardess said she smelled marijuana when you exited the first-class cabin bathroom."

His eyes shift nervously to his father for just a moment, then settle back on me. Chin raised—so offended. "I smelled it too. Must have been one of the other passengers."

I make a note on the file, just to amuse myself. *I've passed kidney stones bigger than this kid's brain.*

Justifications and explanations. Some days I feel like I've heard them all. *I couldn't help myself. He made me do it. She asked for it. I was asleep. I was walking the goddamn dog.* It'd be nice if they put at least a little effort into their bullshit. Originality used to mean something.

"Some advice for future reference?" I tell young, entitled Milton. "Don't screw around with the Federal Aviation Administration. They're very sensitive these days and they've got the budget to make your life miserable." Then I turn to the father. "And in answer to your question,

Malcolm, it'd be easier to make this go away if your son could refrain from getting himself arrested every few weeks."

Two DUIs, a disorderly conduct, and an assault in a bar fight—all within just the last three months. I bet you think that's some kind of record.

It's not.

"So you're saying we can't win?" Milton asks, his voice cracking like he's Bobby from *The Brady Bunch*.

My lips slide into a half grin that feels cold on my face.

"Of course we're going to win. You took medication before the flight for anxiety. That's our angle. A bad reaction to the pills, which explains your offensive behavior. A sworn statement from the prescribing physician should be sufficient."

It's almost too easy.

I point my finger at him. "But for the next six weeks, you need to stay home. Keep your name out of the papers and off of TMZ. Don't drive, don't go out to the clubs, don't fart in a public place. You understand?"

Malcolm grins and places his hand on his son's shoulder. "We do." The three of us stand. "As always, thank you, Jake. We're lucky to have you on our side."

"I'll be in touch." And with a handshake, they're gone.

• • •

Two hours later I'm sliding into my suit jacket, ready to head out to lunch. I automatically straighten my tie, adjust my collar—to ensure the scattering of tattoos that begins at my collarbone, wraps around my right shoulder, and trails down to the end of my wrist is covered. It's a bitch in the summer, but the presence of ink tends to make my upper-crust clients uncomfortable, and it's never well received by judges.

My secretary, Mrs. Higgens, walks into my office. Mrs. Higgens is the classic little old lady, right down to the pearl necklace and spectacles—the kind you'd expect to be sitting in a rocking chair crocheting blankets for dozens of grandkids. She's terrific at her job. I've been accurately called a coldhearted bastard on a number of occasions, but I'm not sure if even I could muster the level of callousness that would be needed to fire her.

"There's a young lady here to see you, Jake. She doesn't have an appointment."

I fucking hate walk-ins. They're unexpected and unpredictable. They screw up my schedule, and my schedule is sacred.

"I'm on my way out."

Mrs. Higgens looks at me sideways and drops an unsubtle hint. "She's very pretty."

I glance at my watch. "Fine. But tell her she's got five minutes and five minutes only."

I sit back down and a few moments later a petite, dark-haired woman enters my office. I'd say she's in her late twenties, attractive, with a banging little body under those beige slacks and that prim yellow cardigan. But her shifty eyes and jittery movements dampen the appeal.

Looks matter, but confidence is by far the most alluring accessory a woman can wear.

Mrs. Higgens closes the door as she exits, and the brunette walk-in stands in front of my desk.

"Hi," she says, glancing ever so briefly at my face before staring back at the floor, pushing her hair back behind her ears.

"Hi. Can I help you?"

That gets her looking up. "You don't remember me, do you?" she asks, hands twisted together.

I study her face, more carefully this time. She's neither remarkably beautiful nor outstandingly fugly. Just kind of . . . generic. Forgettable.

"Should I?"

Her shoulders hunch as she covers her eyes, muttering, "Jeez, I thought this was going to be hard enough . . ." She sinks down into one of the chairs across from my desk, perched on the edge—ready to run. After a beat, she adds, "We met last month at the Angry Inch Saloon? I was wearing a red dress?"

Nope, doesn't ring any bells. I've met lots of women at that bar and when available, I go for blondes. They're not more fun . . . just hotter.

She brushes her dark bangs to the side and tries again. "I asked you to buy me a drink, and you did. A cosmopolitan."

Still nothing.

"We went back to your place after I told you about walking in on my boyfriend having sex with my best friend?"

I'm drawing a blank.

"While he was wearing my favorite pink nightie?"

And we have a winner. Now I remember. Made me think of Marv Albert, the sportscaster with a penchant for women's lingerie—and assault and battery. And yet, he's still on TV.

Only in America.

"Yes. I remember now . . ." I squint, working on the name.

"Lainey."

"Lainey." My fingers snap. "Right. What can I do for you?" I glance at my watch—two minutes left and I'm out the door.

She's back to nervous and jerky. "Okay, there's no easy way to say this . . . so I'm just going to say it."

Sounds like a solid plan.

She takes a big breath and rushes out, "He didn't just take my best friend and my best lingerie . . . he left something behind, too."

How poetic.

"Syphilis."

• • •

That sound you just heard? That's me thinking, *What the fuck did she just say?* I actually stick my finger in my ear, to clear out the water that's obviously clogged in there from my morning shower, distorting the hell out of my hearing.

But then she speaks again. And it sounds exactly the same.

"Yeah, syphilis."

My stomach seizes, and there's a really good chance I'm about to lose my breakfast.

"I got my test results back a few days ago. The people at the clinic said I needed to contact everyone I've had sex with since him. And that's only you. I remembered your name and you said you were a lawyer here in DC." She flaps her hands. "So . . . here I am."

She might want to move a little bit to the right. I'm definitely going to blow chunks.

She breathes easier now, looking relieved that she got it all out. How goddamn nice for her.

"Do you have any questions, Jake? Anything you want to say?"

Motherfucking hell, I should've just gone to lunch.

2

I wasn't always so committed to structure, dedicated to routine. In my younger years, I was the epitome of the bad boy. The badder the better. I've got the scars, the tattoos, and the sealed juvenile criminal record to prove it. In those days I had a major temper and an even bigger chip on my shoulder—a dangerous combination. And I let both rule me the way crank controls a meth head. It was only after a major scare—a near fucking miss that almost decimated my life—that I went legit. With the guidance of a crotchety old judge who took me under his wing and kicked my proverbial ass, I was able to lock up the bad boy and throw away the key.

Because he saw something in me that I'd never seen. Potential. Promise. The possibility of greatness. Sure, my mother always predicted it, but as far as my screwed-up brain was concerned, she didn't count. All moms think their kid is the next Einstein or Gates or Mozart just waiting to happen.

He accepted me for who I was, scabs and all. But he refused to accept that that was *all* I was. And when someone believes in you, goes out on a limb for you when they have no obligation to do shit—it has an impact. It made me want to look in the mirror and see the man he knew I could be.

And today, that's the fucker who stares back at me. Controlled. Powerful. Top of his game. Sure, once in a while the temper rattles the cage, but I keep that shit locked down tight. The bad boy gets out to play in a limited capacity—on a short, thick leash. Women love a man with an edge; they get all wet and quivery for a tough guy—so that's his playground. 'Cause when it comes to fucking . . . like I said . . . the badder the better.

It's that practiced restraint that allows me to keep my standing lunch appointment, even though eating is the last thing I want to do. But it's a ritual. Me, Sofia, Brent, and Stanton—the current fab four of criminal law. Sometimes it's in our offices, most times it's held at any of the taverns or cafés located within blocks of our firm. We're sitting at one of those places now—at a round, checkered-clothed curbside table, the March air and afternoon sun just warm enough to eat outside. Stanton's morning court session ran over so he's late to the party.

Sofia stands up when he approaches, smoothing down her sleek black skirt, her four-inch heels lifting her to eye level with her boyfriend.

He kisses her with smiling lips and a sappy expression. "Hey, darlin'."

She runs a hand through his blond hair. "Hi."

Brent leans back in his chair, his dark blue gaze glinting with mischief. "I don't get a kiss?"

Stanton pulls out Sofia's chair for her, then sits in his own. "My ass is always available for you, Mason."

"Actually, I was talking to Sofia."

"Her ass is off-limits," Stanton replies, scanning the menu.

Stanton Shaw is a good old boy—in every sense of the term. Originally a Mississippi farm boy, he's honest, loyal, has a low tolerance for bullshit, and exudes an easy, genuine charm that women find irresistible—as do juries. We met in law school and became roommates shortly after that. He's a heavy hitter around the firm—his record is as impressive as my own—and he's got his eye on a partnership. But, unlike me, Stanton has baggage. Cool, sweet baggage, sure, but baggage all the same.

I don't like kids—too needy, too whiny. Stanton's daughter, Presley, is the sole exception. She lives back in Mississippi with her mother, Stanton's ex, but she comes to DC often enough that my friend has more than earned his *Daddy* moniker. And he relishes it. If sunshine took human form, like some Greek myth, she would be Presley Shaw. She's just a great fucking kid.

After we order, talk turns to our latest cases, the goings-on at the firm. Who's stepping on whose toes, who has a figurative knife ready to perform a good backstabbing. This isn't gossip; it's intel. Ears to the ground to gather the information we need to know to make our next move.

Our food arrives and the conversation shifts to politics. DC may be a large city, but when it comes to strategy and alliances, it resembles an episode of *Survivor*. And everyone's salivating to vote someone off the island.

But I'm only listening to them with one ear. My other ear is still ringing with the revelation of my unexpected visitor. Lainey. Not likely to forget her name again. I try to stay calm about it, but my sweaty palms betray me. And unless I'm hitting the bag at the gym or running my seven miles a day, I don't fucking sweat. I consider the odds that I'm actually infected and what that means for me. I think about how I came to this point—the choices I should have made differently to avoid the sick feeling in my stomach that makes me leave my meal untouched.

Brent's voice pulls me out of my head. "What's wrong with you today?"

I meet his inquisitive stare with a bland one. "Why would you think something's wrong?"

He shrugs. "You've gone way beyond the strong silent type and are approaching selective mutism. What gives?"

Brent is a talker. A sharer. He comes from a family of extreme wealth going back several generations. But his parents aren't the cold, silent aristocrats you'd imagine. Sure, they're kind of eccentric, which I find entertaining as hell, but they're also warm, funny, giving people and they passed those qualities on to their son. Because they don't actually work, Brent's family members have way too much time on their hands—so they're also way too involved in each other's personal lives. There are no secrets in the Mason clan. Last month his cousin Carolyn emailed the family newsletter with her ovulation date attached, so everyone could keep their fingers crossed for her.

And I'm not even kidding. They'd make a fucking hysterical reality show.

When he was a kid Brent was in an accident, hit by a speeding car. He survived, minus the lower half of one leg. But he's good with it—*self-pity* is not in his vocabulary. His pretty face probably helps in that regard—and the fact that women practically beg for him to screw them doesn't hurt, either. He's also a big believer in therapy. I suspect he's dished out more cash to therapists over the years than he paid for his house.

I am not a sharer or a talker. But we still get along—a yin-and-yang kind of thing. Brent has a knack for dragging me out of my shell in a way that doesn't make me want to punch him.

But not today.

"I don't want talk about it."

His eyes lock on me like a fighter pilot on a target. Or an annoying younger sibling. "Well, now you *have* to talk about it."

"Not really," I say flatly.

"Come on—spill. Tell us. Tell us. You know you want to. Tell us."

Stanton chuckles. "You might as well just come out with it, Jake. He's not gonna stop until you do."

I offer an alternative. "I could break his jaw. Having it wired shut would stop him."

Brent strokes his newly grown, manicured beard. "Like you'd do anything to mar this priceless work of art. That would be a crime. Just tell us. *Teeeeeell us.*"

I open my mouth . . . then pause . . . staring hesitantly at Sofia.

She reads me loud and clear, and rolls her hazel eyes. "I grew up with three older brothers. And I live with him." She points at Stanton. "There's literally nothing you could say that I haven't heard before."

O-kay. I take a breath and force the words from my lungs. "Turns out a woman I nailed last month has syphilis. I have to get tested."

Sofia coughs on her drink. "I stand corrected."

Brent laughs, the bastard. "Man, that's awful."

"Thanks, asshole." I glare at him. "You sound real broken up about it."

Brent reins in his hilarity. "Don't get me wrong, it sucks, but syphilis is cured with a shot—it could've been worse." His voice lowers. "You wanna play, sometimes you have to pay. It happens to the best of us. I had a bad case of seafood critters once myself."

"Seafood?" Sofia asks.

Stanton fills her in. "Crabs, baby."

Her face scrunches up. "Ewww."

Stanton wags his finger at me. "I told you one day that revolving pussy door was gonna pinch you."

"Thanks for not saying I told you so."

"Anytime."

When he was single, Stanton wasn't a monk. But his hookups were more of a slow burn. He *dated*. Had a solid stable of women he felt comfortable calling when he wanted to get laid.

I don't roll that way. It takes too much energy, too much time. A woman's mind and personality don't turn me on. It's her other parts that hold my attention.

I feel the need to defend myself. "It's not like you two are so discriminating. I've seen some of the women you've fucked. Those were some pretty low bars."

"I resent that," Brent tells me. But his grin says he kind of doesn't.

"At least I knew their names," Stanton counters. "A little bit of their background, tastes, history . . ."

"Sure," I argue, "'cause right after 'Nice weather we're having,' a chick is gonna throw out, 'Oh, FYI—I have syphilis.' "

Stanton thinks on that a moment, then shrugs. "She might, actually. You'd be surprised what you could learn if you took the time to talk to women. And even if she didn't tell you, when you get to know a woman, you get a feel for what kind of person she is. That goes a long way in deciding who you don't want to stick your dick into."

I hate to admit he has a point, but he does. And I resolve in this moment—if my tests come back clean—to get to know the next woman I intend to stick my dick into. At least a little. So I'll never—ever—have to deal with this shit again.

Sofia leans forward, bracing her elbows on the table. "Did you call your doctor?"

"Yeah. I have an appointment tonight."

I avoid doctors like the bubonic plague. On some level I know it's ignorant, but I think the stress of knowing you have a fatal disease kills faster than the disease itself. I'd rather not know.

Give me a sudden heart attack in the middle of a fantastic lay or argument in the middle of a courtroom any day. That's how I want to go. Many, *many* years from now.

"You know what the worst part's gonna be, don't you?" Brent asks. The bastard is still grinning.

"This isn't the fucking worst part?"

He shakes his head. "Nope. The celibacy, my good man. No fun times for you for probably about two weeks. Until the test results come back."

"Two weeks? Are you screwing with me?" My dick aches at the idea; it might as well be two years.

He nudges my shoulder and I want to hit him. "Afraid not. You and Hanna are going to be monogamous for a while."

My eyes squint, 'cause I have no idea what he's saying. "Hanna who?"

He waves his palm. "Hanna Hand."

3

Two weeks later

Brent was right. It's been two of the longest, slowest weeks of my life. I've worked out so much I busted my weight bench. Hanna and I have been spending way too much time together. The sex is stale and she's starting to get clingy. Time to kick her to the fucking curb.

I'm not a nympho, I don't need to hump every night, but two weeks is a major dry spell. It hasn't been pleasant—and neither has my mood. With every day that's passed, I've become exponentially more unbearable. I'm tense. Short-tempered. On edge.

Essentially, really goddamn horny.

Stanton has taken to avoiding being in the office with me. The afternoon I threatened to rip his tongue out while he was getting frisky on the phone with Sofia may have had something to do with that.

And even though today is the day I'm hoping to end the fast, anxiety about my test results has me even *more* stressed out. Which is really bad news for the client who just stepped into my office.

Milton I-Can't-Follow-a-Simple-Motherfucking-Direction Bradley.

Milton I-Got-Arrested-Because-I-Was-in-a-Car-That-Got-Pulled-Over-with-Ten-Bags-of-Heroin-in-the-Glove-Compartment Bradley.

The door rattles on its hinges as I throw it closed behind him and level my darkest glare at him. He puts his hands in his pockets and walks to a chair like he's strolling through the park, not a care in the world.

Not today, dipshit.

As he slouches in the chair, I sit behind my desk and fold my hands to keep from punching him.

"What did I tell you?" I ask him.

"It wasn't mine."

My voice gets lower. Sharper. "What. Did I. Tell you?"

His eyes drop, like he's a submissive dog. "You told me to stay home, but—"

I hold up my finger. "There is no *but*. I told you to keep your sorry ass home, and you're too much of a fucking idiot to listen."

He stands up, his face turning from white to an angry pink. "You can't talk to me like that! My father pays your salary."

I stand too—and I'm a lot scarier at it than he is. "Sit. *Down.*"

He does. I stay standing. "I *did* just talk to you like that, asshole. And lightning didn't strike me, so get over yourself. As for your father, no, he doesn't pay my salary. But even if he did, I wouldn't hesitate to call you the stupid, dickless moron you are."

He gets more flushed with every word.

I sit back down, my tone turning more philosophical. "Do you know what happens to boys like you in prison, Milton? Wealthy, pretty, sweet-smelling boys?"

And he goes from pink to pale in no time flat.

"Unless you have a secret fantasy about getting your ass torn apart, you need to get it through your thick skull that the only thing standing between you and a cellmate named Chewbacca is me."

He finally looks frightened.

"And because it's my job, I'm going to keep your undeserving ass out of prison whether you want to cooperate or not. Got it?"

He nods and smartly keeps his mouth shut.

"Now—are your fingerprints on any of the heroin bags?"

He shakes his head. "No. I never touched them."

Perfect. Chances are I'll be able to work around his latest arrest.

I take out a business card from my top drawer. "When you leave my office, go straight to this address."

He examines the card. "What is it?"

"It's a monitoring company. They'll fit you with an ankle monitor that will tell them if you leave your house. If you do, they'll notify me."

He opens his mouth to argue.

"Not a fucking word, Milton. This is your last chance—you screw this up, it's plan B all the way."

"What's plan B?" he asks, like it's an option he'd rather consider.

"I beat the ever-loving shit out of you. You can't get into trouble if you're in traction."

He swallows so hard, I hear it. "O-okay," he stutters. "For real this time, I'll listen."

My expression remains stony; I'm not giving an inch. "For your sake, you damn well better."

• • •

Two hours later, I'm in an exam room at my doctor's office, sitting on the table with that stupid paper crinkling under my beige slacks. I check my watch. He's late. As if my mood wasn't black enough, I really hate to be kept waiting.

With nothing better to do, I glance around the walls of the room. Framed medical certificates from Yale, a poster on proper hand-washing technique, an advertisement for the flu shot, and a reminder to get your prostate exam.

Just shoot me now. Put me out of my misery.

And for the thousandth time in two weeks, I swear I'll never find myself in this position again. No more nameless hookups. No more jilted girlfriends with self-esteem issues looking to lose themselves in a stranger fuck. From here on out, it's dating only. I'll get to know them. I'll become goddamn *choosy*, no matter how unappetizing it sounds.

Finally the door to the room opens, and in walks an unfamiliar face in a white coat. Light brown hair, tiny dark eyes, a smooth chin that appears to have never met a razor.

He looks fucking twelve.

"Can I help you?" I ask.

He glances up from the file in his hands, smiling. "Good morning, Mr. Becker, I'm Dr. Grey."

I fleetingly look at the door, expecting his father to walk in behind him. "You sure?"

Good-natured teeth flash. "Yes, I'm sure I'm a doctor. I'm new to the practice. Dr. Sauer had a family emergency so I'm covering for him today." He turns a page in the file, scanning the contents. "Before we discuss your test results, let's go over the recommended protocols for safe sexual intercourse, including condoms, spermicidal lubricants, birth control—"

I hold up my hand. "Let's not. I'm good with all that. Just give it to me straight—are my results good or bad?"

• • •

I raise my bottle of beer, clinking it against the three raised glasses. "Clean as a whistle." I haven't smiled this much since I won my first case. I'm practically giddy, for Christ's sake. My cheeks are getting sore.

"Congratulations," Sofia tells me happily.

"Healthy, wealthy, and wise," Stanton says. "Here's to stayin' that way."

"Damn straight." I take a drag from the bottle. I don't usually drink at lunch—and I never get drunk, even on the weekends. I've always associated being wasted with weakness, a lack of control, hazy thoughts, and regrettable actions. But this is a special occasion.

"So what's your plan now?" Brent asks. "As if I didn't already know, you randy bastard. I've seen the way you've been leering at poor Mrs. Higgens. Desperate much?"

I flip him off. Mrs. Higgens is pretty much the only female in my radius who's exempt. Which leads me to my next question. "So . . . what's the typical schedule with the whole dating thing? How long before one gets to the actual fucking?"

"Three dates," they all answer simultaneously.

My eyebrows rise. "*Three* dates? Seriously? Are you guys, like . . . more religious than I ever knew?"

"You've never heard of the three-date rule?" Sofia puts a forkful of Caesar salad into her mouth.

When I shake my head, Stanton explains. "The first date, you talk, see if you can stand to be in the same room together for more than an hour. The second date is like . . . verification that you're both actually the person you seemed to be on date one. And the third date is the sweet spot—let the good times roll."

Seems like a lot of effort just to get laid. I wonder if the pussy is better if you actually know the girl's name.

"Wait a second," Sofia pipes up. "Does this mean you've never dated? Never had a girlfriend? Even in high school?"

I shake my head. "I wasn't exactly boyfriend material in high school. And the girls I hung around with weren't interested in that kind of thing."

"That's kind of cute, Jake," she teases. "It's almost like you're a virgin."

I frown. "Except, not at all."

"I've got a date on Friday," Brent tells us. "With Lucy Patterson from Emblem and Glock."

Emblem & Glock is another DC firm with whom we regularly compete for clients.

"Sleeping with the enemy, huh?" Stanton asks him.

Brent shrugs. "She's smart, gorgeous, and doesn't think I'm a prick when I complain about a newbie prosecutor who refuses to make a deal. Plus, the professional competition thing is kind of hot." He looks my way. "I could see if she has a friend. We could double."

I do the calculations in my head. "That means the earliest I'll be getting any is Sunday. And that's only if I blow my whole weekend on a woman I haven't even laid eyes on yet."

That doesn't work for me.

"You have an alternative?" Brent asks.

As a matter of fact, I do.

• • •

Some guys have a problem hooking up with a woman they work with. They're afraid it could turn awkward. Complicated. But not me. And especially not in this case. I figure already knowing each other's names, having seen each other come and go for the last seven years, shaves at least one date from the three-date rule. Gotta love the efficiency.

Camille Longhorn works in the billing department of my firm. Single, five ten, about a hundred and twenty pounds, long legs, fantastic rack, dirty-blond hair, and a face that resembles a young Elle Macpherson. When I asked her out to dinner four hours ago, I was desperately hoping her hair wasn't the only thing dirty about her.

But that was then.

Now? Not so much.

Because after listening to her drone on about things I could never care about; after hearing the high-pitched snorting laugh that makes me flinch involuntarily every fucking time she does it; after watching her compulsively twirl her hair and scratch her head, to the point where *I* feel like I'm crawling with an infestation of angry invisible spiders—I'm just not interested anymore.

At all.

It's like that fat-suit Gwyneth Paltrow movie a few years back. Now she's hot . . . now she's not.

"And then I said, that's above my pay grade!"

Squeak-snort.

Squeak-snort.

Squeak-snort.

Oh god. Please, stop talking.

I try to block it out. To focus on the important things—like the round fullness of her tits straining against her beige sweater. I imagine how they would feel cupped in my hand, between my lips, under my tongue with her thighs around my waist and—

And there's spinach in her teeth. Or arugula, maybe.

My dick hangs his head. And yet I somehow manage to keep my face impassively polite as I point at her mouth and say, "You have a . . . something . . ."

"Oh! Thanks."

She lifts a knife and picks her teeth in the reflection.

I never realized that the downside of getting to know a woman before I screw her is the possibility that I might not want to screw her after I know her. That a personality could have such a devastating effect on desirability. It's depressing. My whole worldview is blown to bits.

When the check comes Camille starts to take her wallet out of her purse, but I wave her off. I toss a couple fifties on the table and together we stand, put on our coats, and head out onto the sidewalk. We walked here after work, so the good news is, I don't have to drive her home.

"Thank you for dinner, Jake." She smiles up at me. "This was fun. We should do it again sometime."

I open my mouth to tell her no thanks. Honesty has always been my policy. I don't have the time or will for sugarcoating. But I stop myself—because this is dating. Spin, half-truths, white lies, keeping options open and bases covered are what you do when you're dating. And maybe she's having an off day. Maybe the next time I see her she won't be annoying and I'll actually want to fuck her brains out. It could happen. And I'd hate to shoot myself in the cock if that is even the slightest possibility.

So I go with the old standby. "I'll call you."

Camille reaches up on tiptoes and kisses my cheek. "Good night, Jake."

"Bye, Camille."

And I walk back to my empty apartment alone. Reminding myself that it could actually be worse. I could be alone with syphilis.

• • •

The next day goes by in a bit of a blur. I spend it reviewing discovery—mostly medical reports—for an upcoming domestic violence case. Senator William Holten is a career politician with his hands in all kinds of cookie jars. That makes him a formidable enemy—and an even more powerful ally. He's charged with several counts of aggravated assault against his wife of thirty years. My boss, Jonas Adams, is Holten's good friend—he asked me personally to take the case. That's a really big fucking deal. This one case could make my whole career at this firm.

Which is why I took it—even though Holten has flat, emotionless eyes that I find unsettling. Even though reading the files, seeing the photographs and details of his wife's injuries going back years, makes me uneasy. Makes my stomach twist with the familiarity of it all.

By five o'clock, I could use some air. I walk out onto the sidewalk and down the block, stretching my legs. It's cooler out today, the sky a dirty gray, with a breeze that blows back the jacket of my navy suit. Still, the cold wind feels good after being inside all day. I close my eyes and inhale deeply, feeling the icy oxygen expand my lungs . . . and then I collide with something waist-high and warm.

It bounces off me with a soft, "Oomph!"

I look down into big cobalt eyes, brown curly hair, pale skin with freckles. He can't be more than nine or ten. He stares at me for a few seconds from where he's sprawled on his ass on the sidewalk, lips parted, breathing hard with surprise. Then he turns on his side, scrambling to bury his hands in his backpack, making sure nothing fell out of the many pockets.

"You all right, kid?" I ask, offering to help lift him up.

His eyes dart to my hand, and he pauses before taking it. I pull him to his feet.

"Yeah, I'm good. Sorry, mister." He drops his chin to his chest and hoists his brown leather backpack up on one shoulder.

"Watch where you're going," I say. "If I'd been on a bike, you would have taken some serious damage."

He mutters a quick "Okay," then turns and continues down the block.

I keep walking in the opposite direction. But after just a few steps, I realize something feels . . . different.

Lighter.

Off balance.

Immediately my hands go to the pockets in my jacket. My phone is in my right pocket and my wallet . . . my wallet is *not* in my left.

I turn sharply, weaving my gaze through the throngs of stooped pedestrians walking against the wind, until I zero in on the kid, who's now a half block away.

"Hey!" My voice booms like a cannon, and he and several other passersby stop and glance my way.

Even from this distance I make eye contact with him. And the diabolical expression that slowly comes over his face tells me everything I need to know. A confident smirk over straight, baby-white teeth, and a victorious glint shining in catlike eyes because he thinks he's out of my reach.

And he holds his right hand high and flips me off with his middle finger.

Little shit.

Then he hauls ass down the block.

I don't fucking think so, kid.

4

Arms pumping, I sprint up the block, then take a sharp left down the connecting street, trying my damnedest not to take out the pedestrians on the sidewalk. I dodge a honking car and make it across the street in three strides, then up concrete steps in two, entering the door of a mall that empties out two blocks up—onto the street I saw the kid turn onto. I dash past the Gap and through the food court.

"Watch it!" a bowed, gray-haired mall walker yells as I pass, wagging his cane.

I bust through the rear doors to the street.

I look right, then left. And I spot the little shit, still running, his backpack like a beacon in the fading sunlight. Beads of sweat break out on my forehead as I race up the block, jumping over a fire hydrant like a track hurdler. I stretch out my arm, fingers reaching—and grab the little fucker by the back of his white collared shirt.

Gotcha!

He squeaks in outrage, then twists and bucks like a fish on a hook, trying to dislodge my grip. But there's no way that's happening.

"Get off! Let me go!"

I shake him to get his attention and bark, "Cut it out!"

Small closed fists smack against my arm, push at my stomach. So I shake him again. "I said stop! Now." And then in a lower voice, "I'm not going to hurt you."

But he's determined. "Help!" he shouts, trying to make eye contact with the curious faces glancing at us. Like most bystanders, they continue on their way, figuring someone else will intervene—but not them. Then the little bastard calls out the mantra drilled into children's heads by overprotective parents and stranger-danger public service announcements.

"You're not my father! I don't know you! Help!"

I shake him harder now, rattling his teeth. Then I hiss, "You really want to bring attention to us with my wallet in your fucking backpack?"

That settles him down. Panting like a fox in a trap, he stops squirming. And he actually has the balls to glare at me, brows glued together with resentment.

"Is there a problem here?"

The question comes from the uniformed police officer who just stepped up to my right. He takes in the scene with an authoritative expression—until he looks at me, and his face melts into recognition.

"Hey, Becker."

Most cops instinctually don't like defense attorneys. I can understand their issue; they spend their days risking their lives to get scum off the street, and those in my profession bust their asses to get them back out, frequently Monday-morning quarterbacking the cop's own actions—how they conducted the arrest, if they had probable cause—to find grounds to spring our clients. It's a naturally antagonistic relationship. Oil and vinegar.

Personally, I like cops. Sure, they're hard-asses and they can be authoritarian pricks, but by and large, they're decent people trying to do a really difficult job.

Paul Noblecky is a beat cop who works out at the same gym as me. We've played basketball a few times and had a couple beers afterward.

"How's it going, Noblecky?"

He cocks his head pleasantly. "Can't complain." He points to the kid I'm still holding by the scruff of his neck, like an errant puppy. "What's this about?"

And before I can answer, the puppy says, "I was just messing around. Becker's my babysitter. I told him I was faster than him and he said I wasn't."

My first instinct is to laugh, 'cause the kid definitely has a knack for bullshitting. Wonder if he's ever considered a legal career—or a political one. My second impulse is to call him on it—rat him out—and toss him over to Noblecky. To walk away and wash my hands.

But something in his face . . . won't let me. The look in his eyes—a mixture of desperation and bitterness. He's hoping for my help, my mercy, but at the same time he hates that he needs it. And there's an innocence about this boy that's unlike the jagged exterior of true street kids. Something that tells me he's still saveable.

And that he's worth saving.

So I rub his head, messing up his hair, putting on a good show. "I told you I could take you."

Noblecky laughs. "Someone actually let you watch their kid?" He glances at the boy. "My condolences."

The kid flinches in response. It's quick, almost unobservable. But I notice.

Noblecky nudges me with his elbow and says jokingly, "What do you charge?" He has a five-year-old at home. "If I don't take Amy out to dinner soon, she's going to divorce me."

I shake my head. "It's a one-shot deal. Kids aren't my thing."

He turns to go. "All right, see you around, Becker."

"Take it easy," I call as he walks away.

As soon as Noblecky is out of earshot I drag the kid across the sidewalk, closer to the wall of a building. I hold out my hand. "Give it back."

He rolls his eyes, digs into his backpack, and slaps my wallet into my hand. I don't think he had enough time to lift anything from it, but I check my cash and credit cards just to be sure.

Satisfied, I slide it into my pocket. "What's your name?"

He glowers up at me. "You a cop?"

I shake my head. "Lawyer."

"I'm Rory."

"Rory what?"

"McQuaid."

I look him over. White button-down shirt, beige pants—a private-school uniform. Add in the two-hundred-and-fifty-dollar sneakers and J.Crew backpack and I have to ask, "Why'd you steal my wallet, Rory McQuaid?"

He kicks at the pavement. "I don't know."

Of course he doesn't.

His shoulders lift. "Just to see if I could do it, I guess."

Here's the moment when I wonder what the hell I'm supposed to do with him now. Keeping him out of the system feels like the right move, but letting him skate scot-free doesn't. He needs to learn stupid actions have consequences—bad ones—and he needs to know it now. If not, there'll be worse decisions in his future, with more severe penalties than he'll be able to pay.

I gesture with my hand toward the end of the block. "All right, let's go."

Rory stays right where he is. "I'm not going anywhere with you. You could be a child molester."

I scowl. "I'm not a child molester."

"Said every child molester ever."

My eyebrows rise. "A pickpocket and a smartass, huh? Perfect. Must be my lucky day." I raise my arm toward the end of the block. "I'm driving you home. I'll tell your parents what you did, and they'll deal with you."

My mother used to get frequent house calls in the same vein—from teachers, guidance counselors, benevolent police officers. It never changed my attitude or my fucked-up behavior, but she always appreciated knowing what her son was really up to, even though she had to work too many hours to do anything about it.

A shadow falls over Rory's face. "You don't have to do that. I'm not going to steal anymore."

"Said every thief ever."

That gets a short, grudging laugh out of him. But he still hesitates.

"Look, kid, either I take you home and you face the music with your parents, or I bring Officer Noblecky back over here. It's your call."

He kicks at the sidewalk again and curses under his breath. Then he hoists his backpack higher on his shoulder and meets my eyes. "Where's your car?"

• • •

When we get to my Mustang, Rory climbs into the backseat and buckles his seat belt without being told. He gives me his address—only about ten miles outside the city—and we head out.

"Is your name really Becker?" he asks after a few minutes.

I meet his eyes in the rearview mirror. "Yeah—Jake Becker." Then I ask a question of my own. "How old are you, kid?"

"I'll be ten in five months."

I nod slowly. "Also known as nine."

He smirks. "And you called me a smartass."

Otherwise, he's quiet during the drive, staring out the window. But after we turn off Rock Creek Parkway, when huge, ancient oak trees line the road and the street names turn to *Whitehaven*, *Foxboro*, and *Hampshire*, and the driveways become gated and long, Rory turns even more sullen. It comes off him in brooding, hostile waves, in the clench of his hand and the tensing of his shoulders.

"They're not gonna come down too hard on you, are they?"

I mean his parents. Just because he seems to be well-fed, clean, and injury free doesn't mean it's impossible that something more sinister might be waiting for him at home.

"No," he answers without fear. "I'll be fine."

When I pull up to Rory's address, the wrought-iron gate opens automatically. The extensive driveway is flanked by lampposts and cherry trees and curves around into a horseshoe. The house is a majestic brick Georgian, completely restored with black shutters and detailed white moldings around its fourteen windows. There's a three-car attached garage, a large front courtyard surrounded by a natural-stone wall, and bright green shrubbery.

I kill the engine and stare at the house, thinking he might be trying to pull one over on me. "You live here?"

"Yeah."

"Are you, like, the gardener's kid?"

Rory frowns with confusion. "No. It's my parents' house." Then, softer, under his breath, "Was . . ."

He doesn't elaborate but instead hops out of the car, backpack in tow. I take long strides to catch up and we stand before the massive oak door. I put my hand on the back of his neck, just to be ready in case he makes a run for it. Then I ring the doorbell.

A protracted string of yappy barks ensues immediately after. There's a shuffling from inside, then the door swings open.

And the air rushes out of my lungs.

She's five five, maybe five six, with long, toned legs in snug black leggings. The outline of a trim waist teases beneath the cotton blouse, with buttons at the top that strain to encase full, firm, perfect breasts. Her neck is elegant, creamy pale, and her face—Jesus—it puts the Victoria's Secret Angels to shame. A stubborn chin; high cheekbones; plump, ripe, gloss-free lips; an impish nose; and two ice-blue eyes that sparkle like fucking diamonds on a sunny winter day. Multifaceted auburn hair is piled high on her head, with a few escaping strands around her face. Dark-rimmed, square glasses frame those striking eyes, giving a sexy-academic, sultry-librarian kind of impression.

I try to swallow, but my mouth just went dry.

"Rory," she breathes with relief, focusing on the boy beside me. And then she's pissed. "Where have you been? You were supposed to be home hours ago! And why isn't your phone on?"

The kid pulls out of my grasp, walks across the black-and-white-tiled foyer, and marches straight up the stairs, not even looking at her.

"Rory! Hey!" she calls after him. Futilely.

Her knuckles turn white where they grip the door frame, then she turns to me. "Hello?"

It's more of a question than a greeting.

"Hi," I respond, just staring. Enjoying the view.

Fuck, I'm horny.

Then I shake my head, snapping out of the idiot stupor of being denied sex for too long.

I start again, extending my hand. "Hi. I'm Jake Becker. I'm an attorney." It's always good to volunteer this fact because—as with police officers—there's an instant trust that's afforded to those of us in legal professions, even if it's not always deserved.

"Chelsea McQuaid." My hand encapsulates her small one as she shakes it with a warm, firm grip.

"I drove Rory home."

Her head tilts and her lips purse with suspicious curiosity. "Really?"

"I need to speak with you about your son, Mrs. McQuaid," I tell her, going with the most logical connection between her and the would-be thief.

Her eyes examine me and I can see the judging wheels turning. Debating whether to, in this day and age, let an imposing, unknown man into her house. I have no doubt that my expensive suit and dark good looks help tip the scales in my favor.

"All right." She steps back. "Please come in, Mr. Becker."

I step over the threshold. "Jake, please." She closes the door behind me, reaching up to engage a child safety lock at the top. Then a tiny blur of long caramel-and-chocolate fur surges out from behind her and pounces on my shoes, sniffing and barking, sticking out its chest and snarling.

A clear case of small-dog syndrome if I ever saw one.

"It, stop it!" Chelsea scolds.

The corner of my mouth quirks. "Your dog's name is It?"

"Yeah." She smiles. And it's fucking stunning. "Cousin It. Like *The Addams Family*?"

It gets more riled, looking like a mop gone insane.

I meet her eyes. "About your son—"

"Nephew, actually. I'm Rory's aunt."

My ears perk up. Because by the look of her naked hand, there's a good chance she's Rory's *single* aunt.

Best news I've heard all damn day.

A baby's wail comes from another room, piercing and demanding. Chelsea turns her head. "Could you come with me? I have to . . ."

She's already walking and I'm right behind her.

We pass by the arched entryways of a library and a conservatory with a grand piano, then go into a spacious den with a huge fireplace and cathedral ceiling. The furnishings are tasteful and clean but in earth tones, warm. Dozens of framed photographs of children cover every wall. Chelsea pushes through a door into the kitchen, where the crying gets louder.

The kitchen is about the size of my whole apartment. It has hardwood floors, mahogany cabinets, and a granite-countered center island with a second sink, and it's chock-full of stainless-steel appliances. A round kitchen table for eight fits in an alcove backed by French doors that open out to a stone patio and garden, with a cobblestone path that leads to an inground pool farther back.

An infant seat sits inside a mesh portable crib beside the island with a vocal, unhappy passenger. "Here ya go, sweetie," Chelsea coos, bending over to pick up the pacifier that's fallen to the baby's stomach and plugging it back into his mouth.

At least I think it's a him—it's wearing dark blue pants and a shirt with boats on it, so, yeah, it's male. She caresses his blond, peach-fuzzy head and the crying is replaced with satisfied sucking.

An immense silver pot bubbles on the stove and the air smells of heat and broth.

"Hi!"

I turn to my right, where a toddler—this one definitely a girl, with golden wispy hair and a stained pink T-shirt—sits on the floor, surrounded by books and blocks.

"Hi," I answer, straight-faced.

She gets louder. "Hi!"

I nod back. "Hey."

Her face scrunches, her voice drops lower, and she leans forward like she's about to tell me something serious. But all that comes out is, "Hiiii."

"Is there something wrong with her?" I ask.

"No," Chelsea answers, sounding slightly affronted. "There's nothing wrong with Regan. She's two."

And Regan is back to smiling at me. "Hi."

"Doesn't she know any other words?"

"No. She's only two."

"Hi, hi, hi, hi!"

I give up and walk away.

"So, how can I reach Rory's parents? It's important that I talk to them."

Her face goes tight. Pained. "You can't. They . . . my brother and his wife were in a car accident almost two months ago. They passed away."

And all the pieces fall into place. The comments Rory made,

his unsubtle anger at the entire world. But it's the name that stands out most—the name and the accident. I point at her gently. "Robert McQuaid was your brother? The environmental lobbyist?"

She smiles, small and sad, and nods her head. "Did you know Robbie? DC's such a busy city, but I've gotten the impression it's like a small town too. Everybody knows everybody."

When it comes to political circles, and legal ones, it's exactly like that.

"No, I didn't know him. But . . . I heard good things. That he was honest, sincere. That's a rare thing around here."

And suddenly she seems younger somehow. Smaller and more . . . delicate. Is she on her own in this huge house with the kids? Just her, Rory, One Word, and Baby Boy?

Chelsea looks up from her hands. "I'm Rory's guardian, so whatever you were going to say to my brother and his wife, you can say to me."

I nod, refocusing. "Right. I drove Rory home because—"

But I don't get the chance to finish the sentence. Because the rumble of feet, like a stampede of rhinos, booms over our heads, cutting me off. Chelsea and I eye the ceiling—like it's about to fall down on us—as the sound travels, getting closer.

And there's screaming. The atom-splitting, banshees-from-hell kind of screaming.

"I'm gonna kill you!"

"I didn't do it!"

"Get back here!"

"It wasn't me!"

Even the two-year-old looks concerned.

The racket reverberates down the second staircase and spills out into the kitchen, and the two screeching, running kids who are making it do laps around the island like a fucked-up *Hunger Games* version of ring-around-the-rosy.

"I told you to stay out of my room!" one of them, a tall girl, yells. She's a curly-brown-haired predator, ready to pounce.

"I didn't do it!" the shorter one squeals, arms outstretched, searching for cover.

Jesus Christ, what kind of madhouse is this?

Chelsea steps between them, grabbing them both by their arms and keeping them separated. "That's enough!"

And now they're yelling at her, pleading their cases at the same time, each trying to be louder than the other. I can't make out what they're saying; it just sounds like: *hiss, blah, she, hiss, squeak*. But the aunt appears to speak the native tongue.

"I said enough!" She holds up her hands, bringing instant blessed silence.

It's impressive. There are sitting federal judges who can't rally that much respect in their own courtrooms.

"One at a time." She turns to the taller girl. "Riley, you first."

Riley's finger slashes the air like a saber. "She went in my room when I've told her a thousand times not to! *And* she went through my makeup and *ruined* my favorite lipstick!"

Chelsea's head turns to the smaller one, who, now that she's not a screaming lunatic, reminds me of a blond Shirley Temple.

"Rosaleen, go."

One Word and I watch eagerly, waiting for the rebuttal . . . but all she comes out with is:

"I didn't do it."

Which, in my professional opinion, wouldn't be a bad defense . . . *if* her mouth and chin weren't completely covered with thick, blazing pink, like she's Ronald McDonald's illegitimate daughter.

"You are such a—" Riley starts to yell.

But Chelsea's raised hand stops her cold. "Tut, tut—shush."

She scoops the little one—Rosaleen—up under her arms and perches her on the counter. "And I'd almost believe you," Chelsea tells her, plucking two baby wipes from a tub next to the sink, wiping the girl's chin, and showing her the pink-stained cloth, "except for the evidence all over your face."

Great minds think alike.

The little girl stares at the cloth with quarter-sized blue eyes. Then, like any defendant who knows she's nailed, she does the only thing she can—throws herself on the mercy of the court.

"I'm sorry, Riley."

Riley is unmoved. "That won't give me my lipstick back, you little brat!"

"I couldn't help myself!" she pleads.

And I unconsciously nod. That's it, kid—go with insanity. It's all you've got left.

"The lipstick was in there, calling to me . . ."

Voices. Voices are good. Always an easy sell.

Her hands delve into her blond curls, ruffling and tugging at them, until they're wild and crazed. "It made me nuts! It's so pink and pretty, I had to touch it!"

Chelsea closes her eyes and breathes deep, making those fabulous tits press against her blouse even more. I enjoy the show, praying for a button to pop or for the sink to spontaneously spurt water all over that white shirt.

A guy can dream.

"Riley, what are your chores this week?"

"I have to set the table for dinner."

Her voice is kind but firm. "Okay. Rosaleen, you'll do your sister's chores for the rest of the week. And when you get your allowance on Sunday, you'll use it to replace the lipstick you ruined. Understood?"

"Okay. Sorry, Riley."

Chelsea runs a tender hand through Rosaleen's messy curls. "Now, go upstairs and wash your face, then come set the table."

With a nod, she hops off the counter and skips past me up the steps.

Her sister vehemently objects. "That's it? That's all you're doing to her?"

Chelsea sighs, a little annoyed. “She’s seven, Riley. What do you want me to do—beat her with a stick?”

“It’s not fair!” she bellows. *So much* fucking louder than necessary.

“Sometimes life isn’t. The sooner you understand that, the better off you’ll be.”

Riley smacks the counter. “I hate this family!”

In a whirl of brown hair and fury, she stomps up the stairs, glaring at *me* along the way. Like I ruined her fucking lipstick.

“Sweet girl,” I tell Chelsea dryly.

“She’s fourteen. It’s a tough age.” She looks wistfully up the steps. “She’ll be human again . . . eventually.”

5

Sorry about that," Chelsea says, grabbing a block that was kicked across the floor during the skirmish and handing it to the toddler. Next she walks back to the stove, dumping a heap of chopped greens from a colander into the boiling pot. Her movements are effortlessly graceful, and I wonder if she's a dancer. "You started to tell me about Rory?"

"Right. He—"

But of course I don't get to tell her. That would be too easy.

Instead I'm cut off by the appearance of a young boy walking through the kitchen door—a boy with Rory's face. He's slightly thinner, a little taller, with round, wire-rimmed Harry Potter glasses perched on his nose.

I can't keep the horror out of my tone. "There's *two* of him?"

Chelsea grins. "If that's your way of asking if Rory has a twin, then the answer is yes."

"I see you've met my brother," the boy says, apparently used to this reaction. "Don't judge me just because we share the same DNA. You've heard the term 'evil genius'?"

"Yeah."

"Rory's the evil. I'm the genius."

"How many kids live in this house exactly?" I ask the aunt.

It's starting to feel like they're cockroaches—see one, and you can bet there's fifty more crawling around inside the walls. I shiver at the thought.

"Six."

Six? I'm guessing Robert McQuaid didn't have many hobbies.

The boy retrieves a black skateboard from the corner and tells his aunt, "I'm going to Walter's next door."

"Okay. Make sure you put your helmet on, Raymond."

The kid groans. "It makes me look like a dork."

"And when you're in a coma after fracturing your skull on the pavement, you think you'll look . . . cool?"

Rory's smartassness is obviously genetic.

"No," Raymond whines. "It's just . . ." He turns to me. "You're a guy—you understand what I mean. Explain it to her."

"Yes"—Chelsea crosses her arms—"explain to me how having a penis excuses you from the laws of gravity."

"Oh my god!" Raymond hisses, his ears and cheeks blooming fire-engine red. "Don't say that."

"What?" She looks from him to me. "What'd I say?"

I shrug because I have no fucking clue.

"Penis?" she guesses.

And Raymond does a fabulous impression of a tomato. "Oh my god! You're so humiliating!" He grabs his skateboard and flees.

"Helmet, Raymond!" Chelsea calls. "Or that skateboard will be roasting in the fireplace tonight!"

She looks at me with a sigh and a smile. "It's the little joys that get me through the day."

And I have the urge to laugh. Chelsea's not only hot, she's . . . entertaining, too.

She moves back to the stove and starts to lift the heavy gargantuan pot, and I quickly step closer and take it from her hands. "I got it."

"Thank you." She directs me to a ceramic bowl on the counter and I carefully pour the hot broth, with its white chunks and strips of green, into the bowl. Then we stand just inches apart, those crystal-blue beauties fixed on me.

"So . . . how did you meet my nephew, Mr. Becker?"

I give it to her straight, like ripping off a Band-Aid. "He stole my wallet, Chelsea. Right on the street. Bumped into me, slipped his hand in my pocket, and then took off."

Her eyes slide closed and her shoulders hunch. "Oh." After a moment, she rubs her forehead, then lifts her chin and looks up at me. "I am so, so sorry."

I wave my hand. "It's okay."

Her voice goes soft, with a ring of sorrow. "He's taken it really hard. I mean, they all have, of course, but Rory is just so . . ."

"Angry," I say, finishing for her.

She nods. "Yeah. Angry." Her voice drops, a trace of hurt seeping in. "Especially at me. It's like . . . he resents me. Because I'm here and they're not."

"How old are you? If you don't mind me asking."

"Twenty-six."

"Do you have any help? Your parents? Friends?"

Rosaleen walks back into the kitchen as her aunt shakes her head. "My parents passed away a few years ago. All my friends are back in California. I was in grad school there . . . before . . ."

Her voice trails off, eyes on her niece as she grabs a stack of plates from the counter.

"When I first moved in, I called an agency for a part-time nanny, but—"

"But she was a bitch," Rosaleen interjects.

"Hey!" Chelsea's head turns sharply. "Don't talk like that."

"That's what Riley said."

"Well, don't you say it."

As soon as the girl walks out to set the table, Chelsea turns to me.

"She *was* a bitch. I wouldn't leave Cousin It with her, never mind the kids."

"What about social services?"

She shakes her head. "Our social worker is nice, she tries to help, but there's all this administrative stuff. Required checklists and meetings, surprise inspections and interviews, sometimes it feels like they're just waiting for me to mess up. Like they don't think I can do it."

"Can you?" I ask softly.

And those gorgeous eyes burn with determination. "I have to. They're all I have left."

"You mean, *you're* all *they* have left," I correct her.

Her shoulder lifts and there's an exquisite sadness in her smile. "That, too."

I rub the back of my neck. "You should get the kid in therapy, Chelsea."

Normally I wouldn't suggest such a thing, but Brent's kind of made a believer out of me. Particularly when it comes to childhood traumas. He swears that if he'd had to deal with the loss of his leg without therapy, he would've ended up a miserable, raging alcoholic.

"I know." She adjusts the fuck-me glasses. "It's on the list. As soon as I get a minute to research it, I'll find a good therapist for all of them."

"The list?" I ask.

She points to the refrigerator, where a magnet holds a handwritten list of about a thousand items. "My sister-in-law, Rachel, was the ultimate multitasker. And she had a list for everything. So I started one too. Those are all the things I have to do, as soon as possible."

A to-do list that never gets smaller—that may be my new definition of hell.

"Okay." I did what I came for. Now he's her problem—they're all her problem. Not mine. "Well, I should get going."

Her head tilts and a delicate wisp of hair falls across her cheek.

"Thank you so much for bringing him home. For not pressing charges. I . . . would you like to stay for dinner? I feel like it's the least I could do."

I glance at the bowl. "What are you having?"

"Miso soup and grilled cheese sandwiches."

Sounds like something they serve in prison to cut down on costs.

"No thanks. I have some work to finish up . . . and I'm more of a meat-and-potatoes kind of guy."

Chelsea walks with me out of the kitchen toward the front door. "Well, thank you again, Mr. Becker."

We pause, facing each other on the shiny black-and-white-tiled foyer floor. And I feel four sets of eyes on the landing above us—watching, listening, burning holes in the back of my head.

But—screw it—why not?

I slip a business card from my wallet. "Here's my card." Chelsea takes it, looking down at the raised black print, stroking her fingertip against one corner. "If you have a free night, want to grab some dinner, a drink or . . . something . . ."

The oldest girl—the one who hates her family—lets out a short snort of disbelief. "Did you just ask her out on a date?"

I keep my eyes on Chelsea's face. "Yeah—I did."

And her cheeks turn the loveliest shade of pink.

Then it's blond Shirley Temple's turn. "But you're so old!"

I tear my eyes from Chelsea's blush to blast the kid with a grumpy brow.

"I'm thirty."

The grumpy brow fails to intimidate.

"Thirty!" Her hands go to her hips. "Do you have grandchildren?"

A laugh bubbles in my chest but doesn't make it past my lips. This kid's a piece of work.

"Thirty is not old enough to have grandchildren, Rosaleen," Chelsea explains. Her attention swings back to me and her voice drops lower.

"I doubt I'll have a free night any time soon, but . . . it's nice to be asked."

"Right." I nod. "Good night, Chelsea." A fleeting look at the four peering faces has me adding, "And . . . good luck."

She's definitely going to need it.

6

On Saturday, I take Brent up on his offer to set up a double date. The way I look at it, this dating thing is kind of like fishing. The more lines you toss out, the greater the likelihood you'll bag a catch that's edible. When you're hungry—and I'm definitely hungry—even a battered trout seems appetizing.

And Lucy Patterson's friend—a fellow attorney at Emblem & Glock—is most definitely not a trout. She's cute. Short, dark hair; tall, toned, athletic body—she mentioned she's an avid tennis player, and from the looks of her ass, she wasn't bullshitting. It turns out to be a pleasant evening, but not an I-can't-wait-to-get-in-your-pants-let's-fuck-in-the-alley-behind-the-bar kind of turn-on. The four of us meet up at a local place, eat appetizers, and go through a few pitchers of beer. Because we share career paths—deal with the same judges and prosecutors and similar uptight bosses—we mostly talk shop. It kind of feels like a casual business meeting, and before we part on the sidewalk outside the bar, we all agree to get together again next weekend.

For the apparently crucial date number two.

And if I'm lucky, maybe I'll get my dick wet by the end of the month.

Great.

When I get home, I can't stop my thoughts from turning long and hard to a certain young, auburn-haired aunt. Emphasis on the word *hard.*

She was feisty—I liked that. Strong-minded but . . . definitely soft in that attractive, feminine way.

She was also way in over her fucking head.

I wonder how she handled Rory after I left—did she ground the little smartass? Make him do extra chores, maybe, like weeding the garden or mowing the lawn? I can say from experience, manual labor leaves a bitch of an impression on even the most stubborn punks. And their lawn was massive.

Grabbing my laptop, I Google Chelsea's brother, Robert, for reasons I can't explain. But the pull of information literally at my fingertips is too strong to resist.

Most lobbyists are bottom-feeders. Smarmy, self-important deal makers who are drunk on their power over the powerful—not unlike the pencil pushers who run the Department of Motor Vehicles. But, as I told his sister, Robert McQuaid had a reputation as a straight shooter. A good guy who genuinely cared about the cause he was paid to champion.

There's a wealth of information about his career—and his death. He was at a charity dinner with his college sweetheart turned wife of seventeen years, Rachel. On their way home, a truck driver fell asleep at the wheel and veered into their lane, too quickly to avoid a head-on collision. His obituary lists his professional accomplishments and his survivors: six children, Riley, Rory, Raymond, Rosaleen, Regan, and Ronan, as well as a sister, Chelsea, of Berkeley, California. There are pictures—a few of the kids through the years, with their attractive parents at various family-friendly events around DC. And one of Chelsea, head bowed, in a black dress and large dark glasses, beside a double grave site. Looking tragically beautiful.

And very much alone.

Feeling like a fucking creeper, I end up closing my laptop and going to bed.

• • •

Like I said before, I'm a fan of routine. Strict time management and an impenetrable schedule. I spend Sunday morning at Sofia and Stanton's, having a breakfast of coffee and delicious Brazilian cheese balls that she makes so very well. Brent jokes about popping my dating cherry and recounts our mutually sexless evening. Stanton mentions that Presley has a few days off from school next week and is coming for a visit.

It's just after noon when I leave their town house and head straight for the Brookside Retirement Home, like I do every Sunday. Because that crotchety old judge who pulled my fifteen-year-old ass out of the fire—who literally saved my life, straightened me out, and made me believe I could actually be a man of significance? That's where he is.

I don't like being beholden to anyone. I don't have many debts. But the few I do owe, I gladly pay.

"Good afternoon, Jake."

"Hi, Mildred."

"Hey, Becker."

"How's it going, Jimmy?"

It's important to stay in the good graces of the lower staff at any facility—be it a hospital, law firm, school, or retirement home. They're the ones who do the actual work, and if shady shit is going down, they'll be the ones who let the cat out of the bag, while the owner and upper-echelon administrators are focused on damage control. The staff at Brookside and I are on a first-name basis. I sign in at the front desk and greet the orderlies and nurses traveling down the hall, some carrying trays of medication to the private rooms, others pushing their feeble charges in wheelchairs to their physical therapy sessions, art classes, or daily afternoon bingo games.

I've played bingo with these senior citizens. They take that shit seriously. They might be old, but if you get I-22 when they were waiting for B-6? They'll bust your fucking kneecaps as quick as any backstreet bookie, without an ounce of remorse.

Brookside is a private facility, top of the line. Its rooms are tasteful, generically comfortable, like a hotel chain. Its employees are educated and well compensated, so they treat the clients here with the respect, care, and dignity they deserve. Other places, for those on public assistance, those who don't have pensions or family with the funds to pay, they're . . . well . . . let's just say there's nothing golden about spending your "golden years" in a damn warehouse.

I step into the Judge's sunlit room. He's in a leather reading chair by the window, dressed in tan slacks and a burgundy sweater, brown loafers on his feet. His thick, gray hair is clean and combed neatly.

His name is Atticus Faulkner, but to me, he's the Judge. He wasn't always the way he is today. Ten years ago, he cut an imposing figure—tall, strong for his seventy years, and active, with green eyes that seemed to see straight into your soul. He was a living, breathing lie detector with a brilliantly intimidating legal mind.

And he was my hero.

Everything I wanted to be. Everything my real father never was.

But life's a bitch sometimes. Six years ago, he was diagnosed with advanced Alzheimer's. He'd done an impeccable job of covering the early signs. Little tricks—hidden notes and reminders—so no one could tell he didn't know what day it was. Sometimes he'd walk home from the courthouse, but only because he couldn't remember where he'd parked his car. Then, later, he'd spend hours in a coffee shop because he'd forgotten his address.

I was busy then—practically just out of law school—making my bones. I should've seen that something was off, but I missed it. So, eventually, when he didn't have any other choice and told me what was going on, it felt like things went downhill really fast. And the hard-ass I knew, the man I feared in the best sense of the word, just . . . slipped away, practically overnight.

The Judge was a lifelong bachelor. Married to his work, respected and esteemed by friends and enemies alike. No children, just a string of "lady friends"—some younger than others, some smarter than others, but all of them gorgeous. And all of them casual. A good time.

Casual lady friends aren't usually interested in visiting a man who no longer recognizes them, who can no longer keep them entertained with a handsome face, a sharp wit, and amusing stories. So I'm the Judge's only regular guest. Which means come hell, high water, sweltering temperatures, or freak blizzard, I'm here, every single week.

I read him the paper—keep him up to speed on the intrigue and ridiculousness of Washington, DC. Sometimes I talk to him about my cases, the fucking lowlifes I keep out of prison. Most of the time he just listens, nods, tells me how interesting the story sounds without any real understanding. But every once in a while, there's a spark, a glint of recognition in his eyes; sometimes it lasts a minute, sometimes ten, but for that brief time, he's himself again. He remembers me. It's good to know that even on the worst of days, he's in there, somewhere.

Today he turns from gazing out the window when I walk in and watches as I pull up a chair from across the room and sit down. "Good afternoon, Judge. How's it going?"

"It's going well, thank you. How are you?" His tone is hesitant and polite. The way you'd speak to a stranger—and right now, that's what I am to him.

"I'm doing good." I unfold the newspaper from under my arm. "The Supreme Court heard oral arguments on Thursday for that health care case. We talked about it last week, do you remember?"

His eyes squint and his finger presses against the lines surrounding his lips, his hand trembling slightly. "No, I can't recall. Which case was it?"

I open to the front page. "I'll read it to you. It's a good article. Lays it all out."

He leans forward attentively, and I begin to read.

• • •

After the newspaper, we kick back and watch the basketball game. The judge grew up on the south side of Boston, so he's a die-hard Celtics fan. Or . . . he used to be. As the game winds down, I talk about my week—Milton Bradley and the epic-fail dinner with Camille. And then I tell him about Rory McQuaid.

"He gets halfway down the block, looks me right in the eyes, and gives me the finger." I chuckle, because it seems a lot funnier now. "Little bastard."

The Judge smiles. "I knew a boy like that once."

My chuckles quiet and my smile slows. "Did you?"

His whole face lights up. "Oh yes! He was delightful. Smart and stubborn—a real tough nut to crack—with gray eyes like a storm cloud. He got into some trouble, and that young boy stood before my bench with his chin raised, just daring me to send him away. Like he was ready to spit in the devil's face. But I could see, deep down, he was terrified."

And I had been. For the first time in my life, I knew what real fear tasted like.

"There was something special about him, a diamond in the rough. So I had him serve his probation under my supervision. For three years, I owned that kid."

Yep, three long years.

"I had to teach him to control his temper. He had a short fuse. So I started with the lawn. Each time he finished mowing, hot and sweaty, I'd go out and inspect his work." He wags his finger. "And I always found spots that he missed. So I'd make him . . ." He starts to cackle, the son of a bitch. "I'd make him go back over the whole lawn with . . . with . . ."

"Garden shears," I fill in for him.

"Yes! Garden shears." He laughs loud. "Oh, he hated me those first few months. Probably thought of ten different ways to murder me."

It was closer to twenty.

"After the yard work, I taught him how to organize, how to repair things around the house. It was good for him—channeling all that energy. And even though he was a very hard worker, I'd always say, 'Do it right . . .' "

Or don't bother.

" '. . . or don't bother.' Then I started to teach him about the work I did. How to research, how to read the statutes. After his probation was up, I offered him a job. A paid intern." The Judge taps his chin and shakes his head. "He could look at a page once and remember every word. So intuitive, great instincts." He sighs.

Then he covers my hand with his age-spotted one. "Do you think . . . do you think you could find him for me?"

And I can't breathe past the lump that clogs my throat.

"I'd like to make sure that boy's all right. See if he needs anything." His green eyes earnestly look into mine.

I clear my throat loudly. "Um . . . I, ah . . . I did find him for you. I checked up on him. He's doing really well—you don't have to worry. He's on his way to making partner. And he . . . asked me to tell you how grateful he is, for everything you did for him. All the things you taught him." I blink against the burn in my eyes. "He hopes . . . he wants to make you proud."

The Judge gives me a peaceful, relieved smile. "I'm sure I would be proud. He was always a good boy."

The two of us fall quiet again, watching the game. Until there's a knock on the open bedroom door. And Marietta—one of the volunteers here—walks in with a smile and a tray of dinner for the Judge.

"Good evening, Mr. Atticus and Jake. How you are you two doin' tonight?"

Marietta is originally from Jamaica, with large midnight eyes, dark skin, and long black hair that falls in a cascade of braids down her back. Her father was once a resident here, and after he died a few years ago, she started volunteering.

"Hey, Marietta."

She sets the tray of food down on a corner table with wheels and brings it between us.

"How was his week?" I ask her quietly, the judge's attention still on the television.

"Not too bad," she tells me. "He was agitated Wednesday and Thursday night—couldn't settle down enough to sleep. So the doctor changed his bedtime medication. He's been good since then."

I nod and grasp his shoulder. "Judge." He turns my way and I gesture to the food. "It's dinnertime."

He looks over the meal and makes a face. "I'm not hungry."

I shake my head. "Don't bust my balls, old man. You need to eat." I stir the beef stew in the bowl. "I know it's not Smith and Wollensky, but it smells good." I push it closer to him. "Dig in."

His hand trembles as he slowly picks up the spoon and shovels in a mouthful of beef and carrot. While he chews, he glances at the tray, eyeing a dish of chocolate pudding covered with thick whipped cream under clear plastic wrapping.

"I want that." He points.

"You can have the pudding after you finish your dinner," I say automatically.

When he brings another shaky spoonful to his mouth, a bit of stew clings to his lower lip and chin. I pick up his napkin and gently wipe his face before it drips on his clothes.

"It's really good for him that you're here, that you spend time with him," Marietta tells me, smiling. "It means a lot."

I shrug. "It's not a big deal. I'm just . . . working through a lifetime of favors I'll never be able to return."

The Judge grins at me and I smile back. "Besides," I tell Marietta, "he doesn't have anyone."

She puts her hand on my shoulder and squeezes. "Of course he does. He has you."

• • •

Wednesday is a slow day. I lean back in my desk chair and peer out the window at the sun-filled street below. A frustrated dog walker struggles with three four-legged clients as they tangle their leashes, fighting for the lead. A double-decker tourist bus rumbles past, leaving a cloud of black exhaust in its wake. A jogging father pushes an orange running stroller; he nearly takes out one of the yapping dogs but turns onto the grass at the last second.

Maybe it's the baby in the stroller, maybe it's the long-haired, rug-like dogs—maybe it's the fact that I haven't gotten any in almost three weeks—but the enticing image of Chelsea McQuaid slides into my mind.

Again.

It's the sole image I've conjured every single time I've jerked off—which has been pathetically often.

Those striking blue eyes; the quick-to-smile pink lips; her long, pale neck, which begged to be licked; her lithe limbs, which I just bet are oh so flexible; and most important, her firm, perfectly sized tits. I mentally kick myself for not getting her number.

She's too old—too hot—to be a virgin at twenty-six, but there was something about her that seemed . . . pure. Untouched. Undiscovered. And that's a course I would love to chart.

I rub my eyes. I need to get laid. This getting-to-know-a-woman-first shit is turning out to be a bigger hassle than I ever anticipated. Is risking contraction of an STD really such a big deal?

And then I remember how it felt waiting for those test results. The sharp, cold terror of being saddled with a disease—possibly for life. Or, even scarier, with one that could cut my valuable life short. Hell yes—it's a big deal.

No fuck—no matter how spectacular—is worth dying for.

That should be the tagline in every high school safe-sex campaign.

My secretary opens my office door, and I'm grateful for the distraction . . . until she informs me an unscheduled client is here asking to see me. Remembering how this went down the last time, I'm about to tell Mrs. Higgens to tell them to fuck off.

Until she adds, "Miss Chelsea McQuaid is her name, Jake. And she's got a whole brood of little ones with her."

My smile is wide and slow and completely gratified. If I believed in signs, this would be a big, flashing neon one.

I straighten my tie. "Show them in, Mrs. Higgens."

7

Mrs. Higgens heads out of the office and a few moments later, Chelsea and her fidgeting, noisy gaggle of nieces and nephews come into my office. She's wearing a casual outfit—definitely "mommy wear," but on that body it screams sexy. A dark green sweater that highlights the red in her auburn hair. Snug blue jeans tucked into high brown boots accent those endless legs—and the tight swell of her supple ass. That's a pleasant surprise—I didn't notice her ass the first time we met, but it's fucking gorgeous.

She adjusts her grip on the baby carrier and her smile is strained. "Hello, Mr. Becker."

I stand up behind my desk. "Chelsea, it's good to see you again. What brings you . . ."

My eyes scan each of the faces that crowd my office, and I realize one is missing.

"Where's Rory?"

Chelsea sighs. Before she can speak, the grouchy girl—fourteen-year-old Riley—answers for her. "The idiot got arrested. He stole a car."

"A car?"

In a week, the little shit went from mugging to grand theft auto. That escalated quickly.

The small towheaded one, Rosaleen, continues. "And then he crashed it."

The two-year-old supplies sound effects. "Brooocshhh."

The smart one, Raymond, adds, "And not just any car—a Ferrari 458 Italia Limited Edition. The starting price is around nine hundred thousand dollars."

I look to Chelsea, who nods. "Yeah, that's pretty much the whole story. He's in juvenile detention—serious trouble this time."

This time implies there's been other times—my almost-robbery notwithstanding.

Jesus Christ, kid.

Chelsea explains in a strained voice, "My brother has dozens of attorneys in his contact list, but none of them are defense attorneys. I had your card . . . and you seem like a good lawyer."

Out of curiosity, I ask, "What makes you think I'm good?"

She raises her chin and meets my eyes. "You look like a man who knows how to win a fight. That's what I need—what Rory needs."

I take a few moments to think—to plan.

Chelsea must interpret my silence as rejection, because her voice turns almost pleading. "I don't know what your typical retainer is, but I can afford—"

My lifted finger stops her. "I don't think that's going to be necessary. Wait here." Then I point to Raymond. "Come with me." And to the oldest girl. "You too, Smiley."

As they follow me out the door, the brooding teen corrects me. "My name is Riley."

"I know. But I'm going to call you Smiley."

"Why?" she asks, like it's the stupidest, most vile thing she's ever heard.

I smirk. "Because you're not."

Let the eye-rolling commence.

I lead them into the office next door. Sofia Santos's head is bent over her desk, her perfectly manicured hands scribbling rapid notes on a document. She looks up as we enter.

"Hey, Sofia." I hook my thumb at the sullen girl behind me. "This is Smiley McQuaid—her aunt is a new client and we have to head downtown for a few hours. Is it okay if she hangs with you?"

Stanton's daughter, Presley, is almost thirteen. I figure if anyone is adept at dealing with a teenage female, it's Sofia.

"Sure. I'll be here all afternoon."

Riley moves to my side. "My name is *Riley*."

Sofia smiles. "Hi, Riley." Then she points to a chair in the corner, next to a wall outlet. "The phone charger's over there."

Riley almost cracks a grin. *Almost.* "Swag."

I turn to Sofia's office companion, who's staring at images on his laptop. "Brent, this is Raymond. Raymond, Brent. Can you keep him out of trouble for a few hours?"

Brent nods. Then, with the excitement of a boy allowed to watch his first R-rated horror movie, he asks Raymond, "You want to see pictures of blood splatter?"

The boy steps forward. "Is it as cool as it sounds?"

"Waaay cooler."

"Sure!"

And my work here is done.

I pop my head back into my office and crook my finger at Rosaleen. She looks up at her aunt, who nods permission, and Rosaleen steps out to join me in front of Mrs. Higgens's desk.

"Mrs. Higgens, this is Rosaleen. Can you mind her for a bit while her aunt and I head to the courthouse?"

Rosaleen looks down shyly, and Mrs. Higgens pulls up a chair beside her. "Of course. I have a granddaughter about your age, Rosaleen. I keep coloring books right here for when she visits. Do you like to color?"

Rosaleen nods eagerly, climbing into the chair.

I stride back into my office, where Chelsea and the two youngest rug rats await. I point at them. "You two look like the real troublemakers in the group, so you're coming with us."

"Hi!" the two-year-old replies with a deceptively sweet smile.

"Oh no, you're not roping me into that again."

I take the baby carrier from Chelsea's hands—and almost drop the thing. "Wow," I say, glancing down. "You're heavier than you look." He gurgles back with a mouth full of drool.

I turn to Chelsea. "You grab Thing One. Let's go."

Her voice stops me. It's a whisper, quiet and inquisitive.

"Jake?"

It's the first time she's said my name. One small syllable that makes my gut tighten. That makes me want to hear her say it again—in a moan, a gasp. A pleasure-spiked scream.

"Can I ask you something before we go?"

"Sure."

She searches my face with an honest curiosity that could pierce body armor. "If it's not the money . . . why are you helping us?"

It's an interesting question. I'm not the noble type. I'm more of an "every man for himself" kind of guy. So why the hell *am* I helping them?

Because I want in her pants, of course. Doing Chelsea a favor is the most direct route to doing her. Really not that complicated.

I shrug. "I'm a sucker for a lost cause."

And because I just can't hold back any longer, I reach out one hand and gently stroke the ivory skin of her cheek. It's softer than I ever could've imagined.

"And for a pretty face."

• • •

We walk out to the parking garage and as Chelsea buckles the kids into their seats, I check out her truck. Her gigantically large dark blue truck. She notices my gaze and remarks, "It's my brother's truck."

I lift an eyebrow. "Your brother—the environmental lobbyist—drove a gas-guzzling Yukon XL?"

She climbs up into the driver's seat. "With six kids, a bicycle wasn't gonna cut it."

I give her directions to the Moultrie Courthouse, where Rory was taken after his arrest this morning. I don't have a lot of experience in family court, but I'm familiar enough with the process to fill her in.

"Rory will be assigned a probation officer who'll review the charges and his history, and make a recommendation to the OAG. The probation officer decides whether he's released to you today or has to remain at the Youth Services Center until trial. They're also the ones I'll talk plea deal with."

The good news is, I know one of the probation officers at Moultrie intimately. We used to bang frequently until she got engaged. Our parting terms were friendly.

A soft V forms on Chelsea's forehead. "The OAG?"

"Office of the Attorney General. That's who would prosecute his case, but don't worry—it's not going that far."

Juvenile cases are very different from adult ones. The system still has hope for delinquents—it's all about rehabilitation and redemption. Saving them before they've gone too far down that dark, wrong road to nowhere. In criminal courts, the main question is, *did* you do it? In family court, it's all about *why* you did it. An orphaned nine-year-old dealing with his parents' deaths by stealing a car will garner a shitload more leniency than an eighteen-year-old boosting a joyride.

The Moultrie Courthouse is an intimidating concrete building with a cavernous maze of hallways. After passing through security, we're ushered into a waiting room with a dozen nondescript tables and chairs scattered around and vending machines along one wall. A few other visitors occupy the room, heads huddled, speaking in hushed whispers.

Chelsea and I sit at an empty table. I put the infant carrier with its sleeping cargo on the table, and the blond, baby-haired Regan squirms on her lap. A guard opens a door across the room and walks in with Rory, who's still wearing his school uniform: tan slacks, a white button-down shirt, a navy blazer.

His young lips are set in a hard frown, his dark blue eyes so full of resentment you can practically hear the "screw you" thoughts. This is not the face of a sad, little soul who knows he messed up—it's the face of an angry cherub, desperately trying to look badass, who'd rather go down in flames than admit he was wrong.

For a second, I reconsider helping him—a few days in juvenile detention could be just what the doctor ordered.

But then Chelsea wraps her arm around him and kisses his forehead, looking both elated with relief and like she wants to strangle him. "Thank god you're okay! Everything's going to be all right, Rory, don't be scared. What the hell were you thinking? A car? You're *never* leaving your room again—ever!"

I lean back in my chair, just watching.

He brushes her off with a rough shrug. "Get off. I'm fine. It's not a big deal."

"Not a big deal?" She grimaces, and I see a flash of hurt feelings, too. "You could've killed yourself—or someone else."

"Well, I didn't, okay? So stop freaking out."

I've seen enough.

"Chelsea, go get Regan a soda or juice." I pull a couple of bills from my wallet and hand them to her. She hesitates. I tilt my head toward Rory. "Give us a minute."

Still looking unsure, she sets the two-year-old on her feet and leads her away.

Once we're alone, Rory sits down. "What are you doing here?"

"Your aunt wanted a good lawyer. Lucky for you, I'm the best—and I happened to have the afternoon free."

"Whatever."

I pin him with an assessing stare. "You're in deep shit, kid."

So sure he knows everything, he scoffs, "I'm nine. What's the worst they can do to me?"

"Keep you here for the next nine years. At least," I tell him simply.

For the first time since he walked into the room, his confidence wavers. His cheeks bloom nervous pink and his voice rises half an octave as he says, "It's not so bad here."

It's a tiny crack in the façade—but still a crack.

I don't waste time telling him he's full of shit. I lean forward and explain, "Here's what's gonna happen. I'm going to call your aunt back over, and you're going to apologize for the way you spoke to her."

He wasn't expecting that. "Why?"

"Because she doesn't deserve it."

He lowers his eyes, almost ashamed. Maybe there's hope for the punk yet.

"Then you're going to sit there"—I point at him—"and let her hug you and kiss you all she wants."

His chin rises, not ready to give up the fight. "And what if I don't?"

I look him right in the eyes. "Then I'll let you rot in here."

And I will.

He doesn't look happy, doesn't like being backed into a corner. He wants to come out swinging—to do the opposite of what I'm ordering, simply because it's an order.

I know what he's feeling. I know this kid through and through.

He needs an out—a way to give up the battle without feeling like he's lost the war. So I give him one.

"You don't need to show me how tough you are, Rory—I can see it. I was a lot like you when I was your age—a tough, pissed-off little asshole. The difference is, I was smart enough not to shit on the people who cared about me." I raise my eyebrows. "Are you?"

He watches me. Looks deep inside with that sixth sense that all children have, to see if I'm being straight with him or just fucking patronizing. After a moment, he gives the briefest of nods and says in a small voice, "Okay. I'll apologize to Aunt Chelsea. And I'll let her kiss and hug me if it makes her happy."

I smile. "Good. Smart *and* tough. I like you more already, kid."

• • •

I leave Chelsea with the kids and head upstairs to the probation offices. I knock on Lisa DiMaggio's door, even though it's open. She swivels around in her desk chair, her long blond hair fanning out behind her.

"Jake Becker." She stands, giving me a perfect view of tan, toned legs beneath her black skirt, and hugs me. Parting on friendly terms most definitely has its benefits. "What are you doing in my neck of the woods?" she asks, stepping back with a smile. "Or is this a social call?"

"I'm here about a client."

"Since when do you play in family court?"

"Long story." I shrug. "And its name is Rory McQuaid."

"Ah." She retrieves a file from her desk. "My car thief. I did his intake this morning. Said he took the car because, and I quote, he 'wanted to see if driving was as easy as Mario Kart.'" She shakes her head. "Kids these days."

I lean back against the wall. "That's not why he took the car. There are extenuating circumstances."

"Enlighten me. I haven't had a chance to interview the parents yet."

"The parents are dead," I tell her. "Robert and Rachel McQuaid were killed in a horrific crash two months ago, leaving Rory and his *five* brothers and sisters in the care of their aunt—their only living relative."

She sits down in her chair. "Jesus."

"The kid's been dealt a shitty hand and he's not dealing with it well. But he doesn't belong in lockup. Talk to his social worker; I'll bet my left nut he was a saint until his parents died."

"That's really saying something—I know how precious your nuts are to you."

I nod.

"Unfortunately," Lisa sighs, "Rory picked the wrong person's car to steal." She names a cranky, influential former presidential hopeful. "And he wants the boy's ass in a sling."

"Fuck that," I growl. "Besides, a public servant has no business owning a car like that."

I don't know if it's because I have a hard-on for his aunt or because he reminds me so much of myself, but if anyone wants a piece of that kid they'll have to come through me first.

"Okay," Lisa says. "Then what are you offering?"

"Court-mandated therapy, once a week. Monthly progress reports."

"Twice a week," she counters. "And I want to pick the therapist. No feel-good quacks permitted."

"Done."

Lisa's gaze travels over me, head to crotch. "I'm surprised by you, Jake. I don't remember you being so . . . soft."

I move forward, bracing my hands on the arms of her chair—caging her in. " 'Soft' isn't in my vocabulary—I'm still as hard as they come." I smirk. "And after."

Her eyes settle on my mouth. "Good to hear. Particularly since Ted and I broke up." She holds up her ringless left hand.

Lisa definitely falls under the "known" category, which means no awkward first-date dinner conversation, no twenty goddamn questions that I don't want to ask, let alone answer. Nope—it'll be straight to the fucking.

Excellent.

"It's a long story," she says. "Which I'm sure you have no interest in hearing."

Yes, Lisa knows me well.

"You still like tequila?" I ask.

"Absolutely. You still have my number?"

"I do."

Her smile is slow and full of promise. "Good. Use it."

I stand up and walk toward the door. "I'll do that."

"And I'll get started on the paperwork."

• • •

A few hours later, after approval from child services and a quick compulsory appearance before an indifferent judge, Rory walks out of the courthouse with us. We head back to my office to gather his many siblings. They all seem happy to see him—if the affectionate "stupid idiot" and eager questions about his stay in "jail" are any indication. The sky is dark by the time I escort Chelsea and her charges back out to her car. I wait next to the driver's-side door as she gets them loaded and buckled in.

Then she comes around and stands in front of me, all warm eyes and soft gratitude. And I'm struck again by the smooth flawlessness of her skin beneath the glow of the streetlight.

Fucking gorgeous.

This close, I notice the adorable dusting of freckles across the bridge of that pert nose and wonder if she has them anywhere else. It'll take a slow, exhaustive search to find out. And I'm just the guy for the job.

She pushes her hair behind her ear. "Thank you, Jake, so much. I don't know what I would've—"

"Aunt Chelsea, I'm starving!"

"Can we get McDonald's?"

"Do you know what they put in McDonald's? Even insects won't eat it."

"Shut up, Raymond! Don't ruin fast food for me!"

"You shut up!"

"No, *you* shut up!"

"Aunt Chelsea!"

"Hiiiiiii!"

I can't help but laugh. And wonder if she owns earplugs.

Chelsea blows out a breath through her perfect, smiling lips. "I should go before they start eating each other."

"That might not be a bad thing. There are enough of them to spare."

She shakes her head and climbs into the truck, then rolls down the window to say, "Thank you again. I owe you, Jake."

I tap the side of the truck as she slowly pulls away. "Yes, you do."

And that's a debt I can't wait to collect.

Soon.

8

Scorching lips suck at the skin along my neck—teeth nipping, tongue-laving suction. Nails scrape along my abs, across my chest, blazing a hard trail of need that leads straight to my cock. Deft fingers work the buttons on my shirt and hot blood pools in my pelvis.

It's been so long—too long—but the dry spell ends tonight.

Fucking finally.

I cradle her face in my hands and move my mouth over hers roughly. My tongue plunges and swirls, tasting tequila. So good.

Friday afternoon, I got around to dialing Lisa DiMaggio. Because I learn from my mistakes, I asked about her and Ted's breakup—it wasn't because of cheating. Then I asked if she'd been tested recently. Miraculously she had, and she was clean. It was like the universe was telling me, "You've suffered enough, poor man."

We made plans for her place on Friday night, and I brought a bottle of Patrón for Lisa and a bottle of red wine for me that I ended up leaving in the car.

Lisa peels open my shirt, running her palms across my pecs and over my shoulders. "God, your tattoos." She moans appreciatively, tracing the ink first with her hands, then with her lips. "These are so fucking hot. They're my favorite part."

I work on her earlobe, flicking at it with my tongue like it's a clit. And I chuckle. "I thought my cock was your favorite."

She giggles against my skin. "Guess I need my memory refreshed."

Works for me.

I'm just about to start doing some unbuttoning of my own when my phone lights up, vibrating on the coffee table near the couch we're sitting on. I glance at the screen but don't recognize the number and let it go to voice mail.

I palm her tit over her blouse. Her blond hair slides over her shoulders as Lisa arches her back, moaning.

And the phone rings again. Same number.

What the fucking fuck?

I pull back. "I should answer that."

Lisa shrugs and pours herself another shot of tequila, licking her hand and dashing it with salt as I stand and bring my phone to my ear. "Becker."

"Hey, Becker! It's Paul Noblecky, how ya doing?"

I was doing a hell of a lot better two minutes ago.

"I'm in the middle of something." My eyes zero in on Lisa's shapely thighs beneath her black dress—that's really where I'd like to be in the middle of. "Make it quick. What do you need, Paul?"

"Well, we broke up a beer party out on Cambridge Place tonight. A high school thing, parents were away. A few of the kids were pretty wasted so we brought them to the station to dry out and call their parents. One of the girls, she won't give us her name—only your business card. Says you're her lawyer, Becker."

My eyes roll closed. And I just know.

"Let me guess—brown curly hair, about five two, blue eyes, piss-poor attitude?"

Noblecky chuckles. "That's her."

I rub my forehead, feeling a migraine coming on—because the blue balls has most likely traveled to my brain. "Her name's Riley. Her aunt's the legal guardian." I rattle off Chelsea's phone number, which I got from her on Wednesday.

"Thanks, Becker—I'll call the aunt, have her come get the kid."

It's late—after midnight. But I'm not going to think about how Chelsea will have to get all those other kids out of bed, including the baby and the little two-year-old. Put their coats on, buckle them in the car. In the dark.

All by herself.

That's not my fucking problem. My problem is the rock-hard dick between my legs that will probably strangle me in my sleep if I don't get him some action soon.

I hang up the phone and lean back on the couch beside Lisa. She grins, slightly buzzed. "Work stuff?"

"Yeah—nothing important."

She palms my junk. "Not like this—*this* is really important."

I thrust against her hand and lean over. "I do like a woman who has her priorities straight."

Then we're kissing again. And it's nice.

But . . . I still can't shake the image of Chelsea and the kids. The tiny blonde with the big blue eyes, Raymond squinting wearily as he puts his glasses on. I imagine them down at the precinct—it's not the safest area to be in, especially after midnight. I imagine them driving, Chelsea yawning, possibly not noticing an oncoming car that's swerved into her lane, not until—

"Shit!" I pull back, breathing hard. "I have to go."

"What?" Lisa whines. "No . . . no, stay. Important things, remember? All the fabulous fucking we were going to do. *Important.*"

"I know. I'm sorry." And I mean I'm really, really fucking sorry. "There's a thing and I have to handle it myself."

Lisa flops backward, resting her head on the arm of the couch, still hot and bothered. "You're killing me, Becker."

I stand up, rebuttoning my shirt. And my cock is furious. "Rain check?"

"Sure." Lisa sighs. Then she smirks flippantly. "At least you got me all warmed up for Mr. Pink. I'll be thinking of your gorgeous tattoos when I play with him."

"Mr. Pink?"

"He's my most favorite vibrator."

I groan at the mental image. "Now *you're* killing *me*."

She winks. "That was my evil plan." Then she stretches up and kisses my cheek. "Call me."

"Will do."

Outside Lisa's apartment, I pull out my phone as I walk to my car and dial Chelsea's number.

She answers on the first ring. "Hello?"

"Chelsea, it's Jake."

"Hi." Her voice is hushed but alert, and I deduce that the kids are still sleeping—and somewhere close by.

"Did Officer Noblecky call you about Riley?"

"Yes. I'm just giving Ronan a bottle, then I'm going to get the kids up and in the car and—"

"Don't bother. I'm on my way there now. They'll let me sign Riley out as her legal counsel."

For a moment, the only response on the other end is the soft sound of Chelsea's breath. Christ—even her breathing is sexy. If I wasn't still hard, I sure as shit would be now.

"You don't have to do that, Jake."

"Yeah, I know I don't have to, but I am," I bite out—harsher than I mean to. "So just say thanks and hang up the phone."

"O-kay. Well . . . thanks. And even though you bit my head off for no reason, I'm gonna let it slide since you're doing me a humongous favor."

I chuckle. "It's been a . . . frustrating evening."

"Ah—now, that I can relate to."

I bet she can.

"I'll see you soon, Chelsea."

"All right. Drive safe."

• • •

I arrive at the precinct, sign some quick paperwork, and wait at the front desk for them to bring Riley out. Noblecky's there—he makes a few stupid comments about my babysitting career, and I don't really listen. But his jokes do get me thinking. What the hell am I doing here? I don't do complicated, I avoid distractions, and up until this point, that strategy has served me well.

Chelsea McQuaid is a fine piece of ass—but her nieces and nephews are turning out to be more distraction than she's worth.

Riley is escorted out from the back room. She's as white as a ghost and unsteady on her feet. Her hair is stringy—wet—and I vaguely wonder if she got puke in it. Dark bruises of mascara shadow bloodshot eyes. She grips a bottle of Gatorade and a paper upchuck bag like the ones so thoughtfully tucked into the seat backs on airplanes.

"Hi," she rasps in a scratchy voice. "Thank you for coming to get me."

The first stirrings of pity echo in my chest. Not only do I remember how it feels to be sick drunk—easily the most miserable experience ever—I also remember what it was like to be fourteen.

It sucked.

"Come on, Smiley, let's go."

She doesn't even have the energy to roll her eyes at me.

I guide her to the car, warning her just before I close the door, "You puke in my car, you'll be walking home."

I slide into the driver's side and the engine roars. Riley squeezes her eyes closed, like the car's vibrations are making her queasy.

"Why didn't you give them your aunt's number?" I ask to distract her.

"Aunt Chelsea already has so much to deal with. I didn't want to bother her."

But it was just peachy to bother the shit out of me.

I pull out of the parking lot. "What were you drinking?"

"Jägermeister." She groans, bringing the bag closer.

And I laugh out loud. "Hope you enjoyed it—chances are you'll never drink it again."

When it comes to mild alcohol poisoning, the body may forgive but the stomach never, ever forgets.

She holds her own against the urge to vomit, breathing slow and deep. "Is this when you lecture me about the dangers of underage drinking?"

I roll to a stop at a red light. "Nope. You already know you were stupid—you don't need me to tell you that. I am curious though—what brought on the sudden binge?"

Her words are slow and careful, like she's afraid if she talks too loud it will offset the delicate balance that's keeping her from retching. "Matthew Applegate threw the party. He told me about it in school today. He's a senior. He's gorgeous and perfect and he seemed interested in me."

Anger sparks, like the flick of a match—because I have no doubt the little prick was interested in some part of her.

"But when I got to the party," she whispers, "he was all over Samantha Frey."

"I'm gonna take a wild guess and say Samantha has a reputation for putting out? Big boobs, nice face—probably a cheerleader?"

Riley nods. "She was the homecoming queen."

Oh man.

"And that's when you made friends with the Jäger?"

She wipes at her cheeks. "It made me feel happy. I didn't care about Matthew or my . . . I didn't care about anything."

I blow out a long breath and decide to hand out some advice. "Riley, boys your age . . . are really not worth your time. They're selfish and stupid. It's not their fault; they're just programmed that way—but they're still a lost cause. I think you should stay away from all of them until you're at least . . . twenty-five. Or . . . have you considered being a lesbian?"

She looks at me blankly. "That is so offensive."

I raise one hand. "Just trying to be helpful."

Riley turns to stare out the window. After a few minutes her chin quivers and her shoulders tremble.

Here's the thing—I don't have a lot of experience with crying females. I've made a concentrated effort to avoid any situation that involves me, women, and tears. In case you haven't noticed, empathy isn't my strong point. And crying teenagers? This feels kind of like a bigfoot encounter—I've heard about it on TV, read about it in the papers . . . but this is the first time I've actually seen one close-up.

She wipes her face on the sleeve of her sweater. "I miss my parents."

And my chest feels weighted. Heavy. For her.

"I know you do."

"I wish they were here." She sniffles.

"What would you say to them if they were?" I pull up the McQuaid driveway and put the car in park.

Riley thinks about my question and then the corner of her mouth tugs. "I would ask them how come Matthew doesn't like me. They were always really honest with us, you know? They would tell me the truth."

I look at her face. She's a pretty girl, even tired and grieving. But there's a fire in her, a fierceness, that will serve her well when she's grown. I've seen it in women I've worked with—women like Sofia. One day, Riley McQuaid will be a force to be reckoned with.

"I can tell you the truth about that," I say with a shrug.

She turns to me.

Gently, I wipe a tear from her cheek. "It's because Matthew is an idiot."

• • •

Chelsea opens the door before we knock. Looking just-fucked gorgeous with bed-mussed wavy hair and her do-me glasses on her face. She's wearing a black tank top and silky red pajama pants. My dick is still pretty pissed, but the sight of her breasts peeking above the top of her shirt makes him consider speaking to me again. Eventually.

"We really need to stop meeting like this," she says, her plump lips sliding into a familiar smile.

Riley hugs her aunt forcefully. "I'm sorry, Aunt Chelsea."

She runs her hand down the back of Riley's hair. "I know." Then she turns her head in disgust. "Did you vomit in your hair?"

"Yeah," Riley groans, sounding miserable.

Chelsea holds her cheek. "Let's get you into bed—we'll talk about this tomorrow. There will be grounding in your future."

She tilts her head toward the family room. "Come on in, Jake. I'll be down in a few minutes."

And she doesn't have to tell me twice.

About twenty minutes later, Chelsea walks back into the living room.

"It was kind of cold, so I started a fire." I gesture to the flickering flames that glow inside the brick fireplace. Heat seeps into the room like a mist, the crackle and scent of live fire comforting. "Hope you don't mind."

She gazes at the fire like a woman staring at a chocolate cake the day after she got off her diet. "I don't mind at all—thank you. You'll have to show me what you have up your sleeve . . ."

Up my sleeve, down my pants. I'll show her anything she wants to see.

". . . I haven't been able to get it going—the logs smolder but don't really burn for me." The orange flames dance in her eyes as she turns to me, teasing. "I was a terrible Girl Scout."

"Would you like a glass of wine?" I indicate the bottle of Merlot resting on the corner stone-top table.

She looks confused. "Robbie and Rachel didn't keep any alcohol in the house."

"I had it in my car."

A smile tickles her lips. "Wow. Wine, a fire—you're like seduction on wheels. Do you keep candles in the trunk?"

"I just figured you might enjoy a drink, maybe a little conversation."

I get the feeling Chelsea hasn't had a conversation with an adult in a long time.

"I'll enjoy that more than I can say." She sighs. "I'll go grab the glasses." Chelsea walks toward the door that leads into the kitchen but stops before exiting. Looking over her shoulder back at me, her reddish hair glowing like gold in the firelight, she raises an eyebrow. "So . . . you're not trying to seduce me?"

I meet her gaze head-on. And wink. "I didn't say that."

"Good to know."

Then she turns back around with a flip of her hair and walks into the kitchen with an extra swivel of that fine ass.

• • •

Later, I add another log to the fire and we're both working our way through glass number two. Chelsea's long legs are tucked snugly beneath her; one hand holds her glass and the other elbow is propped against the back of the couch, her head resting in her hand. The position exposes the smooth expanse of her neck, and I'm fascinated by the pulse that thrums beneath her skin. It makes me feel like a vampire—I want to put my mouth right there, I want to taste her and feel that spot throbbing against my tongue.

I asked her about what she was getting her master's in, and the fucking crazy thing is, I'm actually interested in what's coming out of her mouth—not just fantasizing about what I'd like to put in there.

"I'm an art history major."

I snort. "So you paid thousands of dollars in tuition to look at pretty pictures?"

"No, Mr. Cynical. There's so much more to it than that. Art tells us about culture, what was important to the people of that time. The things they valued, the things they hated or feared—their image of what was beautiful."

I frown. "You sound like a philosopher."

She frowns back. "And you sound like you don't respect philosophy very much."

"All philosophical questions can be answered with one concise statement."

Chelsea refills her glass. "Which is?"

" 'Who gives a fuck?' "

She laughs, and it's an amazing sound.

"Do you do . . . art . . . yourself, or just study other people's work?"

Her cheeks blush. "I sketch, actually."

My eyes are immediately drawn to the framed pencil sketch to the right of the fireplace. It's an incredibly realistic likeness of young Riley, holding twin babies on her lap. I noticed it when I first walked in—you can practically hear the childish, smiling voice.

"Is that one of yours?" I point.

Chelsea nods, still shy.

"You're good." I don't give compliments lightly.

Later, later—she talks about her brother.

"Robbie was fifteen years older than me. I was my parents' midlife-crisis child. My dad had a heart attack when I was about Riley's age. My mom passed a year later when I was in high school." She sips her wine, a mischievous shine in her eye. "I was kind of a wild child after that."

I raise my glass. "Weren't we all?" I drink the Merlot. "So, you lived with your brother after your parents passed away?"

She nods. "Not here though. We were in a smaller place off Cherry Tree. It was just Riley and the boys then—and me, Robbie, and Rachel."

"You and the kids kind of grew up together, then?"

"Yeah. Rachel was like a big sister and a second mother all rolled into one. She was incredible." And there's a mournful note in her voice.

Then she blinks, brightens. "She was the one who really pushed me to travel. Study abroad. I spent a semester in Rome, summers in Paris . . ." Her eyes drop from mine self-consciously. "God, I sound so spoiled. Poor little rich girl, right?"

I shake my head. "No. There's a difference between privileged and spoiled."

And Chelsea McQuaid doesn't have a spoiled bone in her body. She knows she's fortunate, and she appreciates every blessing.

"I'd love to take the kids to Europe one day. To show them how big the world really is."

I chuckle, thinking of a Liam Neeson movie. If some idiot criminal tried taking one of the McQuaid kids, it'd be an hour, tops, before he'd be begging to send them back.

We continue talking, drinking—I lose time admiring the way her skin glows in the firelight. And before I know it, it's almost four in the goddamn morning. Chelsea sets her empty glass on the coffee table and yawns.

"I should get going," I say, even though I don't want to. "I've kept you up past your bedtime. When does the human alarm clock usually rise?"

"Ronan wakes up around six. But . . ." Her eyes trail over my face, down my chest and lower. "But this was worth losing sleep over. Thank you for the wine—the conversation. I had a really great time, Jake."

She has no idea the kind of *great time* I'm capable of giving her.

But not tonight.

"Me too." I stand up and Chelsea walks me to the foyer.

Beside the door, we stand facing each other. And there's a pull—like a fucking magnet—dragging me closer. "Chelsea . . . ," I whisper—with no idea what I'm about to say.

I just like the taste of her name on my lips.

My heart hammers . . . and I lean forward . . . she raises her face and closes her eyes and—

"Aunt Chelsea!"

The blond pixie's voice washes over us from upstairs, like a cold shower.

Goddamn it.

"I had a bad dream! Will you lay down with me?"

Chelsea steps back with a resigned groan, and I feel her pain. Literally.

"I'll be right up, Rosaleen." She shrugs at me apologetically. "Duty calls."

I rub my lips together, making a frustrated smacking sound. "Yeah."

She puts her hand on my chest; it's warm and electrifying. "Thank you again. I really owe you now. Multiples."

And I just can't resist. "That's my line."

Chelsea giggles. "Good night, Jake."

"Bye."

I walk out the door and head home.

9

On Sunday, during breakfast at Sofia and Stanton's place, there's an expected visitor. "Hey, Sunshine," I greet her, walking into the dining room.

"Hey, Jake!" Presley Shaw wraps her arms around my waist.

Presley's almost thirteen now, and in the year or so since I last saw her—when Brent and I visited Mississippi for her mother's wedding—she's lost some of the cute baby roundness in her face, moving one step closer to a full-fledged golden-haired southern beauty.

Her teen years will be fun. Stanton's gonna lose his fucking mind—and probably his hair.

We sit down to eat and he asks, "Remember that band manager I represented last year? The DWI."

There are nods all around.

"Turns out he works with One Direction now, and they're in town. He sent me four front-row seats to the concert tomorrow. Sofia and I were gonna take Presley."

"Who's One Direction?" I inquire, but don't actually care.

Presley's eyes bug out. "Who's One Direction? What, y'all live under a rock?" She holds up the magazine she's been flipping through and flashes me a picture of four punks in skinny jeans. "*This* is One Direction. I'm so excited!" she squeals. "The concert is gonna be *so* on point."

My eyebrows rise to Stanton. "Have fun with that, buddy."

Stanton chews a cheese ball, his green eyes alight with humor. "Soph and I were talkin'—we thought instead of tossing the fourth ticket, it might be nice if you came with me and Presley instead. You and that Riley girl."

"Are you nuts?" I ask, because—*obviously.*

"Please, Jake?" Sunshine begs. "It'll be so much fun havin' a girl my own age there with me." She turns to her father. "No offense, but you and Sofia just don't get it."

Stanton shrugs. "No offense taken. I still know I'm the cool daddy."

Presley puts her hand on his arm. "I love you, Daddy, but whatever you think cool is? It's not that."

Stanton gives her a mock frown.

And her bright blue eyes plead with me. "Come on, Jake. I bet you'll like them. Their music is amazin'—better than the Beatles."

I fear for today's youth.

"It might be good for her," Stanton says, pressing me. Because I told him all about Riley's Friday-night misadventures with Jägermeister.

I sigh, already knowing I'm going to regret this.

But I pick up my phone to call Chelsea anyway.

• • •

The next day, Stanton, Sofia, Presley, and I arrive at Chelsea's house after work. She hasn't told Riley about the concert yet, wanted it to be a surprise. And she said she didn't want to risk Riley's shattering the windows with her screams of excitement.

Oh—and Brent tagged along too. Because I've mentioned Chelsea and the kids at lunch and he wants to meet them. Also, because he has no life.

We gather in the foyer and I make the introductions. Chelsea greets each of my friends warmly. She's wearing a casual, pale blue shirtdress that displays miles of smooth, succulent legs. And I fantasize about Stanton taking the girls on his own, and Sofia and Brent taking the rest of the rabble. Far, far away.

"Hi," Regan says to Sofia, toddling into the room and holding a stuffed bear who looks like he's seen better days.

"Hi," Sofia replies, smiling.

"Hi!" Regan squeaks.

"Hi!" Sofia laughs.

And here we fucking go again.

For my own sanity, I've gotta teach this kid another word.

Stanton and Brent pick up their conversation from lunch—the ongoing "perfect murder" game. "Drowning," Brent says insistently, ticking off his points on his fingers. "Chances are the body will be too decomposed to retain any useful evidence, and there's a built-in alibi because the defendant can always claim the person slipped. It worked like a charm for Natalie Wood's husband."

Stanton shakes his blond head. "I'm still stickin' with an allergic reaction."

Raymond adjusts his glasses and jumps into the conversation. "Are you guys talking about the best way to off somebody?"

They nod and Raymond's face turns eager. "I know a way. You make a high-powered bullet out of ice. And fire it from a sniper's rifle. After it passes through the heart, it'll melt. No fingerprints. No footprints."

We're silent. Shocked.

And kind of freaked out.

"I just got goose bumps." Brent shivers. "Did anyone else get goose bumps?"

Rosaleen steps forward, her eyes focused on Brent. "Why do you walk like that?" she asks innocently.

"Rosaleen!" Chelsea chides. "That's rude."

But from experience, I know it's fine and I tell her so.

Brent explains to the seven-year-old. "I got hit by a car when I was a kid, lost part of my leg." He lifts his pant leg, showing off his titanium prosthetic. "So be careful riding your bike."

She regards him with a tilted head. "So they gave you a fake leg?"

"Yep."

"Can you take it off and show me?"

"No." Brent shakes his head.

Rosaleen considers this. Then she asks, "You wanna come see my playhouse outside? It has curtains."

"Sure." Brent checks his watch. "I've got time."

Riley comes down the stairs, her eyes taking us all in. I introduce her to everyone. She smiles at Presley with a friendly, "Hey." And Presley waves.

"Sooo"—Chelsea grins—"Jake has a surprise for you, Riley." She gives me a look, tilting her head toward Riley, nudging me on.

I clear my throat and stick the tickets in the teenager's hands, trying not to make it a big deal.

"Oh my god!!!" Riley screams.

And Cousin It howls in response.

"These are One Direction tickets! *Front-row* One Direction tickets!" Huge blue eyes brimming with elation look up into mine. "Are you serious?"

"Unfortunately."

The twittering, enthusiastic, unintelligible chattering between her and Presley begins. And goes on.

And on.

Rory smirks at me. "You have to go to a One Direction concert?"

I nod reluctantly.

"Ha!" He laughs, pointing his finger. "Sucker."

I glower. "Shut up, kid."

• • •

Four and a half hours of screaming girls later, I can't hear jack shit. Even driving back in Stanton's car everything is muffled—the shouting, singing girls in the backseat sound like they're annoying me from underwater.

The four of us walk in the front door and find Brent, Sofia, and Chelsea having coffee in the den. Sofia holds Ronan, asleep in her arms, and a fierce, hungry look crosses Stanton's face as he gazes at her.

"How was it?" Chelsea asks, grinning at me in a fuck-hot, teasing sort of way.

I hold up my hand. "Don't make me relive it. I'm trying to block it out."

But that cat's already been sprung from the bag. Presley and Riley tell Sofia and Chelsea every single detail, talking together and over each other. They're big on terms like "OMG" and "can't believe," "best ever," and . . . "*OMG*."

"And then . . . ," Riley screeches, grabbing her aunt's hand, "Harry looked right at me!"

I squint Stanton's way. "Which one was Harry again?"

"The one who needs a haircut."

I try to distinguish them in my mind, but they all need a haircut.

"Daddy," Presley asks, "can Riley sleep over?"

"Yeah, Aunt Chelsea—can I sleep over at Presley's?" Riley asks at about the same time.

Because apparently One Direction's superpower is instant friendship. Someone should ship them to the Middle East so they can get to work on that Israel-Palestine thing.

Stanton gives the go-ahead and Chelsea says it's fine. And then there's *more* screeching—*yay*—before they charge up the stairs to get Riley's stuff.

"Where are the other kids?" I ask Chelsea.

"They're asleep," she gladly informs me. "Brent tired them all out with flashlight manhunt."

Brent pats his own back. "I'm the reigning champion."

When the girls come back down carrying a sleeping bag, pillows, and a duffel bag, Riley stands in front of me, looking genuinely, sparkling happy.

"Thank you, Jake. This was like . . . the best night of my life."

I could say it was my pleasure . . . but that wouldn't be true. "Don't mention it."

Sofia hands Ronan to Chelsea and she gently lays him down in the small dark green portable crib in the corner. As they get ready to leave, I decide to hang around a little longer. Or a *lot* longer. Chelsea and I won't exactly be alone, but minus one child is better than nothing.

Until Brent shoots my plan to shit. "Stanton's car only seats four, so I need a lift home, Jake."

Fuckin' A.

I glance at Chelsea and it's like she can read my mind. Because she's smirking at me with humorous disappointment. "Thanks again, Jake. Good night."

I reach out my hand, brushing her hair back from her face. "Good night."

Then Brent slips in front of me. He bows slightly, takes Chelsea's hand, and lifts it to his lips, kissing the back. "Thank you for a lovely evening—you were the hostess with the mostest."

She giggles, while in the back of my throat, I snarl.

And the idea of breaking his jaw seems even more attractive than it did a few weeks ago.

Chelsea closes the door behind us and we walk toward my car, Brent skipping as best he can. It's fucking annoying.

"Well . . . ," he breathes slowly, suggestion strong in his tone, "Chelsea seems *nice*."

I say nothing.

"And that ass," he goes on admiringly, "*mmm, mmm, good*—I could bounce quarters off that tight—"

My hand lashes out, twisting the front of his shirt, dragging him forward till we're nose to nose. "Shut *up*."

He searches my eyes, his smile slow and knowing. "You like her."

I drop him like a Hot Pocket straight out of the microwave and brush past him to my car. "Of course I like her. She's a nice girl."

Brent sticks close to my side, wagging his finger. "Nooo, you *like* her—not just in the sense that you want her riding reverse cowgirl on your dick. You *like* her, like her."

"What, are you twelve?"

"Age is just a number. Or at least that's what my uncle said when he married lucky, nineteen-year-old wife number three." He nudges my shoulder. "But seriously, you've got this whole knight-in-shining-armor vibe going on."

I shake my head. "My armor was tarnished a long time ago, Brent."

"A knight in tarnished armor is still a knight."

When I don't respond, he pushes—because he actually believes I won't punch his pretty face. "Then let me know when you're done. I'd like to see if I can hit that."

I step toward him. "She's off-fucking-limits to you. Now, during, and after. Don't even think about it."

And the son of a bitch looks pleased with himself. He smiles wider. "Yeah—you definitely like her."

• • •

On Tuesday night I'm working late at the office, finishing up a motion for Senator Holten's domestic abuse trial. I loosen my tie, rub my eyes, and crack my neck. Just as I'm about to dive back in, my cell phone rings.

And Chelsea's name lights up the screen.

I smile just seeing her name. It's fucking weird and completely unlike me. I barely smiled when I graduated law school.

I wipe it off my face as soon as I realize I'm doing it. I tap the accept button and bring the phone to my ear. I start to ask the age-old question *What are you wearing?* But I don't—thank Christ—because a high-pitched voice pipes up from the speaker.

Rosaleen's voice.

"Hi, Jake!"

I lean back in my chair. "Hi, Rosaleen."

"Whatcha doin'?"

"Working. What are you doing?"

"I'm making chicken soup." There's pride in her voice.

"That's nice. Is your aunt around?" I ask, because I have a sneaking suspicion Chelsea doesn't have a clue about what her niece is up to.

"She's in the bathroom. She's sick."

I frown. "What do you mean, she's sick?"

"She's throwing up *everywhere*. They all are, except me. And Ronan—but he spits up all the time anyway, so he doesn't count."

Faintly, the sound of Ronan's wailing comes through in the background.

I sit up and press the phone harder against my ear. "Is that your brother crying?"

"Yeah. He's hungry. I'm going to heat up his bottle as soon as I'm done with the soup."

I'm about to ask her if she's using the stove or the microwave for the soup . . . but the loud, piercing shriek of the fire alarm, which wipes out any other sound from her end, pretty much answers that question before it's asked.

"Whoops!" Rosaleen shouts into the phone. "Gotta go. Bye!"

"Rosaleen, wait—"

But she's already hung up.

Shit.

I call back. It rings and rings, then goes to voice mail.

"Fuck!"

10

It's not my problem. It's none of my business. I have my own shit to worry about.

That's what I tell myself as I put my phone aside, push my chair forward, and refocus on the document in front of me. On the hours of work I still have to finish tonight.

Be smart. Prioritize.

They're fine. People get sick all the time . . .

And then they die.

Fire alarms go off every day . . .

As houses burn to the ground.

"God*damn* it!"

I pick up my phone and dial again. Still nothing.

I shake my head and put my fingers on the keyboard . . . but the only thing I can picture is Chelsea passed out on the bathroom floor.

"Son of a bitch!"

I throw in the towel and pack my briefcase with my laptop and files. I make it to my car in record time and wonder if calling 911 would be an overreaction. It's touch-and-go for a while, but I hold back—I'll be there in ten minutes.

Seven minutes later, I tear up the driveway, throw my car in park, and stomp to the front door. My mouth is dry and my palms are wet with concern. I bang on the door, but the only answer is Cousin It's yap from the other side. I cup my hands and peer through the window, but I don't see anyone.

"Chelsea! Rosaleen!" I try knocking again. "It's Jake."

When there's no response, I contemplate busting the door down. But then I remember to check under the mat—and lo and behold, there's a shiny silver key. And I'm in.

• • •

Cousin It dances around my legs as I walk into the foyer—just as Rosaleen is coming down the stairs, carrying a tray that's bigger than she is. She smiles when she sees me.

"Hi, Jake. When'd you get here?"

Placing the key on the front table, I take the tray from her hands. "Where's your aunt?"

"She's upstairs in the bathroom. She told me to get Ronan's bottle from the refrigerator."

My eyes cut to the upper landing. "Okay. You go do that, I'm going to check on your aunt."

I walk up the stairs and down the hall, following the sound of someone barfing up their stomach lining the way Hansel and Gretel followed bread crumbs. I stand in the bathroom doorway, casting a shadow on Chelsea's crumpled form as she hunches over the toilet, holding on to the sides of the bowl like her life depends on it. She's in a loose-fitting black T-shirt and sweatpants. Her hair is pulled back, a few strands damp with perspiration clinging to the back of her neck.

I crouch down next to her, my hand on her back.

Once her heaves subside, she wipes her mouth with a tissue and groans at me. "What are you doing here? How did you get in?"

"Rosaleen called. I used the key that was under the mat. You shouldn't keep it there."

"You shouldn't be here," she whimpers. "Run. Save yourself."

"When the hell did this start?"

She closes her eyes, panting. "Monday—in the middle of the night. It started with Raymond, and the rest of us fell like dominoes."

"Why didn't you call me?"

"I called the neighbor—Walter's mother. She said she couldn't risk one of her kids catching it. Her daughter has a pageant this weekend. She said she was sorry."

Nice. Because *sorry* is so fucking helpful.

Chelsea drags herself to the sink and splashes water on her face and in her mouth. "I have to check on the kids." She moves toward the door and almost cracks her head on the sink as her knees give out.

But I catch her, scooping her up into my arms. "Whoa—easy." My voice turns firm. Kind of pissed off. "You're not checking on anyone. You're going to bed. Where's your room?"

"No, I have to—"

"Don't fucking argue with me. Where's your room?"

She seems to give in—or she just can't keep her head up anymore. It rests against my arm. "My room's downstairs, but I want to stay up here—in case they need me. Can you take me to the guest room? Last door on the right."

I follow her directions to a plain room with yellow walls and a white bedspread. I lay her in the middle of the bed gently. Her eyes crack open, shiny and miserable, gazing up at me.

"I can't be sick," she whispers.

"It's a little late for that."

"Aunt Chelsea!" one of the boys calls.

And it's like she's been electrified. Her eyes spring open and her head jerks as she tries to pull herself up into a sitting position.

"Lie down," I tell her, guiding her back.

"I have to—"

"Chelsea, I'm here. Let me help you," I bark, ready to shake her at this point. I brush her hair back from her stark-white—but still fucking beautiful—face. "I'll make sure the kids are okay."

She stares at me for a moment, like I'm an apparition. Or a dream. And then slowly, her eyes well with tears. They trickle silently out of the corners of her eyes and down her cheeks.

And every one fucking destroys me.

"Don't cry. Why are you crying?"

She breathes out a shaky breath and wipes her cheeks. "I'm just . . . I'm so tired, Jake. I'm so tired."

For the first time, I think about what it must've been like for her . . . after she got that phone call. How she probably raced around, throwing necessities in a bag, figuring she'd send for the rest of her things later. How she had to withdraw from school, probably break the lease on her apartment—upend her entire fucking existence.

And then she was here—so needed, all the time. Having to make a hundred different arrangements, care for six kids who couldn't possibly care for themselves. And not just feeding them, homework, getting them to school, but helping them navigate an unimaginable grief. She had to keep them from falling apart.

And she had to do it completely on her own.

And I know, without a doubt, that she hasn't taken a second for herself. To process her own pain, get a handle on her own sorrow and loss. There couldn't have been any time. She's been running on that hamster wheel for so long—it was only a matter of time before she completely crashed.

"Then sleep, Chelsea. I swear everything will be okay."

She smiles even as more tears come. She grasps my hand, holding it tight.

"Thank you."

• • •

After that, I do triage. War-zone mode. I check the bedrooms—Rory and Raymond are smooshed together in the bottom bunk of their bed with matching wretched faces, each with his own barf bucket beside him. Riley and Regan are in Riley's bed, with a wastebasket next to them, on the verge of sleep. I pay close attention to the two-year-old, who gazes at me with glassy eyes.

"Hiii," she rasps exhaustedly.

I run my hand through her baby-fine hair. "Hey, kiddo."

Then I head down to the kitchen, where Rosaleen is perched on the counter beside her baby brother, holding a bottle for him. She says she knows how to do it—that she's watched her mother and Chelsea do it a thousand times. Thank fuck for observant kids.

"But you're gonna have to burp him," she tells me, and then explains how it's done. Carefully, I lift him from the seat, holding him with straight arms like a bomb that could detonate at any moment. I follow Rosaleen's instructions and bring him to my shoulder, patting and rubbing his back.

"Like this?" I ask the seven-year-old.

She nods encouragingly.

"You are officially my second in command," I tell her. "You and me together are gonna kick this virus's ass."

She giggles. "Okay."

I feel a ridiculous amount of pride when Ronan lets out a deep, rumbling belch that any grown man would be impressed to produce. I'm not going to tell the others, but I think he's my favorite.

As I congratulate him, I notice his ass feels heavy.

Wet.

I look at his sister. "I think he needs to be changed."

Her face turns wary and she raises her little hands. "Don't look at me. I'm just a kid."

"*Now* you play the kid card?" I ask her.

She shrugs without pity.

Okay. I can do this.

I've been arrested—spent time in lockup with genuinely dangerous guys. I've been in street fights without rules where no one was coming to break it up—and I've won. I've conquered the insurmountable challenge of earning a law degree and dealing with the self-centered jackasses who are my clients without committing aggravated assault.

It's a diaper. How hard could it be?

I carry Ronan to his room, lay him on the pad on his dresser, and look him in the eyes. "Work with me, buddy, okay?"

Then, with one hand on his chest so he doesn't roll away, I Google it.

Gotta love modern technology. Bomb-making and baby-changing diagrams at your fingertips. I get the diaper off, get him cleaned up with the wipes. I squeeze some white pasty shit out of a tube onto his ass, because I'm not sure if he's red, but it's there, so I'll use it. I lift his kicking legs and slide a fresh diaper underneath him.

And then—without warning—a hot stream of piss, like a fireman's hose, arches in the air, coating my shirt with expert aim.

I glare down at the baby. "Seriously, man?"

He just smiles around the hand he's chewing on.

Fucking Google didn't mention this.

• • •

Once I get Ronan settled in his swing, I find Rosaleen in the living room. We walk to the kitchen to check out our supplies, but she stops just inside the kitchen door. Her face goes blank and frighteningly ashen.

"You okay, Rosaleen?"

She opens her mouth to answer—but what comes out is a burst of chunky yellow vomit, like lumpy pancake mix gone sour.

Man down.

She coughs and stares, horrified, at the disaster on the floor, splattered on her shoes and on her sparkly T-shirt. Then she starts to cry. "I'm sorry, Jake."

Something in my chest swells at her tears, making everything feel too tight. I kneel down beside her, my hand rubbing circles on her back. "It's okay. Rosaleen—it's just puke. It's not a big deal."

The dog scurries in like Mighty Mouse coming to save the day. Then he starts to chow down on Rosaleen's vomit.

Robustly.

I gag in the back of my throat but manage to hold it together. "See?" I tell her, trying to sound cheery. "You did me a favor—now I won't have to feed the dog."

• • •

Rosaleen changes into pajamas and climbs into bed next to her sleeping aunt. I do a second check of the wounded and take advantage of the momentary quiet to call my reservists.

"They *all* have it?" Stanton asks with shock—and a lilt of humor.

"They all have it," I declare grumpily. I rub my eyes. "I'm not ashamed to say I'm out of my league here."

"Do they have fevers, too, or just the upchucks?"

"How do I tell if they have fevers?"

"Do they feel hot?"

I think about it for a second helplessly. "They don't feel cold."

"All right. Call the grocery store—they'll deliver. Tell them you need an ear thermometer—the directions will be in the box. You also need Tylenol, saltine crackers, ginger ale, chicken broth, and Pedialyte."

I furiously write down everything he's saying, like it's gospel. "What's Pedialyte?"

"It's like Gatorade for babies. Keep an eye on the infant. If he starts puking, don't mess around—call the pediatrician. The number is probably on the fridge. Babies can get dehydrated really fast. Same goes for the two-year-old—watch her. If she can't hold down a tablespoon of the Pedialyte an hour, you may have to take her in."

"Got it. Anything else?"

"Just keep them comfortable. Little sips when they can drink. Crackers and broth when their stomachs settle. Call us if you need backup."

I sigh. "All right, thanks, man."

• • •

By the next morning, I'm waist-deep in laundry. Sheets, soiled pajamas, cloths for foreheads. I know my way around a washing machine—my mother made sure of it. And since I like things organized and clean, I know how to load a dishwasher and fold a towel, too.

By Wednesday afternoon, the troops are getting restless. They're on the mend but not yet back to full capacity. Because they're getting antsy, they start to argue with each other. *He smells, she's hogging the covers, he's fucking looking at me wrong.*

I transport them all downstairs and corral them in the den. Every couch, recliner, and love seat, and certain sections of the floor, is covered with blankets, pillows, and kids. Chelsea lies on the couch and I sit on the floor, leaning back against it. Ronan lies on his stomach on a blanket beside me. I flick on the television.

And the arguing starts up again.

"Let's watch SpongeBob."

"SpongeBob is stupid. Put on MTV—*16 and Pregnant* is on."

Remember when MTV used to actually play music videos?

"We're not watching *16 and Pregnant*," Chelsea tells her niece.

"How about the Discovery Channel?" Raymond suggests. "There's a marathon on the hunting habits of lions. They eat a ton of gazelles."

"Poor gazelles!" Rosaleen laments.

There's a nightmare in the making.

"Listen up!" I holler. "I have the remote. That makes me master of the universe. And the master says we're watching basketball."

There are complaints and agreements in equal measure.

A little while later, Rosaleen crawls off the recliner, dragging her pillow with her. She plops it down next to me and rests her head on it, regarding me. Her forehead is sickly damp, her eyes glazed. "Will you sing me a song?"

I look back at her. "No."

"Please?" she rasps.

I shake my head definitively. I will not be broken. "Not happening."

Her clammy hand touches my wrist. "It will help me fall asleep."

And just like that, the resolve begins to fissure.

"I don't sing," I explain with a dash of desperation.

Her lip trembles, and the fissure widens. "But it will make me feel better. And I feel terrible, Jake."

I cling to my man-card with straining fingers. "I don't know any songs."

It's doubtful Iron Maiden would be helpful in this situation.

She blinks up at me slowly. "Pretty please?"

And the fissure has now become the Grand fucking Canyon. *Damn it.*

I clear my throat and softly sing the One Direction lyrics that have been buzzing in my head for days like overcaffeinated insects.

"Everyone else in the room can see it . . ."

My voice is too deep and haltingly awful.

The boys groan in tortured unison. Riley perks up from the recliner and turns my way, suddenly interested. Chelsea covers her mouth and I just know she's giggling under that hand. But Rosaleen . . . her baby-blue gaze warms me down to the marrow of my bones. Because it's thankful and adoring and brimming with hero worship.

And for the first time in twenty-four hours, she's smiling.

So I continue. *"Everyone else but you . . ."*

I finish the goddamn chorus. Rosaleen applauds softly and Riley sighs dreamily. "Best song ever."

Chelsea gives up trying to hold it in and giggles out loud.

I glance over my shoulder at her. "I hate myself right now."

• • •

Early Thursday morning, a little over two days after the plague began, Chelsea is back on her feet. She's just out of the shower—her hair is still wet and smells fucking incredible. That clean shampoo scent with a touch of vanilla body wash makes me want to lick her from head to toe and every inch in between. And that's not even a little exaggeration.

She's wrapped in an adorably big pink fluffy robe, cinched at the waist.

We walk down the stairs and stand in front of the door.

"You sure you're feeling better?" I ask.

"Yes. I can take it from here." She nods, her eyes soft with gratitude.

I'm heading out early—I have to stop at home and shower, then be in court in three hours. The kids are better. Still not out of bed or back to school, but they're not puking their body weight into a wastebasket every two hours, either. So . . . progress.

Chelsea rests her hand on my arm, and maybe I'm just really fucking tired, but my skin seems to tingle beneath her touch. I can't imagine how good it will feel on bare skin . . . wrapped around my cock. I'm absolutely going to have to jerk off before I see her again.

"Thank you, Jake. Again." She shakes her head, looking frustrated. "I'll never be able to repay you."

I can think of a few ways.

I wink. "Actions do speak louder than words. And are so much more fun."

"You're right." She squeezes my arm softly. "Which is why I'm going to make you the best dinner you've ever eaten—to show you how much I appreciate all you've done for us. Friday night. Will you come?"

Oh boy, will I come. She has no idea.

But I pretend to think it over. "No tofu, right?"

Chelsea grins. "No tofu."

I lean in, closer to her ear, making gooseflesh rise on the exposed skin along her collarbone. "What were you thinking for dessert?"

Her voice turns sultry as she plays along—and plays well. "What do you like, Jake?"

"I'll eat anything with whipped cream on top."

She blushes, and a laugh bubbles from her lips. "I'll be sure to stock up."

I push her damp hair back behind her ear. "Good. And I'll bring a movie to keep the kids occupied. Riley mentioned they never saw *Goonies*, which is just straight-up criminal."

"That'll be perfect."

I gaze into Chelsea's ice-blue eyes. "I really think it will be."

11

I get out of my car in front of Chelsea's house on Friday night. And not to sound like a total douche, but there's a spring in my step. A lightness in my mood. I'm excited. Looking forward to this evening with Chelsea—and, yes, with the kids too. Sure, they're half a dozen little cockblockers, but they're funny. Smart. In general, pretty awesome.

The fact that there's a really good chance I'm going to finally get laid doesn't hurt, either.

I knock on the door, holding a bouquet of white roses and the movie in one hand.

The door opens, and in front of me stands a tall, tan, lanky guy with strategically tousled dirty-blond hair, a white T-shirt, saggy jeans, and a shark-tooth necklace.

He lifts his chin in greeting. "Hey."

"Hey." Who the fuck is he, and why is he answering the door? "Where's Chelsea?"

He steps back, opening the door wider, turning his head. "Babe! There's a guy here." His brown eyes turn my way. "A big fuckin' guy. What do you bench, two fifty?"

"Something like that."

I step past him, lowering the flowers to my side, feeling like an asshole for having them.

Chelsea comes out from the kitchen, wearing a little black dress with thin straps—sexy in its simplicity—and open-toed black heels. Her hair falls soft and shiny around her shoulders. "Jake!" Her smile is off—kind of forced.

"What's going on?" I ask evenly.

Two more twentysomethings step out behind her: a dark-skinned girl with long dreadlocks and a stunning face, and a guy with long brown hair wearing a trendy, butt-ugly, lime-green paisley shirt.

"My friends from Berkeley came to visit." Her face tightens—broadcasting an apology. "I didn't know they were coming." She steps back, gesturing to the couple behind her. "This is Nikki and Kevin."

Nikki and Kevin both smile at me a little too happily. A little too stoned to play it straight.

"And this"—Chelsea gestures to the blond shark killer—"is Lucas."

Lucas grins dopily. "S'up."

I nod at him, then hand Chelsea the flowers. "These are for you."

She gazes at them lovingly, running her palm over the soft petals. "They're beautiful. Thank you."

So much for dinner. And more important, so much for getting laid.

Fuck.

Rosaleen comes tearing around the corner, her hair parted into curly pigtails, hugging me around the waist. "Jake, you're here! Did you bring the movie?"

I hold it up for her to see and she bounces.

Riley and Rory join us next. Lucas rubs his hand roughly on top of Rory's head. "Little dude, how about you grab me a beer? If we're watching a movie, I'm gonna need a brew."

Chelsea's head tilts. "We don't have any, Lucas. My brother and Rachel weren't drinkers."

"That sucks."

We all walk toward the den, and the muscle in my cheek twitches as I watch Lucas throw his arm around Chelsea's shoulders casually. Cozily. With intimate familiarity.

I really don't like this asswipe. And I'm not the only one.

Rory comes up to my side and whispers, "He touches my head again, I'm punching him in the nuts."

"Sounds like a plan."

"Can we watch the movie in Mom and Dad's room?" Riley asks carefully. "We used to have movie night up there every week. But we haven't since . . ." She ends with a shrug.

"Sure," I tell her.

"I think that's a great idea," Chelsea agrees softly.

"Dude! I just got a greater idea!" Lucas says, turning my way. "So . . . you're like the manny, right?"

"The what?" I ask, my expression heading for hostile.

"Like the nanny, but you're a guy? You can watch the kids, yeah?"

"Sweet!" Nikki squeaks, picking up his train of thought. "So, Mr. Tall, Dark, and Hotty can stay with the babies while the four of us go out!"

I wait for Chelsea to decline.

I wait for her to say she'd rather stay in with the kids.

With *me.*

But she doesn't.

She just turns to me blankly. "Would that work for you, Jake?"

A sharp snort rumbles out of me. Frustration and resentment simmer in my stomach, burning like acid. "Whatever you want to do, Chelsea."

"Awesome." Lucas nods. And he still hasn't moved his fucking arm from her shoulder.

I want to break it off.

Lucas's eyes crawl over her. "You should get changed, babe."

I give him a hard stare. "I think she looks perfect."

His head toggles. "Well, sure, she's smokin'." Then he turns to Chelsea. "But you kinda look like a MILF. Hot and all . . . but still a mom, ya know?"

And now I want to break his mouth, too.

Her face falls, but she agrees. "Okay. I'll get changed real quick and then we'll head out."

Ten minutes later, she comes down the stairs in tight blue jeans and a white halter top. The shirt pushes together her tits in a fantastic way—she looks gorgeous. But different. There's less . . . *elegance* in this outfit. And she seems infinitely more screwable.

Which wouldn't be a bad thing, normally. If I had met her in a bar, wearing that—before—I would've pulled out all the stops to get her to come home with me. It's just the fact that she's going out without me—where other pricks will be looking at her and thinking the same thing—that rubs me the wrong fucking way.

She leads me into the kitchen, rattling off Ronan's feeding schedule and bedtime. Things I already know by now. When she stops talking, her eyes rise from the floor to meet mine.

"I'm sorry about dinner."

"Don't be."

"Jake, I . . ." She licks her lips, shifts her feet indecisively. "I haven't seen them in two months. I didn't know . . ." She pauses again, then seems to find the words she wants to say. "Are you mad at me?"

And her eyes look so hopeful. So . . . vulnerable. My voice softens. "No, I'm not mad at you."

Her douchebag friends, however—that's another story.

"And you're okay with this? Watching the kids for me?"

In trial law, you learn very quickly that words have meaning. Your questions, your answers, are posed carefully and with forethought, because so much of what is said could be open to interpretation. It's made me very good at sidestepping—a useful skill at the moment.

"I planned on being here all night anyway."

And then I think about that hamster wheel again. All the giving of herself she's done, never taking. My hand reaches out, covering hers. "You should go out with your friends, Chelsea. Have fun." *No matter how much I hate the idea.* "The kids and I will be fine."

She smiles, like a weight has been lifted. And I feel just a little less miserable.

• • •

Robert and Rachel McQuaid's bedroom is on the third floor of the house. The staircase to their room begins at the end of the second-floor hallway. Privacy was obviously important to them. And romance—they did have six fucking kids, after all. The room is huge: a sitting area, a spa-like bath, his-and-hers closets as big as some apartment kitchens. The walls are a tasteful red, the furniture dark wood. There's a fireplace in the corner with their wedding portrait above it—they look happy and young, and so eager to start their lives together. On the dresser are pictures of their children—tender, candid shots of first baths, Christmas mornings, days at the beach, and sleeping cuddles.

The kids are quiet when they first walk in, almost like the room is a shrine. But after a few minutes, their natural exuberance and easy comfort with the space take over. They remind me of puppies in a box as they climb on their parents' California-king bed—bumping into each other, lying over one another, until they're all finally settled and comfortable. Riley holds Regan on her lap. Judging by the way Regan's sucking her thumb and her far-off stare, she'll be lucky if she's awake past the opening credits. Raymond scoops Cousin It into his arms like a security blanket, and Rosaleen pats the empty space in the center of the bed.

"Come on, Jake, there's room for you."

I don't know the rules about a grown man lying in bed with kids he's not related to, but their collective, comfortably expectant expressions puts my mind at ease. I slip the movie into the DVD player, grab the remote, and pounce on the mattress, making them all bounce and giggle.

Later, around the time the Goonies tell Troy and his bucket to go screw himself, Rosaleen asks, "Where did Aunt Chelsea go?"

I tense, thinking about exactly where Chelsea is—and who she's gone there with.

"She went out with her friends," I answer, trying to keep the scowl out of my voice.

"I didn't like them," Riley whispers, so as not to wake the sleeping bundle of two-year-old on her lap. "They were smoking weed in the backyard."

"Is that what that smell was?" Rosaleen asks.

"Yep."

My fists clench. Of all the selfish, irresponsible . . . I was young once too, but twenty-six isn't *that* goddamn young. It's too old to be an excuse for sheer fucking stupidity.

"They were dicks," Rory offers.

I don't even chastise him for the language, 'cause I couldn't agree more. Then we go back to watching the movie.

• • •

"That was awesome," Raymond declares as Cyndi Lauper sings over the rolling credits.

"Is there a part two?" Riley asks.

"Nope." I yawn. "In the eighties they knew not to mess with perfection."

Rosaleen jumps on my lap, making me grunt. Then she grabs my face with both little hands, sliding one side down and pushing the other up. "You're kinda like that Sloth guy, Jake. You're big and loud." She gazes down at me thoughtfully. "But you're not as ugly as him."

I'll take what I can get. "Thanks," I murmur though squashed lips.

The kids climb off the bed, stretching and bleary eyed. Rory asks, "Do we have to brush our teeth?"

I walk with them down the stairs to the second floor. "Nah, I think your teeth will survive one night without it. Just go to sleep."

The boys head into their room, and Riley emerges from Regan's after successfully laying her down. She pins me with her judgmental teenage stare, then gives me the smallest of smiles. "This was fun. Thanks."

And a weird, warm feeling tingles in my chest. "It was. You're welcome."

Rosaleen takes my hand and tugs me into her room. It's pink and princessy, with a unicorn border and a rainbow, blue-skyed mural painted on the ceiling. She climbs into her four-poster bed. "Will you lay down with me, Jake?"

I shake my head. "No."

Her teeth chatter dramatically and she pulls the covers up to her chin. "But what if One-Eyed Willie comes to get me?"

I scratch the back of my neck, debating. "Well . . . we can leave your door open and the hall light on?"

Nope—not good enough.

"And . . . I can sit outside your door until you fall asleep." I brought my laptop to get some work done, and the floor suits me as well as a desk. I'm not picky.

"Okay." She smiles. Then she waves me closer with her hand. I lean down and she raises her head off the pillow, pressing the softest kiss to my cheek.

And the weird, warm tingles surge with a vengeance.

"Good night, Jake. Sweet dreams."

I watch her for a moment as she nestles under the covers, the very image of all things pure and good and innocent. And everything in me wants her to be able to stay just like that.

I shake my head at my sentimentality. Because I don't fucking do sappy. Harsh, cynical, brutally honest, yes—but never sappy.

I turn off the light. "Good night, Rosaleen."

• • •

Sometime later—thirty minutes or three hours—I wake up on the floor, my computer open on my lap, chin to chest, my neck aching and my ass totally numb. It's disorienting at first; I'm not sure where I am or why I'm on the goddamn floor. I look around, inhaling deeply, and then I remember. *The Goonies,* Chelsea going out with her loser friends, the kids.

I close the laptop and rub my eyes, wondering what woke me up. Rosaleen's still out cold and all is silent from the other three closed doors in the hall, including the baby's room. I get to my feet and—

Thump.

A sound comes from downstairs, then indecipherable low voices.

What the hell?

My muscles tighten, expecting trouble. Maybe someone's breaking in? I wonder if Chelsea ever moved that key from under the mat.

"Mmm . . . yeah . . ."

That was a male moan. A burglar wouldn't be fucking moaning.

I creep down the stairs, ears straining. And the voices get clearer with each step.

"Lucas!" That was Chelsea.

"You're so fucking hot, babe."

My stomach twists and my fists clench. It's not a burglar.

"I need you so bad," he says.

"Lucas—"

Her voice is low, a harsh whisper because she's thinking of the kids. She's always thinking of the kids. But her words are clear.

"Lucas, get *off.*"

And so are his.

"Don't be a bitch, Chels. I know you want it."

"No. *Stop*, Lucas—no!"

"Shh, relax. Just let me—"

And I fucking lose it.

I round the corner into the living room. They're on the couch, still fully clothed. He's on top, grinding on her, covering her almost completely except for her legs.

Her twisting, kicking legs.

In one move, I pull him off Chelsea by the back of his shirt. I hold him suspended with one hand and punch him in the face with other. My fist makes contact with a satisfying crunch and I feel his nose crack under my knuckles. My vision is tinged white with rage, and my pulse pounds a murderous beat in my eardrums as I pull back and nail him again in the mouth. He raises his hands for protection, and I drop him to the floor.

Just so I can kick him. My boot catches him right under the rib, driving the breath from his lungs.

And I want more. I'm hungry for it—pain, blood, and fucking suffering.

He gasps and wheezes, trying to replace the air. But I don't hear it. I don't even see him, really. The only image playing behind my eyes is Chelsea—sweet and gentle, unwilling and struggling beneath him. Telling him no. Begging him to stop.

He didn't. Why the fuck should I?

I yank him up by his arm and throw him against the wall.

"She said no, asshole! Are you *deaf*?" Then I wrap my hands around his throat.

It's soft. Weak. So easily breakable.

And I squeeze.

His eyes bulge and he claws at my hands. But it's as effective as the brush of a butterfly's wings.

"Jake, please don't."

Chelsea's hand is on my shoulder, and her voice is soft. Pleading. "Don't, Jake. Please stop."

She feels like a harbor, steady and calm amid churning dark, deadly waters.

And so I stop. Not because he deserves it.

Only because she asked.

I release him and the dickhead slides to the floor, coughing and bleeding. I pant, glaring down at him, my heart beating brutally in my chest. I grab his jacket from the chair—mindful enough to take the keys from the pocket, because he reeks like a brewery—before throwing it at him.

"Get out," I growl, sounding as savage as I feel.

He wipes his bleeding face with his jacket and glares up at me with hateful, unrepentant eyes. "I need my keys," he rasps.

Dumb fuck.

"No. You can sleep in your car. When you're sober in the morning, then you can take your sorry ass elsewhere."

He actually opens his mouth to argue, but I don't let him.

"Two choices. Sleep in the goddamn car, or end up unconscious in the hospital. I know which one I'd prefer."

And it's not the car.

He looks over my shoulder at Chelsea, and I bristle that even his gaze is touching her.

"Do what he says, Lucas. Nikki and Kevin will be up in a few hours. Then you can all go."

With a final glare, he walks, hunched over, out the door. Which I slam behind him.

• • •

I turn the lock and the bolt to make sure he stays the fuck out. Or maybe to make sure I don't go out and kill him. My hands shake, my whole body still vibrating with barely restrained fury—and something else that I don't want to put a name to.

From behind me, Chelsea's voice trembles. "I can't believe Lucas tried—"

I whirl around like a roving volcano and erupt all over her.

"Of course he fucking tried! What the hell did you expect? You thought he flew across the country for a hug and a peck on the cheek?"

Arms hug her waist tighter. Her voice goes quieter. "I thought he was my friend."

"The naïve thing is cute, Chelsea—being a goddamn idiot is not."

She rears back like I've raised my hand to strike her. "Excuse me?"

Unfamiliar feelings bubble inside me like black tar, coating my insides, thick and clinging.

And ugly.

"Your friend?" I laugh. And drag my eyes up and down her body. "You dress like that for all your friends?" I click my tongue. "Lucky guys."

Her voice rises an octave. "There's nothing wrong with how I'm dressed."

My questions slice through the air. Sharp and cutting. "Are you drunk?"

"No."

"Are you high?"

"No!"

"Have you fucked him before?"

"That's none of your business!"

My mouth twists. "That's a yes."

"Don't cross-examine me!"

"Do you know what could've happened to you if I wasn't here?" I yell, forgetting about the six sleeping children upstairs.

Because that's the core of it, what has me craving murder. What makes me want to put my fist through the wall—or, more accurately, makes me want to grab that worthless piece of shit outside and put my fist through him. It's the unspeakable things that might've happened to her if I anyone but me had been here.

I've looked into survivors' eyes. I've seen the aftermath. And, sure, maybe they move on. And maybe they get past it. But they never forget.

And they're never, ever the same.

"Yes, I'm well aware, Jake. Contrary to what you think, I'm not stupid. I'm grateful that you were here." Her voice goes from flat to cold. "And now you can go."

I point at the door. "I'm not fucking going anywhere as long as he's outside."

"Fine. Enjoy the couch."

Then I'm dismissed. Chelsea turns around, her back as straight as a soldier's, and walks toward the hallway. After three steps she looks back, and her words hit me like a wrecking ball. "I see now why you're such a successful defense lawyer, Jake. You're so very good at blaming the victim."

For a second I just stand there. Too stunned—maybe too ashamed—to reply.

She walks up the stairs, and I'm alone. With the echo of all the things I shouldn't have said ringing in my ears.

12

Five minutes later I'm in the kitchen, rummaging through cabinets and drawers like an addict who's forgotten where he hid his stash.

And I'm muttering to Chelsea's dead brother.

"Come on, Robert, I've met your kids." I check the back of the fridge, moving aside a jug of almond milk, a block of tofu, and a bag of organic pears. "There's no fucking way you don't have alcohol somewhere in this house."

At this point I'd settle for a bottle of NyQuil.

I burrow in the freezer. And there, below containers of frozen spaghetti sauce, I hit liquid gold. A bottle of Southern Comfort.

I gaze at the label, already tasting relief on my tongue. "Attaboy, Robbie. My kind of guy."

I unscrew the cap and take a swig, too eager to wait for a glass. The cold liquid burns a pleasant, numbing trail down my throat. Before closing the freezer, I grab a bag of frozen peas for my screaming knuckles. Then I take a glass from the cabinet and fill it halfway with the amber-colored alcohol. As I swirl it in the glass, the pitter-patter of sock-covered feet comes down the back staircase.

And a moment later, Rory stands in the doorway, in blue sleeping pants and a white cotton T-shirt, with his brown curly hair sticking up in all directions. But his eyes are alert and wide, telling me he's been awake for some time.

"What are you doing out of bed?" I ask gently.

"I was thirsty," he lies. "Can I have a glass of water?"

I motion for him to sit down at the center island, then fill a glass with cold water from the sink. I slide it in front of him, and for a few moments we sip our respective beverages in the still silence of the dimly lit kitchen.

Until he confesses, "I heard you and Aunt Chelsea."

I just nod.

He peers up at me with a hesitantly probing blue gaze. "You were loud. You sounded . . . mad."

I swallow a gulp and breathe out, "Yeah. I was mad."

Guilt is already eating me up. But when his features tighten with worry, the bite of regret feels particularly sharp. "Are you gonna leave?"

I put my glass on the counter and look him in the eyes. "No, Rory, I'm not gonna leave."

His face relaxes. "Good."

He sips his water, then asks, "Why were you fighting?"

"I . . . lost my temper."

"Were you acting like a pissed-off little asshole?" he asks, using my own words against me.

I snort. The kid's astute—I'll give him that much.

"Something like that."

"My parents used to fight once in a while . . ."

With the stress of so many offspring, I'm not surprised. Actually, if at some point Robert McQuaid had gone full-out "Here's Johnny" from *The Shining*, I wouldn't be surprised.

". . . but they argued in the car."

A grin tugs at my lips. "In the car?"

"Yeah." He chuckles. "I guess they didn't want us to know they were fighting, so they'd go outside where we couldn't hear them. We'd watch them from the upstairs window." His voice goes hushed, smiling with the memory. "My mom's hands would go like this . . ."

Rory's arms flail above his head like an epileptic octopus.

"And my dad would be like . . ."

He pinches the bridge of his nose and shakes his head—the perfect imitation of a man trying to reason with an unreasonable woman.

"What would happen when they came back inside?" I ask.

He thinks a moment before answering. "They'd, like, march around each other. They wouldn't talk or look at each other. But after a while, things would just slide back to normal, you know?"

I don't know, actually. I had a ringside seat for my parents' "disagreements." But I nod and tell him what he already knows.

"They were good parents, kid."

He sighs deeply, with just a shadow of sadness. "Yeah."

I finish off the rest of my drink. "Come on, it's late. Back to bed."

Rory hops off the stool and together we head up the stairs. When we get to the doorway of his room, he feigns a nonchalant attitude I'm now familiar with.

"I'm not a baby, you know. You don't have to tuck me in."

I tap his back. "Yeah, I know."

But I walk in the room with him anyway.

As Rory crawls into the bottom bunk I glance up to where Raymond snores in the top one and pull up the covers that he's kicked off. Once Rory's settled, I smooth out his covers too.

"Night, Rory. Sweet dreams."

"Night." He turns on his side, snuggling into the pillows. I walk to the door, but before I step out, Rory's quiet voice stops me. "I'm glad you're here."

And with shock, I realize . . . so am I.

I turn around, finding his small frame in the darkness, a shy smile on his lips. And I tell him, "Me too."

Then he closes his eyes.

However, there's someone who's probably *not* so glad that I'm still here at the moment. And I head straight for her room. Because she and I need to talk.

• • •

I've heard people talk about anxiety. Nerves. But that doesn't happen to me. I don't get nervous before an opening statement or a closing one, not when my boss calls me to his office for a meeting, and sure as hell not before a hookup. I guess I just never cared about anything—or anyone—enough to be anxious about things not working out. I always figured I'd be able to fix it or find an equal option to replace it.

You know what I'm going to say next, don't you?

Yes: standing outside Chelsea's tightly closed bedroom door, I'm fucking nervous. My palms are sweaty, my stomach is clenched, my skin kind of itches, and I can feel my heartbeat in the back of my throat.

How do people live like this?

It's awful. I hate it.

And the fastest way to not feel like this is to just get it the hell over with. Talk to her. Eat shit and smile as I chew. Which I'm fully prepared to do.

If I could just bring myself to actually knock on the door.

But that's where the evil anxiety comes into play. It won't let me knock on the door, because . . . what if she tells me to screw off? What if she doesn't accept my apology? What if she's concluded that I'm a violent asshole who's unfit to be around her and the kids?

Shit.

A low movement catches my eye and I look down—Cousin It is staring coolly up at me. He's not wagging his tail, and his eyes are mocking. I can almost hear him telepathically calling me a pussy.

"Shut up," I snarl.

He turns from me in disgust and trots away.

I push my hand through my hair, take a breath, and knock twice. It's a soft enough not to reach any of the twelve ears one floor up, but it's decisive; women respond to confidence. The door opens faster than I anticipated—and only just far enough to frame Chelsea's face. Her eyes are red-rimmed and wet.

I put my hand on the frame, leaning in. "Are you okay?"

Her chin rises, all stoic with attempted indifference, but she's as bad at it as her foul-mouthed, car-stealing nephew is. "I'm fine."

Then she shuts the door in my face. She doesn't slam it—but I get the feeling she really wants to.

I knock again.

And again it opens—same width, same expression staring at me.

"I acted like an asshole to you." I thought it best to skip the formalities and get right to the point.

This time her eyes travel up and down, gauging my sincerity. Her beautiful mouth remains in that firm fuck-you line. "Agreed."

And closed goes the door.

When I knock again and the door cracks open again, I wedge my foot in there good to keep it open. "I'm sorry, Chelsea."

Can she hear the strain? The regret that sounds absolutely nothing fucking like me? Does she know this new voice is reserved only for her?

Of course she doesn't, idiot—'cause you haven't told her.

"I was angry that he—that anyone—would try to hurt you. I took it out on you, and I was wrong."

Chelsea blinks and her countenance thaws a couple of degrees, but it's still chilly. She shrugs—and I almost laugh. Because I see exactly where Riley gets it from.

"Just forget it, Jake. It's fine."

"It's not fine." I press my face into the crevice between the frame and the door, feeling like a fucking moron but laying it all on the line.

"And part of the reason I was pissed, even before you left with them, was because . . . I was jealous."

Her jaw drops. "You were?"

I nod. "Can I come in? I feel like a jackass talking through the crack."

"Oh." She moves back, opening the door wide. "Sure."

I step inside and close the door behind me, and I'm surrounded by all things *her*—her scent in the air, her clothes lying across the corner chair, the jewelry that's graced her delicate neck on the dresser, a framed picture of her in a graduation gown flanked by her brother and sister-in-law on the nightstand, and her sketchbook open on the bed. The sensory overload of these intimate sights and scents literally makes me weak in the knees.

She stands in front of me, waiting. She's changed her clothes—gone are the sexy halter and skintight jeans. In their place is an even sexier royal-blue LA Dodgers jersey and tiny white cotton shorts. Her face is flawlessly makeup free, framed by soft auburn waves. My hand twitches with the insane impulse to run my fingers through those waves—to count every shiny shade of color I find.

"You're sure you're all right?" I ask.

She unfolds her arms and nods. "Yeah. I've dealt with overeager guys before." She sits on the bottom of the bed, toying with the blanket. "I just never expected Lucas to be one of them."

I don't want to ask, but the masochist inside me needs to know. "Was he . . . like . . . a boyfriend?"

"No, it was never like that. We were . . . friends. Casual, you know?"

Yes, yes I do.

She shakes her head. "They texted me from the airport after they landed—a surprise. But as soon as they got here, I knew it was a mistake. How much everything—the way I look at things, my idea of a good time—all of it's changed." Her eyes crinkle with grief. Grief for her brother, for the carefree girl she used to be. "I guess responsibility will do that to you."

I sit down on the bed beside her. "I'm sorry."

I'm sorry your brother died. I'm sorry you had to grow up overnight. I'm sorry you're carrying the weight of six worlds on your slender shoulders.

My hand travels to her knee to give comfort, but when my palm makes contact with her warm skin, it changes into something else.

And she feels it too.

Her thick lashes flare a bit, her eyes meeting mine. She leans my way—inching closer.

"Why were you jealous of Lucas, Jake?" Her tongue peeks out, wetting her bottom lip. I don't think she realizes she's doing it—but I can't notice anything else. "I mean, he's still a boy, mooching off his parents, partying every night. You have an actual life; you have an amazing career."

"But he had you." I don't even think before I speak, because something about Chelsea McQuaid makes me want to . . . give. More. I reach across with my other hand and cup her cheek. The silky strands of her hair dance across my fingers. "At least for tonight, he did. How could I not be jealous?"

Chelsea leans closer and I dip my head, until we're just centimeters apart. So close I can taste the sweet mint of her breath.

"Is that what you want?" she asks quietly. "Do you want me?"

I lose myself in those clear blue eyes. Endless and cerulean, like tropical seas. And my voice is barely a whisper. "All the time. I can't remember *not* wanting you anymore."

We close the wisp of distance together, and our lips fuse. *Jesus.* It's slow at first, a gentle exploration. And then my fingers grasp firmer, pressing into the back of her neck, pulling her nearer. My mouth covers hers; it's pliant and soft and so fucking eager. And it feels . . . electric . . . and important. Like every kiss before was just a dress rehearsal to prepare me for this. To bring me here, to this moment, where I can't taste her deep enough—can't get close enough.

I press harder against her and she's right there with me—head arching, meeting me touch for touch. I drag my tongue across her lips, tasting mint and her. Chelsea opens her mouth and I slide my tongue inside its wet depths, delving and groaning, ready to devour.

With our mouths still joined, she rises to her knees, hovering above me. Her fingers scrape my jaw, touching my cheek. We move up farther on the bed, and she lies back, her hands guiding me to her—keeping me close. I settle between her open thighs, feeling heat and clenching, grinding desire. Her nipples are hard and hot beneath the jersey. They press through the fabric against my chest like two sharp flames, and I fucking moan into her mouth. Because I want to stoke those flames with my tongue, suckle that fire. She tilts her head, swiping her tongue slowly against my own.

And her hips slowly, deliberately rise.

Fuck me. I thrust against her in a long tight stroke, because it feels too goddamn good not to. She answers with a gyrating moan, low, guttural, and as decadent as the taste of her tongue. My hand glides up her bare, smooth thigh to her hip. I grasp her with harsh fingers, holding her steady so I can slide against her again.

But then she turns her head away, breathing hard. "Jake, the kids . . ."

Shit. The thought of the half-dozen sleeping demons just yards away should put a damper on my desire. But it doesn't. The stiff, hot erection straining between us whispers, *You can be quiet. They're asleep. You have hours and hours until morning,* he whines. *Just think of what we can do with all that time.*

And as if the baby can actually hear him, Ronan's cry squeaks out from the monitor on the nightstand.

Double dog shit fuck damn it.

That wasn't me. That was the dick talking.

I roll off Chelsea. My forearm covers my eyes and my breath comes out in forceful puffs, like I've run a marathon.

She says my name again, and I pant out, "It's okay—you're right. Just . . . just give me a minute."

Or an hour. Possibly a day.

Chelsea laughs breathlessly, with a hint of frustration. "My nephew has incredible timing. Incredibly bad timing."

I lift my arm and glance her way. Her cheeks are satisfyingly flushed, her lips swollen. It's a damn good look on her.

She sits up to tend to the hungry baby, and I roll to my side and pull her flush against me. "Let me take you out tomorrow night," I say.

Her fingers skim across my brow. "I don't have anyone to watch the kids. I can't just grab a sitter out of nowhere. They're a lot to take on."

"I've got that covered." I happen to know the toughest, most capable, patient child raiser ever. She got me to adulthood in one piece— and I was a shitload worse than all the McQuaids put together.

Chelsea leans back. "Yeah?"

"Yeah. So say yes."

She kisses me—fast and hard, the way I like it. Then she hops off the bed because Ronan is winding up to full volume.

"Yes."

13

At six p.m. Saturday night, I stand in Chelsea's foyer, wearing black slacks, a gray button-down shirt, and a black jacket. Chelsea is still upstairs getting dressed. I didn't go to my prom, but if I had, I imagine it would've felt something like this. Eager excitement. Thrilling possibilities. It's a new, rare feeling and I kind of like it.

When a knock comes from outside, I open the door—and there, before me, stands the kid whisperer. Luckily, she was good with short notice.

"Hey, Mom."

My mother is a tiny woman—five foot nothing, one hundred pounds, exotic gray-blue eyes that see through all types of bullshit, and a timelessly attractive face. What she lacks in physical stature she more than makes up for in a supersized personality. She flings herself at me, arms around my neck. "Honeybear! I've missed you!"

Out of the corner of my eye I spot Rory and Raymond, two sides of the same snickering coin. Raymond elbows his brother. "*Honeybear?*"

Internally I sigh. This could get ugly.

Behind my mother, Owen, her long-term boyfriend, walks in, hauling overloaded shopping bags in both hands. Owen's in his fifties, sports a noticeable beer belly, and has been just a hair or two away from totally bald for years. Together, they're an odd-looking couple—the kind who would make people say, *Is she really going out with him?* But Owen is a hell of a guy—patient, kind, hardworking—and he's worshipped the ground my mother walks on since the day they met.

He places one bag on the ground and shakes my hand. "Good to see you, Jake."

"Oh!" my mother exclaims, the Alabama accent she's never totally lost shining through, "I have to get the other two bags in the car—can't forget them."

Owen taps the air with his hand. "I got 'em, G. Take it easy."

The kids, minus Ronan, are lined up at the entrance to the den. Riley holds Regan on her hip. "That them?" my mother asks me, nodding her chin.

"That's them."

She approaches them slowly, regarding each one by one. "Hey there, children. I'm Jake's momma and your babysitter for the night. You can call me Gigi." She hooks her thumb over her shoulder. "And that's Owen."

"What's in the bags?" Rosaleen asks.

"Well, aren't you just adorable on legs." My mother crouches down to eye level with her. "In the bags are what we'll be doin' tonight. Ingredients for all kinds of cookies. Chocolate chip, sugar, peanut butter bliss, and some that haven't even been invented yet."

Two of the five lick their lips.

My mother stands back up and turns to Riley. "You're Riley?"

"Uh-huh."

"Any allergies in this bunch that I should be aware of?"

"No, Gigi, we don't have any allergies."

"Perfect!" She walks down the line and stands before Rory. His mouth is set and his eyes squint appraisingly. "You're Rory?"

"Yeah."

"I hear you're the tough one."

"You heard right."

She folds her arms. "You ever heard of salmonella poisoning, Rory?"

He thinks for a moment. "You get it from, like, raw eggs, right?"

"That's right. You know what's in raw cookie dough?"

"Eggs?" Rory asks—still sounding like a smartass with the one short word.

"Yep. So, maybe since you're so tough, you can play Russian roulette with salmonella and be our dough taster. What do you think?"

And he cracks a smile. "Sure."

"All right, then! Everyone grab a bag and show me where the kitchen is."

They do as they're told and follow my mother with her cookie bags like she's the Pied Piper. All except Rosaleen, who stays in the foyer with me. I move to the bottom of the staircase, one arm resting on the oak railing. Waiting.

Then Chelsea appears on the landing. And it's—*boom*—instant slow motion. Like every cheesy fucking teen movie from the eighties that I never watched. Her royal-blue dress swishes as she descends, giving teasing glimpses of creamy thigh. The soft fabric cinches at her waist and the deep V of her neckline exposes a tantalizing hint of perfect, pale cleavage. Her curled, glossy hair bounces with each step . . . and so do her boobs.

Rosaleen's little blond head swivels from me to her aunt, then back to me. "Are you gonna kiss her?" she asks curiously.

My eyes continue their travels. And I breathe out, "Oh, yeah."

Rosaleen scrunches her nose like a bunny that ate a bad carrot. "That's disgusting, Jake."

• • •

After reminding the kids not to be idiots for my mother, I take Chelsea to the Prime Rib—a high-end supper club in the heart of DC. It has an elegant, old-school kind of feel—candlelit tables, dark-paneled walls, excellent red wine, and an adjoining room for dancing to the soft tunes of the piano man singing bluesy versions of classic songs. I step in front of the maître d' and pull out her chair myself. After rattling off the specials, he goes to retrieve the bottle of Cabernet Sauvignon I ordered as we scan our menus. For a second, a horrifying thought occurs to me.

"You're not a vegetarian, are you?"

"No," Chelsea scoffs, gazing back at the choices with anticipation. "I love a good piece of meat."

"Happy to hear it." She detects the smirk in my voice and meets my eyes over the menu with a playful laugh.

After placing our orders, we drink our wine . . . and I can't stop looking at her. She's just so fucking gorgeous. She takes a sip of wine and a crimson drop glistens on her upper lip. She swipes at it with the tip of her tongue and I ache to lick it off with mine. Suck on those lips. Drink wine from the hollow of her throat.

I adjust myself below the table and take a swig from my own glass. Christ, this is going to be a long night. Everything she does, everything she says, makes me think of sweaty, slow, hard, deep fucking.

"Your mom isn't anything like I imagined."

Except that.

"What were you imagining?"

"Well . . . a larger woman, I guess. How did she even survive you—you must've been a huge baby. And . . . she looks so young." Chelsea points a finger. "That means you have good genes; you should thank her."

"My father was a big guy; I take after him build-wise. And my mom looks young because she *is* young. She had me when she was sixteen."

"Sixteen?" Chelsea repeats, probably thinking, *That's only two years older than Riley*. Pretty fucking young.

I nod, sipping my wine.

"So, your parents are divorced?" Her tone is hesitant; she doesn't want to wander into uncomfortable territory.

"Yeah." I shrug. "He left . . . when I was eight."

Her face pinches with sympathy. "I'm sorry."

"Don't be." And I couldn't be more honest. "It was the nicest thing he ever did for me."

Our food arrives. Chelsea stares wide-eyed at her porterhouse, 'cause it's larger than her head. "Now, that's a big piece of meat."

And she says it so innocently, there's no way I can let it pass.

"Mine's bigger."

She tilts her head and there's exasperation in her giggle.

"What?" I laugh, gesturing to my plate. "It *is* bigger. Unless you thought I was referring to something else?"

Her answer is an adorable pink blush.

"Dirty, dirty mind."

Chelsea picks up her knife and fork and gets to work on her meat. I get a depraved kind of enjoyment watching her fork slide between her lips, how she closes her eyes and moans on every other buttery mouthful. Before she's a quarter of the way finished, I'm readjusting my cock again—trying to make room in the ever-tightening confines of my pants.

"Did you grow up in DC?" Chelsea asks between bites.

I tip the wine bottle, refilling her glass. "We moved around a lot when I was younger. After my father took off, my mom didn't have a lot of options. She was twenty-four, with a kid, didn't even have a high school diploma. So she joined the army."

"Wow. It's hard to picture her in the army."

I shake my head, cutting my steak. "Believe me, she's tougher than she looks. She got her GED and became a military mechanic. We lived on a few different bases when I was a kid. She was never deployed, but they shuffled us around wherever they needed an extra hand."

"So you were an army brat?"

"Kind of." You'd think army kids would be disciplined—well behaved—but that's not always the case. I was forever the new kid, in places where strength was respected above all else. "Kill or be killed" was a big theme. Where the quickest way to prove your worth was to step on everyone else around you. "After she was discharged, we settled in Baltimore."

Chelsea nods, taking another drink. "And that's where your mom met Owen?"

"Yeah. He's a mechanic too—has his own shop. They run it together now." I smile. "They met when I got into a fight with a couple kids outside his place. He broke it up, called my mother, one thing led to another, they've been together ever since. Owen's good people."

Chelsea zeroes in on one detail of my explanation. "You got into a fight with a *couple* of kids?"

"I was a big kid. One-on-one wasn't really a challenge."

She grins. "Sounds like you were a troublemaker—like Rory."

"*Troublemaker* is an understatement. Rory is a fucking saint compared to me."

"Becker?"

I turn at the sound of my name and Tom Caldwell approaches our table, smiling. Caldwell's a bright-eyed, brown-haired, young but hungry prosecutor with the US attorney's office. A real by-the-book, straitlaced, goody-two-shoes kind of guy. He's also the prosecutor on my upcoming assault trial against Senator Holten.

"Caldwell." I nod, shaking his extended hand.

"I thought it was you. How's it going?"

The interactions between prosecutors and defense attorneys are bizarre. Inside the courtroom, we do our best to eviscerate each other. Outside of it, it's all friendly handshakes and weekend softball-league games. We're not supposed to take anything personally—because it's really not personal. Just business—part of the game.

"Pretty good," I reply vaguely. "Yourself?"

"I'm good—I'm here with my parents. Showing them around DC." His gaze turns to Chelsea—and lights up with interest. He probably thinks I don't notice, but I really fucking do.

Etiquette says I should introduce them. And etiquette can kiss my lily-white ass—pointless set of rules as far as I'm concerned.

But like I said, Tom's not the type to let much stand in his way. He holds out his hand to Chelsea. "Hi, I'm Tom Caldwell."

She shakes his hand. "Chelsea."

"Are you a client of Becker's?"

She smiles. "No. He's represents a few members of my family though."

"They're in good hands. Becker's a fine attorney."

"And your life would be so much easier if I sucked," I say.

He snorts. "That's true." Tom glances toward the entrance. "Well, I should be going. Enjoy your dinner. It was lovely to meet you, Chelsea." He taps my shoulder. "Jake, I'll see you in court."

"Have a good night, Tom."

As he walks away, Chelsea asks, "Is he a friend of yours?"

I shake my head. "Not particularly."

We finish our dinner and split a slice of cheesecake for dessert, but no coffee—neither one of us wants to diminish the pleasant buzz of good wine. There's more moaning, more fruitless readjusting as Chelsea slowly swallows a mouthful of the white, creamy concoction. *Fuck*—and I accused her of having a dirty mind. My dick pushes against the fabric of my pants the way an inmate strains against the bars of his cell, begging to be set free.

Chelsea's skin radiates the flushed, cheery glow of alcohol. Her eyes are hooded and happy but shield her thoughts, making her harder to read than usual. She leans back in her chair, regarding me, running her finger around the rim of her glass. "So if you started out as such a troubled youth, how did you become"—she gestures to me—"this? Successful. Honorable. Respectable."

I pour the last of the wine into my glass. "'Respectable' is probably pushing it a little bit . . . but the story goes like this: I was fifteen, running around with some real dipshits. Older guys. One night we thought it'd be brilliant to break into a sporting goods store, because that's the kind of losers we were, only I didn't know one of them was carrying. He ended up shooting a guard in the leg."

Chelsea gasps just a little.

And my cock twitches a lot.

"We ran out the back, right into the arms of a waiting squad car." I shake my head at the idiot I was. "The prosecutor wanted to charge me as an adult, send me away for serious time—and he could have. I had a hot temper and a record, and aside from my mother, I thought the whole goddamn world was my enemy."

Chelsea leans forward, completely enthralled. "So what happened?"

"The Honorable Atticus Faulkner happened. He was the juvenile judge on my case—a big, mean, scary son of a bitch. And he . . . thought he saw something worthy in me. So he kept me in juvenile court—gave me community service and probation, to be supervised by the hard-ass himself." I chuckle. "At the time, I thought the judge was doing me a favor—going easy on me."

"He wasn't?"

"Depends on your definition of 'easy.' For the next few years I trimmed grass by hand with fucking garden shears. I carried boulders, scrubbed floors, reshingled the goddamn roof—real Mr. Miyagi, wax-on-wax-off kind of shit. He rode my ass—nothing was ever good enough. It made me want to do everything better, just to fucking spite the bastard. And then . . . he had me start doing research. Studying case law, drafting briefs, analyzing opinions—it was fascinating to me. When my probation was up, the Judge offered me a job. By then I'd gotten my head out of my ass and was actually scoring decent grades in high school. With his recommendation and a shitload of student loans, I got through college, then law school . . . and that's all she wrote."

"I think that's amazing," she says softly, watching me.

"Yeah—the Judge is a pretty amazing guy."

Her lips slide into a gentle smile and something like awe shines in her eyes. "I was talking about you."

I'm hardly ever taken off guard. Surprised. But this stunning wisp of a woman just did exactly that.

Chelsea turns her head toward the piano music floating in from the other room. "I love this song."

It's a Van Morrison cover—"Crazy Love."

I toss my napkin on the table and move to stand next to her, holding out my hand. "Would you like to dance?" And I can tell I just surprised her too. The simple delight on her face when her hand slides into mine makes me want to do it again.

We step out onto the edge of the dance floor. I wrap my arm around her lower back, holding her tight and flush against me. One of Chelsea's hands rest on my shoulder, toying with the hair at the nape of my neck. The other is clasped in mine just over my heart. We sway, just looking at each other for a few moments.

"I was going to ask you to dance," she tells me. "But you don't seem like the type who would've said yes."

"I'm not," I answer, staring at her lush mouth. "I was just using it as an excuse to be closer to you."

She give me love, love, love, love, crazy love.

She sighs, practically sinks into my arms. Chelsea's head fits against my chest like she was made to be there. My chin rests against her hair, and I smell clean and sweet vanilla.

"Hey, Jake?"

"Yeah?"

Chelsea lifts her head from my chest. "You don't need an excuse."

I lower my head at the same moment she reaches up for me. And her lips—fuck—they're warm, soft, and move with such innocent daring, I'm practically trembling. Was it just last night that I first kissed her? It seems longer ago. I cup her cheek, stroking her skin with my thumb, kissing deeper, tasting wine and the moan I've been obsessing over all night.

And the absolute craziest part of it all? I haven't gotten laid in three goddamn weeks, but if this is all we do—kissing, with her against me, my arms around her—I'll be grinning in the morning like a guy who banged a whole sorority house full of cheerleaders.

I'm hoping for more. I want everything—all the secret, sweetest parts of her—but if this is all I get to have tonight? It's enough.

She give me love, love, love, love, crazy love . . .

14

With Chelsea inside, I close the passenger door to the Mustang and tip the valet. Then I slide in behind the wheel and pull away from the restaurant.

Moment of truth.

"I set my mom and Owen up in the upstairs guest room, so they don't have to drive back to Baltimore tonight."

"Okay." She nods.

I skim the steering wheel with the palm of my hand. "That means we could go to my place or head—"

"Your place is good," Chelsea says in a rush that makes me grin.

"My place it is."

On the ride over, I think about how it'll go down. Don't want to be overeager—can't jump her the minute I get in the door.

No matter how much I fucking want to.

I'll have to move slow, be smooth. Romance her. Offer her a drink, give her a tour. It's not like I haven't done this before, but it feels different this time. Because I know her.

Because I actually . . . like her—no matter how ridiculously inadequate that sounds.

• • •

I walk in the door ahead of Chelsea, flicking the switch on the wall that turns on the low light of the corner table lamp, illuminating black leather couches, hardwood floors, and bare walls. I'm not much for decorating.

Chelsea closes the door behind us, and I toss my keys on the table. I turn around to her, asking, "Would you like somethin—"

But I never finish the sentence.

Chelsea collides with me, arms around my neck, practically crawling up my torso, pulling me down and locking our lips. It's totally fucking unexpected.

And a total fucking turn-on.

Her breasts press against my chest, her hips gyrate against me—providing glorious friction against the straining boner trapped between us. And her mouth—god—she sucks at my tongue, nibbles on my lip, traps it between her teeth and tugs, one small step above pain that threatens to make me lose my goddamn mind.

When her hand skims down my shirt and rubs against the fabric-covered outline of my cock, I groan. "Jesus, slow down."

She pulls back, panting, "I don't want to slow down."

And she sounds so sure—confident and whimperingly needy at the same time—my heart starts to pound out of my chest.

"Okay."

My hands dive under her dress, grasping hot, firm thighs, just below her ass, and I lift, wrapping those perfect legs around my waist. Her fingers burrow through my hair as I angle my head, covering her mouth with mine. When I return the favor—sucking and biting, scraping those plump lips with my teeth like I've been dreaming about for weeks—a sharp keening sound vibrates from Chelsea's throat, and I swear to Christ, I almost come right then and there.

She lifts herself up and down, writhing against my stomach, as I stumble like a drunk toward the bedroom.

"Clothes," I grind out between kisses. "Too many clothes."

She nods, laughing, trying to drag my jacket off my arms while they're holding her up—which ends up pinning my elbows to my sides, like I'm a hockey player who's about to get his ass kicked in a brawl. Finally, we make it to my room. Chelsea's fingers span my jaw as she kisses me, slipping her legs out from around me, sliding deliciously down my front to her feet.

I rip my jacket the rest of the way off, then I breathe deep, trying to regain at least some finesse. My palms slide up her arms, my lips cover that perfect pulse point on her neck, and a moan echoes through the room.

I just can't tell if it's mine or hers.

I taste her skin with my tongue, licking and sucking—and she's warm, so fucking sweet. Without looking I manage to unzip the back of her dress. She lowers her arms, letting it drop to a puddle at her feet. And then I definitely look.

I step back from her, feasting with my eyes. All that smooth, rich skin beckons, aching to be touched, broken up only by bits of sheer black lace. *Fuck*, I can see her nipples through her bra—hard, pert, pink points. Her waist is flat and narrow, its circumference spanning both my hands, with a hint of toned muscle beneath soft skin. Her legs—Christ—long and lean and silky, like I knew they would be. And at the juncture of her thighs, the tiniest dusting of an auburn landing strip teases through the lace of her panties.

I want to rub my face against that softness, I want to rip that lace with my teeth and fuck her with my tongue until my name is the only word she remembers.

"You're perfect." My voice is low and ragged.

She meets my eyes; hers are impatient. "And you're overdressed."

My mouth twitches with a smirk, and I hold her gaze as I slowly unbutton my shirt. Her eyes go from ice to blue fire as I skim the shirt off my arms and drop it on the floor. She stares at my tattoos, the bulk of my biceps, wetting her lips with that tasty pink tongue. Still smirking, I unclasp my pants and drag the zipper down. My cock springs free from his confines, stiffly bobbing just a bit, and a moment later my pants and black boxer briefs pool on the floor too.

I stand before Chelsea naked and more consumed with lust than I have ever been in my entire fucking life. Her gaze continues to roam and it feels intense. Like a stroking hand—over my corded neck, across my chest, around the ridges of my abs, down the happy trail. When she gets to my cock, jutting out thick and ready, her eyes widen.

And then . . . she giggles.

Not exactly the reaction I was expecting.

"Something funny?"

Chelsea's flush deepens until her cheeks are crimson, and she giggles again.

"You're doing a number on my ego here, Chelsea."

"No, it's not . . ." She takes a breath. "You have *really* big hands."

I frown in confusion. "And?"

"And . . . I was just thinking . . . what they say about guys with big hands is definitely . . . true."

I've heard similar compliments before. What can I say? When God was passing out dick, he gave me extra.

But she sounds almost nervous when she says, "It's . . . it's been awhile for me, Jake."

"What's awhile?"

"Eight months."

That *is* a long time. And sick bastard that I am, the first thing that pops into my head is how incredibly snug she's going to feel around me.

I push those thoughts aside and focus on Chelsea. "Then here's what we're going to do. I'm going to lay you down in my big, huge bed and I'm going to make you come with my mouth and my fingers." I start to stroke my dick while I talk. Because it feels good and because she's watching. "Then we're going to go real slow . . . inch by inch . . . until you beg me to not go slow anymore. Sound good?"

Chelsea's chest rises and falls quickly. "Yeah. I like the way that sounds."

"Good." And it feels like I might actually die if I don't get my mouth on her right now. "C'mere." She meets me in the middle, raising her lips to welcome my mouth. The kiss is slower now but deep and rhythmic. I don't let up until I feel her shoulders relax. Then I move back to her luscious neck. I skim my nose along her collarbone, leaving a trail of wet kisses from her pulse to below her ear and back again. Her head tilts and she moans my name. I pull her bra strap down her shoulder, following it with scraping teeth. My deft fingers work the back clasp, and it falls away from her, leaving nothing standing between my mouth and Chelsea's pale, absolutely perfect tits.

I dip my head and take one peaked nipple into my mouth, working it over with my tongue, making her squirm and grind against my thigh. Then I pick her up, wrapping her legs around me again, before slowly laying her down in the center of the bed. She guides me over her, between her legs, and now we're kissing and rubbing—moaning and grinding. It's fucking fantastic.

Quick gasping curses slip from between Chelsea's lips, and it's so goddamn sexy because she's trying to keep them in . . . and just *can't*.

I slide down her writhing body, kissing and licking as I go. I nibble around her belly button, making her stomach contract. And just as I'm about to dive into pussy heaven, Chelsea whispers my name.

"Jake."

Only . . . it's not the good kind of whisper—not a *Jake, fuck me right now* type of tone. Has more of a *wait* kind of sound to it.

I look up into her eyes and ask against her skin, "What's wrong?"

There's vulnerability in her eyes and she does that flaily thing women do with her hand. "You should know I . . . I don't usually . . . *get there* this way."

"What do you mean?"

"I mean, sometimes it can take a long time for me to get off when a guy is . . ."

"Going down on you?" I finish for her.

And I swear her entire body blushes.

"Yes."

I consider this information while nibbling on the skin just below her hip bone. It's succulent.

"Do you want me to stop?"

Please say no, please say no, please say no . . .

"No, it's fine . . ."

Thank fuck.

". . . I just didn't want you to be disappointed."

I laugh a little, 'cause it's not the most absurd thing I've ever heard, but it's up there. "That's . . . really just not possible."

But now I'm intrigued. I slide back up until I can kiss her mouth and her tits press tight against my chest deliciously. Then I shift my hips, rubbing our lower halves together. Chelsea groans and sucks at my neck, getting into it.

"Why do you think you can't come with my face between your legs?" I ask against her ear.

"Do we really need to talk about this now?"

"I'm a lawyer. Asking questions turns me on. Having them answered is pretty hot too."

"I just . . . ," she pants. "I can't seem to ever relax enough, you know? My mind's always going. Always worried . . ."

I trace her ear with my tongue, blowing softly. "Worried about what?"

She scrapes her nails down my back. "You know . . . the sounds I'm making, what I . . . smell like . . . taste like."

Is she kidding? There's no way in hell I'm letting this go.

"Close your eyes, Chelsea."

She does. And I wrap her hand around my length, stroking slowly.

So fucking good.

"Now say my name."

"Jake."

Christ.

"Again," I grunt. "Fucking moan it."

"Jaaaake."

I grow harder, hotter, in her hand. I rub her thumb on the pre-cum that leaks from the tip, spreading it around the head.

"Do you feel that?" I pant harshly.

"Yeah." She gasps. "Yes."

"That's what your sounds make me feel."

She keeps her hand on my cock as mine skims down her stomach into her panties. She's smooth and swollen and so fucking soaked I have to bite my lip to keep from moaning. I slide my fingers through her lips, where she's warm and wet.

And then I bring my fingers up and run them across her upper lip.

"What do you smell?"

She's breathing so hard from her open mouth, it takes her a moment to answer.

"I . . . it smells clean . . . hot. Oh god, it smells like I want you really bad."

What a great answer.

I dip my fingers back in, circling her opening, teasing us both. Then I trace them over her lips, painting her with her own desire. She gets what I'm doing and slides her tongue out without being told.

"What do you taste like, Chelsea?"

"Sweet . . ." She gasps. "Warm . . . thick . . . like honey."

And I can't hold back a second longer. My mouth crashes onto hers—sucking all that sweetness off her lips. Licking at every drop. When I finally break away, I promise, "Now I'm going to make you come. And it's going to be every bit as fucking good for me as it is for you. Probably better."

Need pushes on me hard. I yank her panties down her legs and spread her wide open. And then my lips are on her like an openmouthed kiss, lapping and sucking, spearing her with my tongue.

Her back arches and her hips buck against me. I grasp her and hold her down, delving my tongue deep inside, tasting heaven. I push against her harder, covering my face in her—fucking drowning. And it's sublime. I eat her like she's the last meal on earth, devour her like the delicacy she is.

My tongue rubs tight, tiny circles on Chelsea's clit and I slide two fingers into her. Her muscles grip as I pump my hand and groan. And then she's coming, hard and long, pulsing around my fingers, against my mouth.

I drag myself up, wipe my mouth against my arm, not giving her time to recover. Not able to wait.

She takes my face in her hands and brings my mouth to hers. I grip my cock firmly, dragging the head through her pussy, teasing her opening.

And then, slowly, I push inside. Just the head.

Fuck me, she's tight. My eyes squeeze closed as her cunt closes around the tip of my dick, muscles clenching—pulling me in deeper.

Wait, my brain screams. *Wait, wait, wait . . .*

Braced above her on my elbows, my body and my mind war for sanity. For some kind of goddamn composure. Because I need to pull away. I need to get a condom.

And it's like she can read my mind.

"I'm on birth control," she gasps, sounding as winded and wound up as I feel. "The patch. I . . . I've been tested—the school clinic. I'm clean. There hasn't been . . . I don't do this. Ever. But I want it to be really good for you . . ."

It's already blown every other past experience out of the water—and I haven't even come yet.

"And . . ."

She caresses my face, gentle and tender. I look down into those beautiful blue eyes.

". . . and I trust you, Jake."

It's not smart—actually it's beyond stupid, especially for me. Especially after all that's happened and the last three weeks of hell. But feeling her bare. Sliding inside her with nothing between us . . . how can I say no to that?

I must've really lost my mind.

Because I don't.

"You can . . . ," I swear. "You can trust me. I won't hurt you."

She nods, eyes locked with mine. And that's all I need.

My hips move forward, pushing into her slowly, inch by torturous inch. It's hell and heaven rolled into one. Agonizingly, mind-blowingly slow.

I feel her stretch around me. Making room. She clenches, so snug and hot it borders on pain. The best kind.

A serrated moan pours from her lips and I almost lose it.

"You're okay?" I gasp desperately. "It's good?"

Chelsea arches up to kiss me, keening against my lips. "Yes . . . so good."

I pull back, just a centimeter, then flex forward again. Pressing and pushing, sliding along that tight fucking channel until I'm fully nestled. Until my balls rest against her ass. So deep. So wet. My eyes roll closed and I'm consumed by the sensation of Chelsea wrapped around me. Her scent, her moans, the taste of her lips, the grip of her hands on my back, on my ass, overwhelms me. Everything else fades away, and I'm lost in this one perfect moment—focused solely on where I'm buried deep inside her.

With almost a tinge of regret, I withdraw. Only to moan when I get to slide back in. This isn't fucking. Or screwing. This is something different—something more—that doesn't have a name.

"Jake . . . oh god . . . faster."

Her hips rise up to meet me and I lose track of time. All that exists is grinding and gasping, kisses and whispers, pounding and pulsing. *Harder and deeper and more.* Pleasure beyond anything I've known.

Electric heat scorches up my spine. I feel Chelsea's muscles throbbing around me, squeezing as she cries out beneath me. And when I start to come, the only word in my mind . . . is her name.

"Chelsea . . . Chelsea . . ."

I picture it, how I'm jerking, pulsing deep inside of her—filling her. And the image makes me come that much harder.

Afterward, the sharp pleasure eventually wanes, smoothes out, and settles into a pleasant hum through my limbs. Awareness returns and I lift my head from the crook of Chelsea's neck—my new favorite spot—to see her smiling drowsily up at me.

And all I can do is smile back.

I run my hand through her damp hair, feel the slick sweat on our bodies that seals us together, as I pull out of her with a grunt, then shift to the side, dragging her against me. I wrap my arms around her and kiss her forehead with more tenderness than I ever knew I was capable of.

15

I can't get enough of Chelsea's skin. It's bordering on obsession. I can't stop touching it, stroking the rough pads of my fingertips up her arm, across her creamy shoulder, down the perfect, pale line of her spine. It glistens like an opal under the glimmer of moonlight coming in from the bedroom window. My lips follow my fingers, soft brushes—she feels like velvet against my mouth, like the deepest cleft of a rose petal.

And she's not exactly idle either. Her tongue swirls around my nipple, she nips at my shoulder, her fingers play with the peppering of hair on my chest . . . and lower. She likes the feel of my stubble against her breast and I love the sensation of her auburn hair sliding across my stomach. For the next hour, it's a silent exploration. An erotic discovery—what tickles, what turns us on, makes me groan, makes her scream.

And then we're at it again. This time I'm on the bed, legs stretched out straight, leaning back on my elbows, watching with rapt attention as Chelsea rides my cock with total abandon. Her knees fall on either side of my waist; her pelvis rocks forward and back with the rhythm of an exotic dancer. The moonlight glowing in the window behind her casts her features in shadow, but her silhouette is nothing short of magnificent. Her hair wild, head thrown back, tits bouncing, lips parted and gasping.

I could stay just like this . . . I could watch her forever.

"Oh god . . . oh god . . . ," she pants, hips moving faster.

I curse, trying so hard not to thrust. Because I'm so deep—buried from base to tip in snug, hot cunt—and it feels incredible. I don't want it to end yet.

I cup her breasts, rolling both nipples between my thumb and forefinger. Pinching until she moans loud and long. It makes her hips sway harder, grinding down on me now in tight circles. And her moan sounded so sweet, I have to take her nipple in my mouth. Dragging my tongue around the velvet bud, flicking and teasing. Chelsea's hands grip my hair, holding me there, as I suction with my lips, then move up and around the soft mounds, sucking at the flesh, leaving a scattering of pink abrasions she'll feel tomorrow.

Her hands flatten on my shoulder blades, keeping me close.

"Jake . . . ," she keens, just to say my name, I think.

"That's it, Chelsea." My voice is both reassuring and demanding. An order and a prayer. And I can actually feel her get wetter, tighter around me. *Fucking A*—nothing has ever felt this good. "Come on, baby. Ride me, make yourself come. You're so close, aren't you?"

She whimpers and nods, her head jerking.

"Let me feel it. It's gonna feel so good. Get there, Chelsea."

And I can't not go with her.

I grab her hips in both hands and push up into her, my pelvis rubbing right against the spot she needs. Her hips push down while I thrust. And with my mouth open, teeth pressing into the skin of her collarbone, she stiffens and comes with the sexiest moan that seems to go on forever.

I let go with a long, broken groan.

For several seconds neither of us move. We're a perfect tangled mess of sweaty skin, harsh breaths, and languid limbs. My orgasm was so strong, I'm still twitching inside her as she leans forward, pushing me onto my back.

Chelsea lays her head over my heart, laughing against my chest, her soft hair falling around my neck.

And I blink at the ceiling, seeing stars. "Holy fuck."

Her back shudders with a giggle. "It was kind of a religious experience, wasn't it?" I feel her lips on my skin, worshipping the inked flesh. "Tell me about your tattoos." She kisses the one just below my collarbone—a string of numbers and letters.

I run my hand down her hair. "That's the docket number from my case with the Judge."

"And this one?" I don't have to look—I feel her lips move over the one that's lower, stretching from my pec to my shoulder. It's an angel, a perpetual child with a smirking face and crooked halo.

"That's for Benny. A kid I knew when I was twelve. He got mugged one night walking home. They hit him with a metal pipe—cracked his head. He died."

Below the angel is a cursive *G*—she places a soft kiss beside it. "This is for your mom?"

I nod. Chelsea brushes her lips against the others—the scales of justice I got after law school, the dragon and roses I got after I lost my virginity, the deep-rooted tree I got in honor of the Judge, and about a dozen more.

She moves lower down to the crook of my elbow, the underside of my forearm. It tickles when she kisses it. "And this?"

It's a spiral tribal design that winds around my arm—sharp swirls with jagged edges. I grin. "I just thought that one looked cool."

I feel my dick softening inside her, but I have no desire to move. And Chelsea must feel the same, because she rubs her cheek across my pec, resting above my nipple. And her breath turns slow and even, exhaustion taking hold of us both, as as we slip into well-earned oblivion.

• • •

Sometime later, I become aware that her weight is missing, the heat from her lush, lithe body is absent. And there's a strange dry, scratching sound that makes me think Cousin It tracked us down and is trying to push open the door with his rough paw. I stretch out my left hand, searching, but there's only empty space beside me. I roll to my side and open my eyes.

Chelsea is in the brown cushioned chair by the window, legs tucked under her, a glow of moonlight behind her. She's wearing my gray button-down shirt—and it's never looked better. She's watching me, her bottom lip caught between her teeth, her hands busy in her lap.

Sketching.

Chelsea is drawing. Me.

"Am I gonna have to pay you a dime, Jack?" My voice is gravelly with sleep and sex.

She smiles. And it's beautiful. "This one is on the house, Rose."

Yeah. Time to remind her I'm definitely not a Rose. I throw back the covers, putting my bare-assness on full display. I sit up, swing around to sit on the edge of the bed, feet on the floor. I lower my hand, wrap it around my dick, and bring him back to life with just a few rough strokes. And Chelsea's drawing suddenly stops short.

"I've never done an X-rated sketch. Are you auditioning to be my first?" she asks lightly.

"I wasn't sure what the focus of the piece would be. I wanted to make sure it's to scale."

"That's so helpful of you."

"How about you? You in a helpful mood?"

There's an edge to my voice that only I can hear. It'll be dawn in a few hours. I don't really know what happens then. But I'm almost desperate to feel her, everywhere, all at once. To not miss a thing or waste a minute—touch every fantasy. Because . . . this may be the only chance I've got.

She sets the pad of paper aside on the chair and comes to stand in front of me.

"I'm in the mood to make you feel good," she says softly.

I rest my hands on her hips, pulling her to me, and press my forehead to her stomach.

"You already make me feel good," I whisper hotly against her perfect skin.

Chelsea slides down to her knees in front of me. "Then let's shoot for better than good."

She leans forward, placing a warm kiss on the tip of my cock.

Oh Christ.

Her tongue peeks out, laving a circle around the head. And my heart goes berserk. She takes me in her mouth—hot and so wet. She slips down on me, as far as she can go, then slowly back up, making the shaft slick with her saliva. Then she grips me at the base, pumping firmly, while her mouth goes to work, sucking hard and fabulously. After a few minutes, I'm clenching my jaw, but can't keep the low grunts at bay—Chelsea answers me with a pleasured hum that makes my balls ache. Then she releases me, looks up, takes my hand, and pushes it into her thick auburn locks.

"Show me what you like, Jake."

Motherfucking god.

She goes back to working me over with her mouth, with her hand, her cheeks hollowing out. And it feels unreal. My hand flexes in her hair, guiding her up and down in my favorite rhythm. It makes me feel powerful . . . and at the same time completely at her mercy. The pressure builds, the blissful tension as her head bobs faster and I climb higher and higher.

With a guttural groan, I grip her hair and pull her off. "Get on the bed." My voice is harsh. Desperate.

Chelsea climbs on beside me and I stand, yanking my shirt from her arms in one swift motion. Because it's in my way—and I want to see. Everything. I hold her by the hips, my thumbs digging into the flesh of her perfect ass, conveying without words exactly how I want her.

On her hands and knees.

I get on my own knees, on the bed behind her. My fingers toy with her cunt, sliding and rubbing where she's already wet. I line my straining dick up and plunge inside with a hard thrust.

Chelsea cries out, back arching, and I have to fucking remind myself to go easy. Short, shallow thrusts make her keen, and then she's pushing back against me—wanting it harder. Deeper. My hand skims the smooth expanse of her back, tracing her spine down to her ass. I knead the flesh with rough hands, gripping, so I can move her forward and back along my cock. And the view—fuck—it's beautiful. Watching my full length disappear into her tight heat, over and over, seeing the fine sheen that covers her skin, hearing her groan my name as her hair sways with every vigorous movement.

I'm close now—so close. The only thing holding me back is the need to watch her go first. I guide her down onto her stomach and cover her with my body, my chest and stomach against her back, my pelvis on her ass, thigh along thigh—not an inch of space between us. I kiss and suck on the silken skin of her neck as our bodies slide, warm and damp with sweat. My hips pump into her deep and fast. I wedge my hand beneath her, finding that magical, hard nub between her swollen lips, rubbing it with my fingers, giving it the friction it needs to make her scream. Chelsea's hands fist the sheets above her head and her muscles clamp down on me as she comes.

"Jake!"

I think it's her voice that pushes me over. With my mouth against her ear, I grunt and growl, thrusting forward one last time, as my vision goes white and the purest pleasure surges from my gut, spreading out to my fingers and the tips of my toes. Robbing me of the will to move, to think, to do anything but keep this gorgeous woman under me.

I pant against her neck and, after a moment roll to the side off her back so she can breathe again. Without a word, I pull her against my chest, holding on tight, my face buried in her hair. Chelsea's heavy breaths eventually slow and just before I fall asleep, I feel her delicate lips press a chaste kiss to each of my knuckles. Then she tucks my hands beneath hers and drifts off.

• • •

My eyes open at five a.m. on the button—even though it's only been two hours since they closed the last time. I stare at the fiery gold of Chelsea's hair, still in my face, her warm body still encased in my arms. Carefully, I pull away and am able to disentangle myself without waking her. Like always, I head to the bathroom, to take a piss, brush my teeth. I stretch, crack my neck, feeling only slightly stiff.

I avoid my reflection in the mirror as I splash my face with cold water and slick back the unruly black hair. Then I pad silently to the closet for a T-shirt and sweatpants, giving Chelsea's angelic sleeping features only a quick glance. I head to the kitchen and turn on the small flat-screen television, keeping the volume low, as I wait for the coffee to brew. When it's done, I step out onto the balcony, watching the streetlights fade and the pink-gray sky of dawn turn to blue.

And I tell myself to breathe. Slow and steady. In and out. There's a sick, churning feeling in my gut—and I tell myself to ignore it.

I step back inside the kitchen to find Chelsea leaning against the wall, squinting, looking adorable in my gray button-down, which almost reaches her knees. "You're not a sleeping-in-when-you-get-the-chance kind of guy, are you?" she asks with a yawn.

"Ah, no," I tell her with a straight face and a shaking head. Then I start the speech—and the words taste bitter. Wrong.

"I'm going for a run. There's coffee in the pot and—"

"Coffee?" Chelsea cuts me off. "No way—I'm going back to sleep." She steps closer to me, running her palm along my abs. "But . . . if you want some company in the shower when you get back from your run . . . I'll definitely wake up for that."

She stretches up on her tiptoes, kissing me quickly. And I imagine her in the shower, wet everywhere, her luscious tits slick with soapy suds. It does seem like a good idea.

She turns to walk back to the bedroom. But my voice stops her.

"Chelsea . . ."

Because direct is always easier. And I don't do complicated. Honesty is . . . shit, I don't remember the rest.

"Yeah?"

I look at her face, so open and giving and real. Her lips, so close to smiling. And I remember words whispered in the dark.

". . . and I trust you, Jake."

"I won't hurt you."

And all I can say is, "I had an amazing time last night."

The smile comes to fruition. "So did I."

• • •

The run is punishing. I sprint farther, push harder. Sweat pours down my forehead, my chest throbs, and my legs burn like my muscles are on fire as I try to figure out a way for the chaos that is Chelsea and her gaggle of kids to fit into my organized life. I have goals, priorities. I didn't get where I am today by getting distracted by a piece of ass—no matter how spectacular the ass may be.

I walk through my apartment door an hour and a half later, still breathing heavily. Van Morrison's "Into the Mystic" is playing from the speakers. I grab a bottle of water from the fridge, chugging it, as Chelsea stands at my stove—looking more delectable than she has the right to—cooking. Still in the gray shirt, she rocks her hips in time to the music—then she uses the spatula as a microphone.

"I . . . want to rock your gypsy soul . . ."

And I have to laugh. That kind of fuck-hot, sexy-cute—it's lethal.

"I thought you were going back to sleep."

Chelsea glances back over her shoulder at me. "So did I. Apparently Ronan has ruined me forever—couldn't fall back asleep. Then I decided to cook breakfast . . . except you don't have any food. Judging by your refrigerator and your cabinets you exist on eggs, pasta, and the occasional beer alone."

"I make a mean macaroni and cheese. Otherwise it's takeout."

She scoops scrambled eggs onto a plate and hands it to me, eyes sparkling with a playful, morning-after contentment. "Bon appétit. Here's the best I can do under these conditions."

I take the plate but set it on the counter. And I forget all about priorities and goals, honesty and schedules.

I just want to kiss her again.

Before I have the chance, my cell phone rings, my mother's name flashing on the screen. Chelsea sees it too and she steps closer to me, her face shadowed with concern. I bring the phone to my ear. "Mom? Everything okay?"

"No, Honeybear, it's not. You and Chelsea need to meet me at the hospital."

16

"I can't tell you how awful I feel. I'm so sorry." My mother looks like she's on the verge of tears—and she's not a crier.

Chelsea rubs her shoulder. "It's okay. These things happen—especially to my nieces and nephews. Riley broke her collarbone when she was two, Raymond broke his leg last year—and my sister-in-law was always on top of them. It's not your fault, Gigi."

"I knew as soon as I heard him yell, somethin' wasn't right . . ."

They continue to talk in the emergency room waiting room, while I crouch down in front of Rory where he sits in an orange plastic chair, cradling his right arm against his chest. Pain has bled his face of color. His eyes droop with agony and he takes in air slowly, every move hurting.

"How are you doing, kid?"

"It hurts."

"Yeah, I know." I brush my knuckles against his knee, not wanting to jostle him, then I glare at the triage nurse and tell her to hurry up, that I think he could be going into shock.

She can tell I'm full of shit but it makes me feel better to try.

The story goes that the kids were playing in the backyard, under

Owen's watchful eye, while my mother made breakfast. Riley bet Rory that he couldn't climb to the top of the oak tree. Which, of course, Rory could—and did. Getting down . . . posed more of a challenge. And here we are.

"Why don't you head back to the house, Mom?" I tell her, rubbing her shoulder. "Owen's probably losing his mind with the other five by now."

"Okay." She nods, caressing Rory's head. "I'll see you soon, sweetie."

"Don't worry, Gigi, I'll be fine," Rory says kindly, proving that my mother has definitely won the kid over.

"Rory McQuaid?" a nurse with a wheelchair announces, ready to actually take us into the ER.

"Thank Christ," I mutter.

• • •

Later, Rory's propped up on an exam table while a George Clooney lookalike explains to Chelsea that her nephew's arm is busted.

"He fractured the ulna. It's a clean break, and we won't need surgery to set the bone—that's a positive."

"Good." Chelsea nods her head, nervously glancing at Rory.

The doctor gestures toward the door. "So, if you could both just step outside, I'll set the bone and we'll get Rory fitted for his cast."

"Step outside?" Chelsea asks, frowning.

"Yes, it's hospital protocol. Closed reductions can be painful, which is upsetting for parents and guardians, so we have them wait outside the room during the procedure."

"I prefer to stay with my nephew."

"I'm afraid that's not possible," George replies.

All her nervousness fades away, and Chelsea is rock-solid, sure. She's poised and polite—but there isn't any way she's taking no for an answer.

"I appreciate your position, Dr. Campbell, and I hope you'll appreciate mine. I will sit next to Rory and I'll hold his hand while you set his bone. Neither Mr. Becker nor I will make a sound or say a word. But I'm *not* leaving him. If necessary, I'll take him to another hospital."

The doctor thinks it over—and then he completely caves.

"That won't be necessary."

Chelsea sits in the chair beside the table and clasps Rory's left hand in hers. Her smile is so loving, so tender, my chest aches looking at her. The doctor adjusts the table so Rory's flat on his back, then he shows me where to brace his shoulders, holding him still. They gave him some pain meds, but even with them, I know from experience, getting two halves of your broken bone rubbed together doesn't fucking tickle.

"Just breathe, Rory," the doctor tells him—like that'll help—and my chest starts aching for a completely different reason. Then he holds the kid by his wrist and near the elbow and starts.

"Ahh!" Rory yells. His voice is sharp and shocked and hits me like a shank to the stomach. "Ahh!" he calls again, trying to grit his teeth.

Chelsea tightens her grip, looking at him earnestly, letting him know she's here, sharing his pain—even if she can't save him from it. And I whisper to him, right against his ear, giving him the only comfort I can, wishing like hell that I could take this pain for him.

"You're doing so good, kid. It's almost done."

"Ahh . . ."

"Almost there, Rory . . . almost there . . ."

• • •

"This cast is totally badass!" Rory admires the camo-patterned plaster that now covers his arm from elbow to hand. I chuckle because he bounced back quickly, and obviously his sparkling personality is intact.

Chelsea gives him the obligatory chiding for his language—but she's smiling too.

"Hey—could you draw a tattoo on my cast? Like yours?" Rory asks, pointing to the tats visible in my short-sleeved T-shirt.

"Sure."

Chelsea looks around. "I wonder what's taking so long with the discharge papers? I'm going to go ask . . . oh, hey, Janet!"

A woman steps within the curtained area where we're waiting. She's a black woman, in her midthirties, with tightly cropped brown hair and a bright smile, wearing a beige suit and white blouse.

"Hi, Chelsea." Her eyes fall to Rory, on the bed. "Hi, Rory, I heard you had an accident."

Rory shrugs, his earlier smile replaced with a distrusting scowl.

Janet looks me over and I notice her gaze pause at the tattoos on my arms.

"Jake, this is Janet Morrison," Chelsea says, introducing us. "She's our social worker from CFSA. Janet, this is Jake Becker, my . . ."

She searches for the word. "Lawyer," I supply, offering Janet my hand. "I'm with Adams and Williamson."

Janet nods her head. "That's right—you negotiated Rory's release with probation after . . . the car incident."

It might just be the nature of my job, but I'm not a big fan of government agencies—or their employees. Too much power, too many people—too many mistakes that can so easily be made without any accountability. That's what has me asking, "So, Janet—did you just happen to be in the area?"

"No." She glances at the open file in her hand. "Whenever a child in our system has an incident at school, at a hospital, or with the police, we're automatically flagged." She turns to Chelsea. "Do you mind if I ask you my questions now before you go?"

"Sure, that's fine."

"Great. The doctor said Rory fell out of a tree. Did you see him fall, Chelsea?"

And I suddenly get a bad fucking feeling about this. Chelsea doesn't appear to share my concern.

"No. I actually wasn't home when he fell out of the tree."

This is news to Janet. "Where were you?"

Chelsea's eyes slide my way. "I was . . . with Jake."

"Your lawyer?"

"It was sort of a working breakfast meeting," I explain smoothly.

"I see." She writes something down on the file. "So who was with the children while you were at your meeting?"

"Jake's mother," Chelsea answers.

Pen poised, Janet asks me, "Your mother's name and address?"

"Giovanna Becker." Then I rattle off her phone number and address and tell Janet it's fine to contact her whenever she wants to.

She closes her file. "That's all I need from you right now, Chelsea. Is it all right if I speak with Rory alone for a few minutes?"

"He's a minor," I tell her.

"In cases like this it's standard to speak with children alone."

"Cases like this?" I ask, schooling my tone. "What kind of case do you think this is, exactly?"

Janet isn't the backing-down type. "It's a case where an injury has been sustained and abuse needs to be ruled out."

"Abuse?" I half-laugh, half-choke. "You think she did this?" I point at Chelsea.

"No, Mr. Becker, I don't. However, if she had, Rory would be much less likely to divulge that information with you both in the room."

And I do actually see her point. I just don't like it.

I look to Rory. "You up to talking, kid? It's your call."

Rory's smart and I can see in his eyes that he senses this is something that needs to be dealt with now. "Yeah, I'll talk to her, Jake. No big deal."

I squeeze his shoulder. "We'll be right outside."

• • •

I guide Chelsea through the curtain and into the hall, out of Janet's earshot.

"What's wrong with you?" she asks once we stop. "Why are you antagonizing Janet?"

I grasp her elbow. "I wasn't antagonistic. But it's important that she knows that you know your rights."

She shakes her head, confusion gripping her features. "Janet is the nicest person I've met at CFSA. She's my social worker. It's her job to help me."

"No, Chelsea, it's not. Her job is to make sure you're a stable guardian for the kids."

For the first time she realizes the difference—the distinction—and her mouth turns tight with worry.

"Do you think . . . I mean . . . could I get in trouble for this? Are they going to give me a problem about Rory's arm? About being with you last night?"

My hands move to her shoulders, squeezing and rubbing at the tension that stiffens them. "No—listen to me—it's okay. You didn't do anything wrong and they're not gonna give you a hard time." I pause then, wanting to make her understand without freaking her out. "But you need to think about how you phrase things. Sometimes how a statement reads in a report doesn't represent the way things actually are."

I see this often in my cases. Words like *terroristic threats* being applied to six-year-olds who shoot finger guns at classmates and claim they're "dead." Or a charge of "possession with intent to distribute" makes some moron sound like a member of a goddamn drug cartel, when in reality they're a slacker fuckup who happened to get their hands on a big stash.

Words matter, and sometimes context can make all the difference in the world.

"When you talk to Janet, you have to think about not just what's true, but how the truth will look in black-and-white. Okay?"

She nods and I pull her in against me. I kiss the anxiety on her forehead, then whisper, "Don't worry. Everything is fine."

She squeezes her arms around me and nods against my chest.

We step apart as Janet comes out, wheeling Rory in a hospital-policy-mandated wheelchair. "We're all set." She smiles.

A nurse comes up and gives Chelsea his discharge instructions and pain medication. Out on the sidewalk, Rory stands, saying he can walk to the car.

Janet shields her eyes from the glaring afternoon sun. "I'll be stopping by the house one day this week, okay, Chelsea?"

"That's fine," Chelsea replies. "I'll be there."

"It was nice meeting you, Janet," I offer just for pleasantries' sake.

"Same here, Mr. Becker."

Rory is between me and Chelsea and we walk to the car, her arm around his lower back, my hand on his shoulder, just in case he stumbles. And even though I don't look back, I feel Janet's eyes on the three of us the whole way.

• • •

Over the next few weeks, Chelsea and I settle into a weird domesticated arrangement. After work, I swing by the house to help her with the kids, hang out, and do whatever needs doing. Then, after the kids are in bed, Chelsea and I . . . hang out together . . . more often than not without clothes.

The sex has been . . . fucking intense. Quiet—so as not to wake the cockblocking interrupters who are all too eager to disturb us—but still top-notch. It's a different situation for me—new—but strangely comfortable. I haven't really let myself think about it too deeply. No labels or discussions or any shit like that. They say ignorance is bliss . . . and my nights with Chelsea have certainly been that.

For now, that's good enough.

And the kids are a fucking riot. Like a funny, sometimes adorable, sometimes ass-pain-causing fungus, they've grown on me. One time, after work, Chelsea needed me to take Rosaleen to her piano lesson. And I did, but . . . it didn't end well:

"We need to add a piano teacher to the list," Rosaleen tells her aunt as we walk into the kitchen.

The TV is blaring in the next room, where Raymond and Rory engage in Mortal Kombat—the video game—but from the sounds of it, they may actually be on the verge of beating the shit out of each other. Ronan rocks quietly in his swing while Regan busies herself with pots, pans, and wooden spoons strewn like landmines across the floor. A big metal pot boils on the stove, giving off a warm, beefy aroma.

Chelsea looks up from the cutting board, where a half-chopped carrot lies in wait. "What do you mean? You have a piano teacher."

"Not anymore." The seven-year-old shrugs.

Chelsea turns suspicious eyes on me.

And I have no guilt at all. "That guy shouldn't be teaching children. Sadistic son of a bitch."

Chelsea places the knife down beside the carrot. Then she takes a deep breath, and I know she's trying not to stress. "Monsieur Jacques La Rue is the best piano instructor in the city. It took months for Rachel to get him to take Rosaleen as his student. What happened?"

I pop a slice of carrot in my mouth. "What kind of guy makes his students call him Monsieur*? He's probably not even French," I grumble. "I bet his real name is Joey Lawrence from the Bronx."*

Rosaleen climbs onto the island stool across from her aunt and eagerly tells the tale. "He hit my knuckles with the ruler 'cause I messed up."

"Exhibit A," I interrupt. "What kind of sick fuck could hit her?" I motion to Rosaleen's joyously precious face. "Rory? He's another story. Her? No way."

Rosaleen continues. "So Jake went out to his car and came back in with a baseball bat. Monsieur La Rue asked him what he was doing and

Jake told him, 'You hit that kid's knuckles again, I'm gonna hit you with this.'"

Chelsea turns to me, her head tilted and jaw slack.

I admit nothing.

"So . . . he fired us," Rosaleen concludes.

I nudge her with my elbow and offer her a carrot. "We fired him.*"*

She pops it in her mouth with a smile.

Chelsea watches our exchange and her face softens. "Okay. New piano teacher. I'll add it to the list."

Another time, the older kids had dentist appointments that conflicted with Regan and Ronan's Mommy and Me playtime. Like I've said before, I fucking hate doctors—and dentists are just doctors for teeth. So I opted to take the little kids to their class. I mean, they're babies—how hard could it be?

Children are everywhere, all shapes and sizes, some climbing, some stumbling, some—like Ronan—getting their "tummy time" on the floor as they try to master crawling. And the parents—Jesus, they're like a frighteningly uptight, Stepford-wife smiling, cooing religious cult armed with cameras. The Mommy and Me playroom is obnoxiously colorful—a rainbow rug, neon slides, blaring padded wedges, and mats that hurt my eyes if I look at them too long. Freakily cheerful music pours from mounted speakers with a forcefully happy teenager in a fuchsia T-shirt running the show.

And don't get me started on the clowns.

They're painted on the walls, marionette versions line the shelves, and stuffed ones with eerily wide-spread arms fill the corners, their red-rimmed, white-teethed mouths opened in the creepiest fucking grins I've ever seen. Like they're just waiting for an unsuspecting kid to wander by so they can bite their heads off.

About ten minutes into free play, I watch Regan navigate an obstacle course. Next to me is a loudmouthed father cheering his son on like the kid's about to reach the end zone in the goddamn Super Bowl. He gestures with his head. "He's the fastest kid here. I got him running the course in forty-five seconds."

Good for you, buddy.

"Which one's yours?"

I point to Regan, where she climbs the slide, her orange jumpsuit sparkling beneath the lights. She chants as she goes, "Hi, hi, hi, hi . . . ," like the Seven Dwarves marching with their pickaxes.

"Is there something wrong with her?" the son of a bitch asks.

I scowl. "No, there's nothing fucking wrong with her. She's . . . focused." Then, for shits and giggles, I add, "And she could totally do this course in under forty-five seconds."

Dickhead scoffs. "I doubt that."

I turn cold eyes on him. "Wanna bet?"

He brushes his brown bangs with an arrogant hand. "Fifty bucks says my boy beats her."

"You're on."

I shake his hand, then I go scoop Regan off the slide and coach her as I carry her back to the obstacle course—like Mickey talking to Rocky Balboa in his corner.

"You got this, Regan. Don't let him distract you—watch his left hook, keep your eyes straight ahead."

She squeezes my nose.

So I try to use words she'll understand. "If you do this, I will hi you forever."

That gets her smiling.

We line them up and the father counts them down. "On your mark, get set, go!"

And they're off . . .

Douchebag and I cheer them on, like gamblers at the horse track.

"Go, baby, go!"

"That's it! Pull away from the pack! Make your move!"

They're neck and neck . . . until the little boy gets distracted by a massive booger hanging out of his nose. He stops to work on it—and the race is Regan's.

"Yes! Fuckin' A!" I yell proudly. I pick her up and hold her high above

my head; she laughs and squeals. And somewhere Freddie Mercury sings "We Are the Champions."

As loser dad passes me the fifty, the teenager busts us. "What is going on? This is a cheerful place—there's no gambling!"

"Right. Well, we're gonna head out anyway."

I grab Ronan in one arm and Regan in the other. On our way out the door, I whisper to her, "Let's just keep this between us, okay?"

She looks me straight in the face and nods. "Hi."

I spend my Saturdays with Chelsea and the kids. I bring work with me, sneak in scraps of time when I can focus. Most Saturdays, if there aren't too many activities to get to, are relaxing. Fun, even. But sometimes . . . well . . . there're six kids. From a purely statistical standpoint, the odds of a bad day are pretty goddamn high.

One morning, as soon as I got out of the car I knew it was going to be a bad day. It wasn't any kind of sixth sense that gave it away.

It was the screaming.

I open the front door, and the impressive screeching sound that only a really pissed off two-year-old can make hits me like a blast of hot air. Regan sits on the foyer floor in front of the closet, a mess of tears and screams and stamping feet, surrounded by shoes, flip-flops, and boots. Chelsea squats in front of her, holding out a sparkly sneaker for the toddler's inspection. Two other pairs of tiny shoes are beside her on the floor.

"This one?" she asks, with a mixture of hope and annoyance.

Regan knocks the sneaker from her aunt's hand, shakes her head, bangs her hands on the ground, and wails.

Guess that wasn't the one.

Chelsea notices I'm here. I raise my eyebrows and try really damn hard not to grin. "Everything okay?"

"No," she hisses. "It's not." She yanks her hair back from her face, the haphazard bun ready to fall. There's stains on her T-shirt—looks like peas—and her cheeks are flushed with color.

That's when I notice that it's not just Regan making a shit-ton of noise.

It's a chorus—a symphony of angry young voices coming from the living room. Somewhere upstairs, Ronan's voice joins the melee. And he does not sound fucking happy.

After another shoe rejection, Chelsea stands up and throws the sandal across the room. "Which one, Regan? What do you want?*"*

Regan just cries and points at absolutely nothing.

Before I can say a word, the twins come crashing into the foyer, arms locked around one another. They drop to the floor, rolling and grunting, teeth bared.

"You knew I was saving it!" Rory yells.

"It was in the cabinet—it's free game!" Raymond growls.

"Stop it!" Chelsea screams. "Both of you, cut it out!" She's kind of screechy now, too.

They totally ignore her.

"You're a jerk!" one shouts.

"You're a dick!" the other replies, and I'm betting that one was Rory.

"Stop!" Chelsea shrieks, and she grabs the one on top by the tiny, sensitive hairs at the base of his skull. Then she yanks him up.

Even I *fucking flinch.*

Rory howls, both hands coving the back of his neck. "What the hell?" he demands from his aunt. "I'm gonna have a frigging bald spot now!"

"Don't fight with your brother!"

"He ate the last chocolate chunk cookie!" Rory fires back. "He knew I was saving it and he ate it anyway."

Standing now too, Raymond taunts. "And it was gooood."

Rory lunges, and I unfreeze from the shock of seeing all hell break loose. I step between the boys, separating them with iron grips on their arms. "Knock it off."

Then Rosaleen comes tearing around the corner, with a livid Riley right behind her.

Of course.

"Give it back!"

“No, it’s mine!”

“It’s not yours, it’s mine*!”*

“No it’s not!”

Chelsea instinctively holds out her arms when Rosaleen cowers behind her.

“What is going on?” she shouts to her oldest niece.

“She has my pen!” Riley screams.

“A pen!” Chelsea shrieks back. “Are you kidding me? You’re fighting over a fucking pen!”

Riley pouts in that scathing way teenagers do. “Nice language, Aunt Chelsea.”

Chelsea grinds her teeth. “Give me a break, Riley.”

“No—you’re supposed to be the adult. Look at us! No wonder this is a crazy house!”

“And that’s my fault? That you’re a bunch of selfish, evil heathens?”

Riley gets in her face. “Yes! It is *your fault!”*

Chelsea raises her hands. “That’s it! I have had enough of this! All of you—go to your rooms!”

Loud with indignation, Rosaleen bellows, “But I didn’t do anything!”

Chelsea spins sharply, facing the little blonde. “I said go! Now!”

Rosaleen draws herself up, her little face scrunched and angry. “You’re mean! I don’t like you!”

Chelsea grabs the seven-year-old by the arm and moves her toward the stairs. “Well, you can not-like me from your room!”

Rosaleen tears up the stairs, crying. Riley marches up behind her, arms folded and shoulders stubbornly straight. Rory gets in one last shove to his brother, then heads up, too. As Raymond turns to follow, Chelsea adds, “Raymond—you go to the spare room. I don’t want you boys near each other.”

He glares. “This sucks!”

And Chelsea glares right back. “Tell me about it!”

After the Four Horsemen of the Apocalypse disappear upstairs, an eerie quiet settles in the house—like a town after a tornado has blown through. Ronan isn't crying anymore from upstairs, probably succumbing to his mid-morning nap. Regan selects two hot pink flip-flops from the pile of unwanted shoes, slides them on her feet, then—sniffling—shuffles out of the foyer.

Chelsea breathes hard, and I approach her with caution.

"You okay?" I ask softly.

Her blue eyes meet mine for a moment. And then she bursts into tears.

And she looks so damn sweet, even unhinged with frustration, that I choke down a laugh. 'Cause she'll kill me if it gets past my lips.

I rub her shoulder and guide her down the hall into the kitchen. "It's all right. Shhh, don't cry—it's all right."

She shakes her head, tears streaming as she settles on an island stool. "It's not all right. They're evil. They're ungrateful little animals."

And I suddenly have the urge to call my mother, to apologize. Not for anything in particular . . . just the first fifteen years of my life.

I grab the Southern Comfort from the freezer and pour her a glass.

She sobs into her hands.

And I pour a little more.

"What happened?" I ask.

"Nothing!" She looks up at me. "Absolutely nothing! They all just woke up like this."

Chelsea swipes at her cheeks and takes a long sip. I squeeze her shoulder. She props her elbow on the counter and drops her forehead into her hand. Her voice is laced with guilt. "Oh, God. I can't believe I pulled Rory's hair. Rachel never would've done that. She and Robbie didn't believe in corporal punishment."

"That explains a lot." Believe me, I'm not a fan of hitting kids. But there are times when a smack on the ass is very much deserved.

"Rosaleen's right. I am mean!" And she's crying again.

And my laugh will no longer be contained. It comes out deep and totally sympathetic. "Sweetheart, I know *mean. Trust me, you're not mean."*

She finishes off her drink.

"I'm not telling you how to raise them, but I know from my own experience that kids need discipline. They want it—even if they don't know it. You should write up a list of offenses and punishments. You know, curse and you lose your phone for the day. Fight, and you have to pick up the dog shit. A McQuaid Penal Code."

She snorts, red-eyed and runny-nosed. "That's not a bad idea."

I step closer, nudging her legs apart to stand between them. I touch her jaw. "Do you feel better?"

Chelsea sighs dejectedly. "No."

I tilt her face up to me and lean down. "Then let's see what we can do about that."

Her lips are warm. She sinks into the kiss, opening for me, taking my tongue with a gasp and gently offering hers. It's just a kiss—it won't lead to more. But if it feels half as good for her as it does for me, than it's done the job.

I pull away, just an inch. "Feel better now?"

And she smiles. "Almost. We should work on that a little more."

I chuckle. "Let's do that." Then I press my lips to hers again.

Some days, I get insanely turned on watching Chelsea. Just the way she moves, smiles . . . bends over to pick toys up off the floor. And if I'm lucky, the opportunity presents itself to act on it. But we have to be sneaky.

There was one evening when Ronan fell asleep early, Riley was reading in the living room, and Rosaleen and Regan were watching Rory and Raymond play Xbox.

I grab Chelsea's arm, dragging her toward the stairs.

"Boys—watch your sisters," I call.

And a few seconds later, I've got Chelsea in the bathroom of the guest room upstairs. I turn on the shower for cover, and the sink faucet, then I press up against her back, running my nose up her neck, inhaling the sweet fragrance of her skin and her want for me. She turns her head, kissing me with tongue-dueling vigor, gripping the sink so hard her knuckles turn white.

"What are we doing?" she pants.

"I can make it quick," I promise. "And I can make it good."

Then I drop to my knees behind her. Lifting her skirt, dragging white lace panties down her legs. And my mouth is on her, enveloping her pussy, pressing into her, licking like a starving man. My nose skims between the delectable cheeks of her ass—goddamn, that ass.

When I have more time, I swear I'll give that particular area all the glorious attention it deserves.

I knead with my hands, probe with my fingers, getting her hotter—making her wetter than she already is. She moans above me, leaning forward. So ready and beautifully fucking eager.

I stand up, unbuckle my pants, and slide into her wet softness in one smooth thrust.

"Christ," I groan. "Nothing should feel this good."

Chelsea whimpers encouragement as I start to thrust against her, the buckle on my belt jingling with every push. She stays upright, her hands reaching back to caress anywhere she can touch, and that angle makes her even tighter.

Splaying a steadying hand across her hip, I cup her face with the other, turning her head so I can kiss her, taste that sweet tongue. Our lips clash and nibble, our moans mingle. Pumping faster, I move my hand to her shoulder, my arm crossing her chest, holding her right where I need her. Chelsea's hand disappears downward, touching herself, rubbing quick circles on her clit as I slide in and out from behind.

And I lose it.

"Oh fuck . . ."

She gets there with a high-pitched whimper, her knees going weak, but

I hold her up, my thrusts losing their rhythm, turning to hedonistic jerks as I come gloriously inside her.

Afterward, we fix each other's clothes, touching and kissing. Chelsea's creamy cheeks are beautifully flushed as she laughs against my mouth. "My God . . . I really like quick."

And I think I just might love her.

17

Although the majority of the night is spent in her bed, I don't actually sleep at Chelsea's. I go home before the kids wake up—we've talked about it; she doesn't want to confuse them or set a bad example. So, early one morning, after my run and a shower, as I'm threading my tie around my neck, my phone lights up with Chelsea's name. I bring it to my ear.

"Let me guess—you've found a nanny who makes Mary Poppins look like a slacker and she's agreed to take the kids for a whole week, so you need me and my hard cock at the house ASAP?"

Her throaty laugh comes through the speaker. "That is a lovely dream—but just a dream. I'm calling about something else—something that's actually more wonderful. Are you sitting down?"

Curious, I sit down on the closed lid of the toilet. "I am now. What's up?"

"Listen to this."

There's a rustling—the sound of her adjusting her cell phone. Farther away I hear her voice. "Regan, did you learn a new word?"

Then, loud and clear, comes Regan's tiny voice. "No."

"Are you *sure*?" Chelsea asks.

"No."

"Regan, say no."

"No, no, no!"

By the time Chelsea gets back on the phone, I'm laughing too. And pride—ridiculous, knee-weakening pride—surges through me.

"What do you think of that?" Chelsea asks, a huge smile in her voice.

"I think we've got a fucking genius in our midst."

• • •

On a day in early April, Chelsea has a meeting with Janet at the CFSA offices. She brings the two little ones with her and I cut out of work early to be at the house when the other kids get home from school. I'm sitting in the front courtyard when Rory and Raymond make their way up the driveway. And before he even reaches me, I spot a bright red welt on Raymond's cheekbone—fresh, but already starting to bruise.

"What happened to your face?"

Raymond's eyes flick to his brother, then back to me. "I fell walking up the stairs at school. Hit my cheek on the metal railing."

I motion to the chair next to me. "Sit down." Then I grab a decent-size rock from the garden, come back, and start tapping his knees—watching them jerk on impact.

He adjusts his glasses. "What are you doing?"

"Checking your reflexes."

"Why?"

"Because you're nine. And unless a person is very old or ill, the body's automatic reflex when falling forward is to protect the face and vital organs from injury by softening the impact with the hands. So . . . before I accuse you of being full of shit, I want to make sure you don't have a brain tumor." After another tap, I put the rock on the wrought-iron table and look him in the eyes. "Everything appears normal. So—who punched you in the face, Raymond?"

Rory exits the conversation, walking onto the front lawn, and his brother sighs. "You can't tell Aunt Chelsea."

"Why not?"

"Because she'll call the principal and we'll have to have a meeting and it'll just make everything . . ."

"Worse." I nod my head, totally getting it.

"Yeah."

I lean forward, bracing my elbows on my knees. "I won't tell your aunt—but you're gonna start talking to me. Right now."

"His name is Jeremy Sheridan. He hates me."

"Is he an athlete?" I guess. "Gives you a hard time to show his friends how awesome he is?"

"No—he's in all my advanced placement classes. The National Honor Society too. He doesn't play sports."

A nerd bully? That's new.

Times have changed since I was in school.

"But my GPA is higher than his. I always score better than him on tests—so he hates me," Raymond explains, his voice melancholy.

"When did this start?"

He thinks back. "January. It was little things at first—him messing with my locker, knocking my books out of my hands, tripping me. But lately things have . . . escalated."

I nod slowly, anger sizzling like a long fuse. "And how do you react when Jeremy pulls this crap?"

He shrugs, embarrassed. "I just try to stay out of his way. I'm thinking of throwing my grades. I didn't want to resort to that, but maybe he'll leave me alone if he can be number one in class."

It's then that I notice Rory, still on the lawn, bending down every now and then, a plastic bag in his hand.

I cup my hands around my mouth. "What are you doing?"

"Collecting It's shit," he yells back.

"Why?"

"So I can put it in a bag and set it on fire in Jeremy Sheridan's locker."

Well . . . that's one way to deal with it.

"Your heart's in the right place, but I don't think that's a smart idea." I wave him back. "C'mere."

I have another strategy in mind.

I look Raymond over appraisingly. "You're thin . . . weak."

"Yeah," he sighs. "I know."

"But . . . if you can be fast, if you know the vulnerable spots to hit . . . that won't matter."

"You want me to hit Jeremy?"

"The next time he comes at you? I want you to break his fucking nose. I guarantee he won't come at you again after that."

Raymond stares at the ground, thinking it over. "My dad used to say violence is never the answer."

"It isn't. But defending yourself isn't violence—there's a difference. Your dad would want you to defend yourself, Raymond."

He seems to agree with that rationale. "But . . . I don't know how to punch."

I put my hand on his shoulder. "I do."

• • •

After Chelsea gets home, I take the boys to my gym. We spend the next two hours hitting the bag—Rory using only the fist that's not encased in a cast. I show Raymond how to aim, how to put his weight behind a punch, how to land one without breaking his thumb. As we walk out and climb into my car, he's looking decidedly more chipper than when he came home from school.

And then my phone rings.

It's the monitoring company.

"Fucking Milton," I spit under my breath. "Where is he?" I bark into the phone.

They give me the address and I hang a U-turn. "Hold on, boys, we have to make a quick detour."

Fifteen minutes later, I pull up in front of a mansion. Not a big house that can be called a mansion—an actual fucking mansion. Groups of twentysomethings and people even younger are gathered in clusters around the lawn, holding red Solo cups and smoking cigarettes. Cars are parked haphazardly along the long driveway, and music pounds out from the lighted windows. Rory and Raymond are behind me as we walk in the front door.

"Stay close to me, guys."

Their eyes go wide with wonder as we pass rooms with half-naked women—girls—walking around, amid screams of laughter. Their necks arch and turn at the sight of guys in baseball caps and expensive jeans snorting white powder from glass tabletops. In the hallway, a pretty blonde wearing nothing but Daisy Dukes and a bra stares at Rory.

She reaches out her hand. "You're sooo cute."

But I grab her wrist before she lays a finger on him.

"Milton Bradley?" I ask in a low voice.

"He's in the card room—in the back."

I drop her hand and stalk toward the back room. And I make sure the boys are with me. We enter the card room, and through a fog of smoke I spot the dipshit himself—seated at a round card table, blond hair falling over his forehead, a tall glass of beer and a stack of black chips in front of him.

His eyes meet mine. "Oh, shit."

He jumps to his feet, ready to bolt out the French doors behind him.

"Don't even think about it," I say, warning him. "If you run it'll just piss me off more—and it'll be that much worse for you when I catch you. And believe me when I say I will fucking catch you."

Rory tries to be helpful. "For an old guy, he's pretty fast, dude."

Milton's shoulders droop.

"Party's over." I crook my finger at him. "Let's go."

Rory and Raymond buckle in in the backseat and Asshole sits in the front beside me. As soon as we hit the road he starts in: "I can explain."

"Which would matter if I was interested in hearing an explanation. I'm not."

But he keeps talking anyway. "I was celebrating! I'm allowed to be happy—they dropped the heroin charges against me."

"No shit, Sherlock!" I have to yell. "I'm the one who petitioned them to drop the charges. And let me just make sure I have this right—you thought it was a good idea to celebrate drug charges being dropped by going to a party where fucking drugs are everywhere? Do you really not see the problem with that?"

He just shrugs.

Twenty minutes of blessed silence later, I pull up in front of Milton's mansion. With the car idling, I ask, "Where are your parents?"

"I don't know," he answers petulantly. "France, I think. Mother said she needed a vacation."

Probably from the dumbass that is her son.

But even still—his parents aren't going to be getting any Parents of the Year awards.

"So . . . you guys, like . . . wanna come in and hang out?" Milton asks.

I rub my eyes. "No, Milton, I don't want to fucking hang out with you." I point my finger at him. "Just go inside, lock the door, and go to bed. Maybe you'll wake up smarter tomorrow."

He pouts. "All right."

I make sure he gets into the house and then I pull away.

After a few minutes, Raymond says quietly, "He seems lonely."

"He's a fuckup." No sympathy from me.

"He seems like a lonely fuckup."

"Watch your mouth," I bark over my shoulder.

"You just said it!"

"And when you're thirty, you can say it as much as you like. Until then, keep the language PG."

"That's, like, the definition of hypocritical, Jake," Raymond argues.

"Your point?" I shoot back.

Rory's unusually quiet during the ride. And I wonder what he thinks about the things he's seen. His family doesn't have the same kind of money to burn as the Bradleys, but they're close. And without even realizing it, I channel the Judge.

"Do you know why he's a fuckup, boys?"

"Because he drinks and does drugs?" Raymond tries. "Only losers do drugs."

There's something wonderfully heartwarming about Raymond's answer. So simply black-and-white—so innocent.

"That's true. But that's not the whole reason." I turn onto Chelsea's street and continue. "Milton promised me he'd stay home. And then he broke that promise. When you take everything else away—money, clothes, nice cars, big houses—all a man has is his word. That he says exactly what he means, and he does what he says. If a man doesn't have his word, he's not a man."

They digest that for a moment. Then Rory asks, "Did your dad teach you that? Did he show you how to be . . . a man?"

There's a hint of worry in his voice. And I wonder if he's concerned about himself and his brothers and sisters growing up without their own father. With no example to guide them. So all I can give him is the truth.

"No, Rory. My dad was . . . the kind of man I didn't want to be." And then I add, "But there was another guy, a friend—the best kind of friend—who wouldn't put up with any of my shit. He taught me everything I needed to know."

• • •

Later that night, hours after the kids are in bed, Chelsea and I writhe between her sheets. It's slow, almost sweet. Her long, pristine arms stretch out above her, glowing with smooth flawlessness. I kiss her neck, worshipping that skin, as my hips flex between her legs. I ride her in smooth, steady strokes, the muscles in my back tense with rising pleasure. She sucks on my earlobe, whispering how good it feels, and my thrusts quicken of their own accord. My body takes over—it's mindless, carnal perfection that I never want to end.

But what a fucking ending it is.

Chelsea's hands grip my ass, pushing me deeper as her own hips rise to take me in. We go over the edge together—she stiffens beneath me as I go taut above her, pulsing inside her, both of us silently gasping.

Afterward, I wrap around her from behind. She laughs at nothing and kisses my hands before tucking them under her cheek, like her own personal pillow. I inhale her scent as I drift off, my nose against the nape of her neck.

But a small, scared voice breaks the quiet.

"Nooo. Noooo . . ."

It comes from Regan's baby monitor. Chelsea jerks, opens her eyes, and starts to drag herself out of bed. Without thinking, I kiss her temple. "Go back to sleep. I'll get her."

I slip on my pants and a T-shirt and pad barefoot up the stairs.

Regan is sitting up in her miniature toddler bed, eyes bleary, hair a mess, her room illuminated by a Cinderella nightlight. She raises her arms up as soon as she sees me.

And my mother's words, from decades ago, come out of my mouth.

"What's the trouble, bubble?"

I lift her up, her warm little body instantly clinging. I rub her back and smooth her hair. Regan's lower lip trembles as she points to the long drapery in the shadowed corner of her room. "Nooo."

"Did you have a bad dream?"

I move the drapes, showing her there's nothing hidden, nothing to be afraid of. She squeezes my shoulders with tiny arms and lays her head down against me. I sit in the rocking chair beside her bed, patting her back and whispering softly.

"There're no monsters, Regan."

In real life there are, but not in this house. Not while I'm breathing.

"I've got you, kiddo. You're safe. Shhh . . . go to sleep."

I kiss the back of her head and rub her back, rocking her until she relaxes in my arms and falls back into a peaceful slumber.

18

A few days later, Rosaleen scares about ten years off of Chelsea's life when she disappears. I'm working late, Chelsea is helping Riley with her homework, and the rest of the kids are scattered around the house . . . doing what kids do. When it's time to start getting ready for bed, that's when Chelsea notices the little blonde is missing. They call her name, comb through the bedrooms, the closet, the playhouse in the backyard, the fucking swimming pool and garden. Chelsea calls the neighbors and they check their backyards too.

By the time she stops searching to call me, she's a mess of frantic tears, ready to call the police and the national guard. In the car, driving to the house, I'm the one who asks if they checked the third floor—Robert and Rachel's room.

In a breathless rush, Chelsea says they didn't—and she bolts up the stairs. There, curled up on the floor of the walk-in closet, wrapped in her mother's robe, is Rosaleen, fast asleep. I get to the house a few minutes after the discovery, when Chelsea is still teary-eyed and shaking. Rosaleen feels bad but says she likes to go into her mother's closet sometimes. To remember what she smelled like.

The explanation makes Chelsea cry more. And just about breaks my fucking heart too.

After an unusually long bedtime, when Chelsea can't seem to pry herself away from her niece's doorway, I broach the subject of the bedroom. It's been months since Robert and Rachel died, and the room stands exactly as it did before.

I don't know much about grieving—I know even less about kids—but it doesn't seem . . . *healthy* to me. Chelsea is adamant—she claims the kids aren't ready for the change, to have their parents' most personal things boxed up and relocated. Or worse, given away. But I don't think it's the kids who aren't ready.

I think it's her.

She shoots the topic down, refuses to discuss it. And when those gorgeous eyes turn icy, I let it drop. Because it isn't really any of my business, so it isn't worth an argument.

• • •

Late on the Wednesday afternoon after Rosaleen's Houdini imitation, Chelsea calls me at the office. "Are you free?"

"Depends. What do you have in mind?" I say, my tone weighted with suggestion about what's exactly in *my* mind. It's right along the lines of what's in my pants.

"Don't get your hopes up." Chelsea sighs. "I'm on my way to pick up Raymond at school."

I check my watch. "Shouldn't he be home already?"

"He should be, but they kept him after. Apparently he got into a fight."

A smile slides onto my lips. "Did he win?"

"What kind of question is that?"

"Ah . . . the only one that matters?"

She chuckles. "I don't know if he won. Principal Janovich would like to see me in his office to discuss it. Do you want to meet me there? I have a feeling your lawyering may come in handy."

And I have a feeling she's right.

"I'm packing up now—I'll meet you there."

By the time I arrive at the ivy-covered grounds of Raymond's private school, the meeting is already under way. A secretary ushers me into a large office, where a dignified, gray-haired man sits behind a presidential desk—awards and accolades line the walls, and dark wood bookshelves are filled with important-looking, gold-leafed, thick leather volumes.

Chelsea sits on the opposite side, an empty chair between her and two very wealthy-looking—very pissed-off-looking—parents. The woman is blond, in a royal-blue suit and pearls, with long bloodred fingernails. The husband looks quieter, smaller—the remora to her shark.

"And you are?" the gray-haired guy—Principal Janovich—drones.

I hand him my card. "Jake Becker. I'm the family attorney."

The blonde raises one scathing eyebrow. "I'm an attorney as well," she tells me—like it's a warning.

"I thought you might be," I volley back.

Takes one to know one.

I sit beside Chelsea. She looks nervous, hands clasped on her lap tightly. "Where were we?"

"They want to expel Raymond," she says in a strained voice.

I lean back and nod. "Interesting."

Janovich clears his throat uncomfortably. "We have a zero-tolerance policy here for fighting, harassment of any kind. Raymond injured his classmate gravely."

"Did he break his nose?" I ask casually.

The principal is a bit taken aback. "No . . ."

Too bad—better luck next time, kid.

". . . but there was excessive bleeding. It was a frightening experience for all involved."

Unable to stay silent any longer, the blond mother rises to her feet. "I do not pay thirty thousand dollars a year in tuition to have my child assaulted in the hallways. I demand this . . . delinquent be brought up on charges!"

"Let's pull the tapes," I suggest.

"The tapes?" Janovich asks, like he doesn't know what I'm talking about.

"The tapes." I nod. "I passed no less than nine hallway security cameras on my way in. There must be video of the altercation. And since it just occurred hours ago, surely the footage couldn't have been recycled already."

The principal's eyes widen—and I almost expect him to say, *Don't call me Shirley.*

"Unless . . . you've already seen the footage?" I narrow my eyes. "I see what's going on now." And it fucking pisses me off.

They won't like me pissed off.

"What do you think you see, Mr. Becker?"

I address the blond viper. "You're booster club people, aren't you? Patrons? You donate money to the school on top of that thirty grand—for libraries, new wings, and things like that?"

The father at last finds his voice. "I don't see how that has anything to do with this."

My eyes swing back to the old man behind the desk. "It has everything to do with this is because Mr. Janovich here thought it'd be easier to hang this whole thing on Raymond—who has a legal guardian who may be too busy to put up a fight—rather than ruffle a benefactor's feathers. Is that accurate?"

"It most certainly is not!" he chokes out. "I don't appreciate what you're implying."

"I'm sure you don't."

He fiddles with his tie. "I have viewed the footage Mr. Becker is referring to. Although behavior on both sides was less than exemplary, I feel given the violence of Raymond's assault, he does warrant harsher punishment."

And now I'm laughing. "So because Raymond is the better fighter, you're gonna come down harder on him?"

He starts to speak, but I wave him off. "Let's put a tack in that for now and discuss your 'zero-tolerance' policy. Where was that policy when Raymond was being bullied since January?"

Chelsea's head turns sharply to me. "What?"

I keep my focus on the principal, and my voice is deadly calm. "I have it on good authority that Jeremy has punched, pushed, tripped, and demeaned Raymond numerous times. Either you've chosen to ignore those instances, or you don't know what's going on in your building, Mr. Janovich. Either way, it doesn't bode well for you."

His face goes red, but I don't let up. I lean forward. "And let me be perfectly clear on this point: if there are any further instances of harassment in any form against Raymond McQuaid from this day on, I will sue the ever-loving hell out of this school and you personally." I tilt my head toward Chelsea. "By the time I'm done with you, she will own every building on these grounds—and your house." I pin him to the wall with my stare. "I don't make threats often, Mr. Janovich, and when I do . . . they are never idle."

I turn my head to the seething blond shark. "That goes for you and your son, too."

And the seething turns to a full boil. "You wait just a damn minute! My son is the victim here! He was—"

"Lady, I hate to break it to you, but your son is a mean-spirited little shit who enjoys lording it over those who are weaker—and smarter—than him. And it stops today."

She stands up. "Jeremy would never do such a thing!"

Oh boy—she's one of those. I see a lot of parents like this in my line of work: people with selectively blind not-my-angel syndrome.

"And if Raymond McQuaid said he did, then he is a filthy, disgusting little liar!"

And now Chelsea is on her feet, too. "I'm not going to listen to you call my nephew names. He is kind and thoughtful, and if your son hurt him in any way—"

She gets in Chelsea's face. "Perhaps if your brother had been a better father, he wouldn't have a son who acts like an animal!"

The breath rushes from Chelsea's body. And her face goes white. "What did you just say?"

"You heard me! Instead of going out and getting himself splattered across the highway, maybe he should have stayed home and—"

I've heard the expression *Fathers will die for their children; mothers will kill for them.* But I've never fully understood it until this moment. Gone is the sweet, smiling woman I know, and in her place is a scrappy cage fighter gunning for the Hulk.

It's hot.

"Fuck you, you mean cunt!"

"Chelsea!" I yell, totally astounded.

I get to my feet and grab her arm, just as she moves to take a swing at the blonde. She struggles to get out of my grip as I push her behind me.

"I'll shove those pearls down your throat, you miserable bitch!"

And the miserable bitch isn't taking it quietly either.

"No, you little whore, fuck *you*! I will end you!" Her husband valiantly tries to hold her back.

Chelsea grabs for her, almost making it past me. "I'll break your face, you plastic-surgery-addicted freak!"

This may be getting out of control. So I pick Chelsea up and throw her over my shoulder, legs kicking and cursing a blue streak into my back as I hold on to her with one arm.

"We'll take a one-day suspension," I tell the principal. "As long as Jeremy gets the same."

"Done," Janovich agrees, more eager than anyone to get us the hell out of his office.

I keep Chelsea out of the screeching hag's reach. "Good luck with that, man," I tell her husband, and walk out the door.

In two chairs lined up against the hallway wall sit Raymond and—judging by the bloody rag held against his nose—the ginger-haired Jeremy.

"Nice face," I tell Carrot Top. Then to Raymond, "Let's go."

Raymond stares aghast at the still-raving woman hanging down my back. "What's wrong with Aunt Chelsea?"

"Oh . . . ," I say, trying to play it off, as we walk down the hall, "she's just lost her mind a little bit."

• • •

By the time we make it out to the parking lot, Chelsea is a little quieter—slightly calmer. "Put me down, Jake! Right now—I mean it."

I set her on her feet.

And she proceeds to walk around me, right back toward the school.

I plant myself in front of her. "A, I've already spent countless unbillable hours keeping members of your family out of jail."

She marches forward, undeterred. I cut her off again. "B, CFSA will not look kindly on you assaulting the mother of your nephew's classmate at his school."

That does the trick. Chelsea looks up at me, eyes blazing with fury . . . and pain. "That woman is a heartless bitch!"

I move in closer, my voice dropping. "I couldn't agree more. And there's not a damn thing you can do about it." I rub her shoulder. "Are you good with that?"

Her breathing starts to level off. And she looks more like the non-crazy version of herself. "Yeah. I'm okay now."

She turns around and heads toward her car, where Raymond stands. Her finger points at him. "You should've told me, Raymond!"

"I didn't want to make it worse," he says.

"I love you! It's my job to protect you and I can't protect you if you don't tell me when someone is hurting you!"

"I told Jake," Raymond yells, gesturing to me. "And he helped me. Everything will be better now."

Chelsea looks at me sharply. Unhappily. And I get the distinct impression things won't exactly be better for me.

She takes a deep breath. "Okay. We have to pick up the other kids. Let's talk about this at home."

Chelsea is rigid and silent on the drive home. She walks over to the neighbor's house and thanks them for keeping an eye on the other kids. As they scatter inside the house, she frowns. "I need to talk to you in the kitchen, Jake. Now."

As soon as we're through the kitchen door, she turns on me. "How could you not tell me what was happening with Raymond?"

I really don't understand why this is such a big deal with her.

"He asked me not to."

Her arms swing out from her sides. "Two days ago, Rosaleen asked me to dye her hair three different colors! We don't always have to do what they ask us! I thought I could depend on you—we're supposed to be a team, Jake!"

I don't know if it's the fact that she's yelling at me or the totally unrecognizable state that is now my life—but I start to get pissed.

"What does that mean?"

"What do you mean, *what does that mean*? It's us against them—I'm already outnumbered; you're supposed to be on my side."

Then she looks at my face. And her beautiful eyes cloud over.

With uncertainty. Doubt.

"Aren't you?"

Feelings of responsibility for all of them sit on my back like a bank vault. Of obligation and baggage—all the things I swore I'd never get mixed up in. And now she's giving me shit? What the hell more does she want from me? Christ, isn't it enough that I think about her—them—all the time? That I'm totally distracted? I go into work late and leave early at the drop of a hat, just to see them sooner.

For fuck's sake it's . . . it's . . . *terrifying.*

I point to my chest. My words come out clipped and biting. "The only side I'm on is my own." I rub my hand over my face. "Don't get me wrong—you're a good time and the kids are a trip, but I'm not Mr. fucking Mom here, Chelsea. This is not my life. I have priorities and plans that, believe it or not, have nothing to do with anyone in this house."

I breathe hard after the words are out.

And Chelsea is . . . silent. Unusually still for several seconds. Then, without looking at me, she all but whispers, "My mistake. Thank you for clarifying that."

She turns away stiffly and starts to take vegetables out of the refrigerator for dinner. As the quiet stretches, I think about my words and how . . . harsh they sounded.

I step toward her. "Chelsea, look, I—"

"Hey, Jake, you want to play Xbox?" Rory asks, sliding into the room.

Finally, Chelsea looks up and I see her eyes. They swim with hurt, shine with pain. And a terrible pressure squeezes my chest.

"Jake can't play right now, Rory. He has to go back to his side of the field."

Rory's eyebrows draw together. "Am I supposed to know what that means?"

She may have been talking to Rory, but she was speaking to me.

"Rory, go in the other room," I tell him, my eyes squarely on his aunt.

Miraculously, he does what I ask. And when he's gone I snap. "Are you seriously gonna pull that shit? Put them in the middle? Holding them over my head?" My finger points hard. "That's fucked up, Chelsea."

She comes at me, eyes blazing. "I would *never* put them between us. Besides, there would have to be an 'us' in the first place, and according to you, there's not! And me not wanting you around Rory right now has nothing to do with this discussion and everything to do with you acting like a dick!"

From the other room, Rosaleen says, "Oooh . . . Aunt Chelsea called Jake the D-word!"

Rory's voice carries into the kitchen. "Dipshit?"

"No."

"Dumbass?"

"No."

"Douchebag?"

"What's a douchebag?"

"Rory!" Chelsea and I yell at exactly the same time.

Our gazes hold and clash, neither giving an inch.

"Maybe I should just go."

It's not a question, but she answers anyway. "I think that would be best."

I'm the one who brought it up, so there's no fucking reason her words should leave me feeling cold inside. Hollow. But they do.

Without another word, I turn and walk out the door.

19

Thursday starts off shitty and goes straight to hell from there. It's raining, and my morning run is crap because I had a terrible night's sleep. No matter how many times I punched the hell out of my pillow, I couldn't get comfortable. I'm late getting into the office because some moron who didn't know how to drive in the rain slammed his car into a telephone pole, backing up traffic to East fucking Jabip. Then, an hour after I finally get settled at my desk to start working through a pile of files taller than I am, I end up spilling hot coffee on my favorite shirt.

"Goddamn fucking shit!"

Stanton swivels around in his chair from his desk on the other side of the office we share.

"Problem?"

I rub at the stain on my chest with a napkin, trying to murder it. "I spilled my coffee."

His eyebrows rise. "Did somebody piss in it first? You've been barking all morning. You even snapped at Mrs. Higgens—and she's as close to a saint as I've ever seen."

I shake my head, not in the mood to share. "Just a bad day."

He goes back to reading the document in his hands. "And it's only just begun."

Fucking tell me about it.

• • •

I don't hear from Chelsea all morning, not that I expect to. And I don't think about her. Not the anger frozen on her face or the hurt in her eyes the last time I saw her. Not her plump lips that kiss so softly, smile so easily, and laugh so enchantingly. I don't think about the kids either—not Riley's wisely perceptive look or Raymond's kind questions. I don't think about Rory's smartass smirk or Rosaleen's giggle. Not Regan's sweet voice or Ronan's drooling grin.

I refuse to think of any of them—at all.

• • •

After a quiet lunch with Sofia and Stanton—Brent was stuck in court—I sit down at my desk and bury myself in case files for two hours. And then there's a commotion outside my office. Raised voices and Mrs. Higgens saying I can't be disturbed without an appointment. For a crazy split second I think maybe it's Chelsea with a few of the kids.

But it's not.

"Mrs. Holten."

She stands in my office doorway, blond hair perfectly coiffed in an elegant knot at the base of her neck. Her blouse is white, just a shade darker than her skin tone. French-manicured nails decorate delicate hands, one of which is still graced with a shiny engagement ring and wedding band. They rest at her sides, against a Democratic-blue skirt.

Mrs. Holten is Senator William Holten's wife. The one he's accused of beating to a bloody pulp in the US attorney's case against him. The case I'm representing him in. And she's in my office.

"I need to speak with you, Mr. Becker."

Mrs. Higgens tries to explain, "I told her you can't see her, Jake. I—"

I hold up my hand. "It's all right, Mrs. Higgens. I'll take care of it." She closes the door as she leaves.

Mrs. Holten lets out a quick relieved breath and steps closer to my desk. "Is it true?"

"Mrs. Holten—"

"I just came from the prosecutor's office. They said at my husband's trial, certain . . . indiscretions . . . from my past could be made public. By you. Is that true?"

I stand up. My voice is even but firm. "I can't speak with you. You are the complaining witness in a felony assault case against my client."

"I need to know!"

My palm moves to my chest. "I could be accused of tampering with a witness. You can't be here."

She grinds her teeth, on the verge of tears, hands shaking—but more than anything she looks utterly terrified. "I married William when I was eighteen years old. I've never had a career—my only job was to be his wife, the mother to our children, his prop on the campaign trail." Her throat contracts as she swallows reflexively. "He's capable of tying up our divorce for years. He knows all the judges. When this is done, all I will have to rely on is the kindness of affluent friends and the admiration of my children. If you know what I suspect you know, and if that comes out at William's trial, they will never look at me the same way again. I will have nothing. Please, Mr. Becker, I just need to be prepared for what's to come."

I scrape my hand down my face and gesture to the chair in front of my desk. Mrs. Holten sits down but remains stiff as a frightened board. "Would you like a glass of water?"

"Thank you, yes."

I pour her a glass and set it on my desk within her reach. Then I sit back down and when I speak, I choose my words so very carefully, doing my damnedest to bend the rules without breaking them, and in the process wrecking my entire fucking career.

"Speaking purely hypothetically and not referring to this particular case at all, it is standard practice for this firm and myself personally to employ private investigators who vet potential witnesses. They look into their backgrounds and recent histories for information which could possibly be used to impeach their credibility."

" 'Impeach their credibility'?" she repeats. "So, once a liar, always a liar—is that right?"

I look into her eyes—they're gentle brown, like a doe's. "Depending on the circumstances . . . yes."

Mrs. Holten sips her water and asks, "So if a potential witness had an affair and lied to her husband, her children, her friends about it? If she developed a reliance on pain medication and had to attend a live-in rehabilitation center? Would you use those facts to impeach a witness's credibility, Mr. Becker?"

She's asking because according to the report in my desk drawer, Mrs. Holten has done all those things.

My stomach twists, angry and sick. But I won't lie to her. "As much as a judge would allow, yes, I would absolutely bring those facts up at trial."

"That's blackmail!"

"That's the law."

She starts to pant, hand to her throat—almost hyperventilating. Stanton approaches her from across the room. "Is there anything you need, ma'am?"

She closes her eyes and forces her breaths back to even. "No, I'll be fine. I'm just . . . I was a fool to ever think . . ." She pats her perfect hair and turns back to me. "Tell William I'll fix this. And I'll come home. Tell him—"

"I can't do that. I can't pass messages. I—"

"It's important that he knows I'm willing to come home!" she says, pushing. "And that I will clean up this mess I have made." She stands abruptly. "I can show myself out, gentlemen. Thank you, Mr. Becker, for your . . . honesty."

And her eyes go flat. Like a death row inmate, just waiting for someone to come along and flip the switch.

Then she sweeps out of my office, closing the door softly behind her. I stare at the closed door for a few minutes . . . remembering.

Until Stanton calls my name. "You all right, Jake?"

I blink and shake my head clear. Then I move closer to my desk and refocus.

"Yeah, I'm good." And my voice is as lifeless as Mrs. Holten's eyes. "Just part of the job."

• • •

A few hours later, after pitch black fills my office window, another commotion stirs outside the door. It opens and the young prosecutor Tom Caldwell stands there, fuming.

His noble steed is probably parked outside.

I tell Stanton dryly, "Must be dramatic entrance day. Lucky me."

I wave Mrs. Higgens away as Tom practically charges my desk. "What did you say to her?"

I lean back in my chair. "I'm not sure I know what you're talking about, Tom."

His finger stabs the air. "You know exactly what I'm talking about! Sabrina Holten came to my office—to recant her allegations against her husband. Said she couldn't risk her indiscretions coming to light."

I shrug. "Flip-flopping witnesses are always a pain in the ass."

"I know she was here!" he rails, eyes burning into me.

"She stopped in, yeah. Seemed pretty distraught."

He leans on my desk. "Did you discuss the case with her?"

I still don't bother to get out of my chair. "Of course I didn't—except to say that I couldn't discuss the case with her. Otherwise we spoke of hypotheticals. And then she left. Stanton was in the room the entire time."

" 'Hypotheticals' . . . ," he spits, like it's a dirty word. "I bet."

From across the room, Stanton asks, "Are you accusing my colleague of something, Caldwell?"

Caldwell addresses his answer to me. "Yes, I'm accusing him of being a scumbag."

I stare him down. "I really don't like your fucking attitude, Tom. It's been a rough day—you don't want to push me."

He backs down, but only a little. His hands are still balled into fists, his gaze still throwing knives. "I told her I could proceed without her testimony—I would submit her statement as evidence."

"Which I would never let you do," I say, interrupting him. "I can't cross-examine a statement."

"She was scared out of her mind, Becker! Doesn't that bother you at all?"

I don't answer. Because sometimes, there's just nothing you can say.

"She went so far as to tell me that she would testify on her husband's behalf if I went forward," Caldwell goes on. "That she would claim she was confused and it was all a political witch hunt against him. I said I could charge her with perjury."

Stanton laughs. "Wow, prosecuting your victims? That's gonna make you real popular with advocacy groups."

"I wasn't going to actually do it," Tom tells him. "I just wanted to see if she'd change her mind. She didn't." He glowers at me for a few seconds, then he asks, "Have you looked at her medical history? She's not his wife—she's his punching bag!"

I rub my eyes. Suddenly . . . so fucking tired. Of all of it. "What are you looking for here, Caldwell? I don't get it—what do you want me to do for you?"

His eyes rake over me, filled with loathing. With disgust. "Forget looking at yourself in the mirror—I just want to know, how do you live in your skin?"

The words hang heavy in the quiet of the room, until Tom shakes his head. "Never mind. It doesn't matter and you're not worth my time."

And he marches out of the office, slamming the door behind him.

I run my hand over the back of my neck. Then I stand and pack files into my briefcase. "I'm heading out," I tell Stanton.

"You want to come over tonight? Have dinner with me and Sofia?"

"Not tonight, man. The faster I get to sleep, the faster this fucking day will end."

• • •

But I don't go home. Instead I drive over to a small hole-in-the-wall kind of place—a real dive bar—with grouchy staff, almost nonexistent clientele, and fantastic scotch. Instead of having to deal with friendly, tip-hungry bartenders and female patrons looking to hook up, here I know they'll leave me the fuck alone. Which is exactly what I need at the moment.

I sit on the threadbare stool as a muscular bartender with a thick, black goatee pours me a double scotch—neat. I toss several bills onto the rotting wood bar, more than needed.

"Just leave the whole fucking bottle."

20

Hours later, I find myself stumbling onto Chelsea's stoop, without any clear recollection of how I got there. I glance back at my car—parked crookedly.

And on the lawn.

Glad that valet gig didn't work out—I obviously suck at it.

The lights inside the house are out, and all is silent at the McQuaid compound. It registers that it's probably too late to show up here, and it's damn straight too late to knock on the door.

Then I remember the spare key. 'Cause I'm a fucking genius.

I lift the mat and see the silver, sparkling little piece of metal. I unlock the door and tiptoe in—as much as my two-hundred-twenty-five-pound frame allows, anyway. The fur ball approaches, tiny nails clicking on the hardwood floor, smelling my feet.

"Hey, Shaggy. Where's Scooby?" I laugh—even though that wasn't really funny.

I walk into the kitchen and grab a bottle of water from the fridge. Midchug, Chelsea jumps through the kitchen door, a baseball bat in her hands, raised and ready.

The panicked look on her face fades when she sees me, shifting to annoyance. But at least she lowers the bat. "Jake? You scared the hell out of me!"

I swallow a gulp of water and slur, "How many times have I told you to move that goddamn key? It's the first place burglars will check. I mean—*sheesh*—look at me. I got in and now you're stuck with me."

Her head tilts and her brow puckers. It's adorable. I want to kiss the pucker. And her whole face. I want to lick her, lather her, rub myself all over her until she smells like me. So anyone who's near her knows she belongs to someone.

Is that as gross as it sounds?

"Are you drunk?" she whispers.

Does she really need to ask? I used the word *sheesh*—of course I'm fucking drunk.

"Oh yeah, off-the-ass drunk, I am."

Thanks, Yoda.

"Are you . . . is everything okay?"

"It was a rough day at the office, honey. I deserved a shitfacing."

"What happened?"

I avoid her question and say softly, "I had to see you. You just make everything . . . better."

She stares at me for a few seconds. Then she props the bat in the corner. Her hand reaches for me. "You have to be quiet, okay? Don't wake the kids."

That would be terrible. I lock my lips with an imaginary key.

But as she starts to lead the way, I yank her hand—turning her around, making her crash against me. Because there's something I have to tell her.

"Chelsea . . . I didn't mean what I said. I *am* on your side."

She searches my face, smiling gently. Her hand runs through my dark hair. "I know you are."

We make it to Chelsea's room undetected. She closes the door while I sit on the bed, yanking at my tie. Chelsea comes to my rescue and lifts it over my head. Then she goes to work on my shirt, my pants—stripping me down to boxers and my T-shirt.

I watch her through hooded eyes, relishing the admonishing smile dancing on her face, the way she moves with effortless grace.

"You're so beautiful," I tell her, because I can't keep the words in a second longer.

She looks up at me from the floor, throwing my socks over her shoulder. "You're not so bad yourself." She cocks her chin toward the middle of the bed. "Go on. Scoot over."

I do as I'm told and she climbs onto the bed behind me. I lie back against the pillow, one arm bent behind my head. Chelsea nestles up close, her cheek resting above my heart.

"What's going on with you, Jake?"

Somewhere deep inside lies the truth. It's curled up into a tight, black ball, under heavy blankets of disappointment. Fear. And shame. But it wants to show itself the way a wounded animal exposes its tender underbelly when it knows it's beaten. Just to hasten whatever comes next.

"I'm not a good man."

The whispered confession echoes in the still room. Chelsea lifts her head and I feel the point of her chin against my ribs. "You're one of the best men I've ever known. In every way possible." There's disbelief in her voice—playfulness—like she thinks I'm teasing her.

I don't bother arguing. She'll know soon enough. *The truth will set you free.* What a fucking joke. When the truth is ugly, it holds you prisoner, and when it's revealed, it tears the whole world down around you.

"Did I ever tell you about my father?"

"You said he left when you were eight."

I snort. "Yeah, he left all right." I shake my head as I dive back into that dark lake of memories best forgotten. "He was a mean bastard, even on a good day. But when he drank . . . he was truly dangerous.

My mother . . . she used to sit so still, I'd watch her chest, just to make sure she was still breathing. It was like she was trying to blend into the wallpaper, so he wouldn't have a reason . . ."

But guys like my old man don't need a reason.

They make their own.

My voice goes flat and faraway. "The last time . . . it was because she sneezed." I see it in my mind. The way he upended the tray, the way his dinner splattered across the TV and clung to the walls, leaving a greasy mashed-potato trail as it slid down. The way he grabbed her. "Can you believe it? She fucking sneezed."

For the first time since I began, I look at Chelsea. She gazes at me with sympathy, sadness. Her brows are weighted, the corners of her mouth heavy with compassion that doesn't feel at all like pity.

"And she was so little, Chelsea. Even as a kid, I could see she was so much smaller than him." I moisten my lips, so the rest of the words can pass. "He threw her down the stairs and I remember thinking he wasn't going to stop this time. He'd told her he'd do it one day. That when it happened, he'd bury her where no one could find her. He'd said no one would miss her . . ." My eyes sting with the memory and my throat squeezes. "No one but me."

I blink away moisture and clear my throat. "So I went to the box under the bed—the dumb fuck stored the thing loaded. And I walked back to the living room and pointed it at him. It wasn't heavy; my hands didn't shake at all. But when I cocked it, the sound it made—it seemed so loud. He stopped, right away—froze. He knew exactly what that sound was. He turned around, slowly, and I kept it aimed right at his chest. I told him to go, to get away from us . . . or I would kill him. And I really fucking would have."

At some point, Chelsea's hand started rubbing soothing circles on my chest, my stomach, but I didn't feel her touch until just now. It gives me the motivation I need to finish.

"I guess it's true what they say about cowards. They only prey on easy targets, the ones who don't fight back. Because he left and didn't come back."

For a moment, the only noise in the room is the sound of our breaths moving in time. Then Chelsea says with admiration, "That's why you do what you do."

"What do you mean?"

"You're a defender. You defend people. Like you defended your mother . . . and Rory. You gave them a chance, to have a new start."

My eyes squeeze shut. "Most people don't see it that way, Chelsea."

Her warm hand cups my jaw. "*I* see it that way."

The look on her face is everything I want it to be. Gentle, adoring—like I'm the hero of the story. And god, I want to be fucking selfish. I want to roll us over, peel her clothes off, and eradicate any chance she'll ever look at me any differently than she is at this moment.

I want to get to keep her.

But ugly truth always comes out eventually. And she deserves to hear it from me.

"Today I defended a man exactly like my father."

Her stroking hand stutters. Stops.

"His wife . . . she's stayed with him for thirty years—took everything he dished out—and she finally got the courage to leave. To tell him to go screw himself." I pause, swallowing. "And I took that away from her.

"He hurts her—I know he does—and because of me, he's going to keep on hurting her." I look into her eyes, hoping that in them I'll find an answer I can live with. "He's a monster, Chelsea, and I defended him. What does that make me?"

Her heartbeat quickens, like a fluttering bird who's only just realized it's in a cage. She searches my face . . . searches for the words to say.

In that quietly confident voice she tries, "Jake . . . sometimes, in life, we have to make hard choices—"

I grip her arms, pulling her closer. "But that's just it. If I was a good man, it wouldn't be a hard choice. Sometimes . . . sometimes things are so right . . . they should be easy."

Something inside me crumbles, under the weight of all the things I want. I want her—this fearless, stunning woman. And I want the kids. Those perfect, awful, amazing children—whom she loves with every inch of her soul. I want them to be mine. Mine to hold, mine to protect and teach. Their joy, their laughter, their love. I want to come home to it, bask in it, be the reason for it.

But even more than that, I want to deserve them.

To be worthy.

And all today did was point out the stark, cold fact . . . that I'm not.

"I shouldn't even be here," I tell her, my voice aching. "You deserve a man who knows what the right thing is, and who does it. I want . . . *Christ,* I want to be that for you."

Wordlessly, Chelsea slides out of my grasp and moves higher up the bed, above me. So she can guide my head against her breast.

She's soft and warm and smells so fucking good. She whispers to me, rubs my temple, the back of my neck, fingers sliding through my hair. And there is nowhere else in the entire world I would rather be.

"It's okay, Jake. Go to sleep. Shhh . . . it's okay."

21

I think he's dead."

"He's not dead—he's still breathing."

"Can you breathe if you're dead?"

"No. Well, maybe. But you'd need a ventilator."

Sniff, sniff.

"He smells like he's dead."

There's pressure against my eyelid. And then it's pried open—revealing Rosaleen's blurry, peering face.

"Are you dead?" she yells.

Apparently she suspects I'm also deaf.

I reclaim my eye with a jerk of my head.

"Yes, I'm dead." I roll onto my side, away from the voices. "Let me rest in peace." *Pounding* doesn't being to describe what's going on in my head right now. It feels like sharp-clawed parasites have burrowed under my skull and are prying it open from the inside. My stomach churns, and although I haven't puked from alcohol since I was twenty-two, today just might be the day it happens again.

"I could make you feel better, you know."

That came from Raymond. I shift slowly to my back and crack open my eyes. The four of them—Raymond, Rory, Riley, and Rosaleen—

gaze down at me, dressed in their school uniforms, with expressions of curious disgust. Mostly disgust.

"How?"

"Our mom was really into homeopathic cures and supplements. I could mix something for you."

"Okay."

And this is how desperate I am—listening to a fucking nine-year-old.

I use the walls for support as I make my way into the kitchen. Chelsea's there—dressed in tight black leggings and a Berkeley T-shirt that makes her tits look fantastic. If only I felt well enough to show my appreciation properly.

She scoops nasty-looking green slop into Ronan's mouth—and I almost vomit all over the floor. He seems to enjoy it. "Oh, you're up," she says cheerily. Then, less so, "You look awful."

"That makes sense," I mutter. "Awful is how I feel."

I sit at the island while Raymond gets out the blender and starts dumping various juices, capsules, and gelcaps into it. Then he turns the blender on. And my head explodes. After two long minutes, the brown, grainy concoction gets plopped into a glass and set in front of me. They stare at me—even the baby—like I'm the wolf man at those freak-show olden-days carnivals.

"Is this really going to work?" I ask Raymond.

"Well . . ." He purses his lips. "It'll either work or you'll throw up. But either way, you'll probably feel better."

He does have a point.

I choke it down, trying not to breathe, in a few gulps. Then I burp nastily and my stomach groans. I put my head on the counter. "Somebody fucking kill me."

"Okay, kids, time for school," Chelsea tells them, passing out lunch bags and backpacks amid disgruntled moans. I hear them trudge down the hall and out the front door. I think I fall asleep for a few minutes, because the next time I open my eyes and lift my head, it's just me and Chelsea in the kitchen.

She sets a tall glass of water in front of me, her expression neutral.

"Thank you."

I don't remember everything about last night, just a few words and images. But I still feel the need to say, "I'm sorry about last night."

"Why?" she asks, stacking dishes in the sink. "It's not like you accosted me."

"No—I definitely would've remembered that."

She glances at me with a quick, fleeting smile.

"Chelsea." There's a desperation in my voice that makes her stop and meet my eyes. "I'm sorry about what I said the other day, too. You're not just a 'good time' to me—you know that, right? You have to know that, you're . . . so much more. And I don't handle . . . more . . . very well."

Her stiff expression melts and her eyes go soft and warm. She licks her lips, considering her words, then says, "I missed you. I know it was only a day, and I know that's probably going to freak you out . . . But I like having you around—and everything that goes with it. We don't have to . . . move forward if that makes you uncomfortable. I'm good with keeping things just as they are. I think they're . . . pretty awesome."

I take her hand, sliding her closer. I press it between my two hands, watching it disappear. So small. So beautiful. "I think they're pretty awesome too."

And her smile grows. "Good."

I yawn and stretch . . . and goddamn, I'm actually beginning to not feel like a dump Death took anymore. Raymond may be onto something with that drink; hope he wrote the recipe down.

"I have to get to work, but before I head home for a change of clothes, I really want a shower."

Chelsea runs her fingers through my hair, massaging my scalp. "There are five showers in this house—take your pick."

I grin. "I like the one in your room."

The hot water feels amazing on my tight muscles. I hang my head under the rain-shower spout, letting the water run over me, and yesterday washes away. My conversation with Mrs. Holten and Tom Caldwell and the feelings they resurrected circles the drain and goes down.

I step out into Chelsea's room with a towel around my waist. She's there, putting sexy scraps of folded lace and satin into drawers. She watches me, staring at the drops of water that trail down my chest, across my abs. My cock preens under her gaze.

And she definitely notices that.

Looking hungrily at the hard outline beneath the towel, she asks, almost breathlessly, "Feeling better?"

I run my tongue along my bottom lip. "Much better."

And the towel doesn't stay on my hips for long after that.

• • •

In the days that follow, Chelsea and I find our rhythm again, in and out of the bedroom. My life goes back to normal—a strange, different kind of normal that includes her and the kids. One day, Chelsea joins Brent, Sofia, Stanton, and me for lunch—and Sofia holds Ronan on her lap the whole time. I take Rory to Little League tryouts and we all celebrate with pizza on the back patio when he makes the team. Rosaleen starts lessons with a new piano teacher who comes to the house—and I supervise to make sure there's not a ruler in sight. Riley discovers 5 Seconds of Summer and One Direction gets downgraded—though to be honest, they all look exactly the same to me. Ronan starts sleeping through the night—a huge plus—while Raymond enjoys his torment-free days at school. And Regan flexes her power with her newly expanded vocabulary, telling us all "no" every chance she gets.

It's pretty great.

But then . . . a day comes along that changes everything. And it all goes to hell.

• • •

After Mrs. Holten's strong repudiation of her statement and her refusal to assist the prosecution in any case against her husband, Caldwell had no choice but to drop the charges against the senator. And that was recorded as a win in my column. It's a big fucking deal for me professionally. I'm now Jonas Adams's pet employee and the favorite guy in the whole world of Senator Holten—a man with considerable influence in DC. Late one Friday afternoon, the senator makes room in his busy schedule to come to our firm, to Jonas's office, for a meeting with me. To hobnob and discuss my future.

To talk about all the deals the devil wants to make.

We sit on the leather couches in Jonas's office, enjoying an afternoon scotch. Holten talks about a good "friend" of his who's being investigated for money laundering. His eyes are dark, bottomless, almost soulless. And it's kind of creeping me out.

As the senator drones on, my phone vibrates in my pocket. I glance at it discreetly—Chelsea's name glows on the screen. I send the call to voice mail. But a few minutes later, the hairs on the back of my neck stand up when her silent call comes again.

My thumb hovers for a second . . . and then I send it to voice mail again. This may very well be the biggest meeting of my career—hearing about how many feet Ronan crawled today is just going to have to wait.

We finish our drinks, and the talk turns to my recent cases—my latest acquittal. And then Veronica, Mr. Adams's private secretary, walks into the office, her voice hesitant at interrupting us. "Pardon the intrusion, gentlemen." She looks at me. "Mrs. Higgens is on line one, with an urgent call for you, Mr. Becker."

My first thought is of the kids, that Rory has gotten himself into some fresh brew of trouble or that one of them, maybe Regan—she's due—has had an accident. Something minor, of course, a broken bone or a cut that needs stitching.

But I cover the concern with a shrug, eyeing Holten and my boss. "My apologies. The cost of being in high demand."

Mr. Adams nods his head. "Use my phone, Becker."

I stand beside his desk as their chatter resumes and press the button under the blinking, waiting light. There's a click over the line, a pause as it connects . . . and then Chelsea's voice.

"Jake?"

I hear a lot in that one syllable. Her voice is . . . off. Somehow flat and high-pitched at the same time. And she's exhaling hard, like when you twist an ankle or slice your hand . . . and have to breathe through the pain.

"What's wrong?"

"Janet's here. With . . . officers. They have an . . . an order . . ."

And the floor drops out from under me.

"They're taking the kids, Jake."

Nausea slams into my stomach and I feel like I'm falling. Grappling, grasping for a perch to stop the descent.

I swallow bile. "I'm leaving right now. Tell them . . ." I choke down a curse. "Tell them I'm on my way."

"Hurry," she begs in a whisper. And the line goes dead.

I replace the phone on the cradle. It takes every ounce of control I have not to sprint out of the fucking room or break my way straight through the wall.

"I'm sorry, I have to leave." My briefcase is in hand and I'm already walking to the door as my boss calls, "Becker, Senator Holten is only available for this afternoon."

Gripping the doorknob, I make myself turn and answer. "Again, I'm very sorry we couldn't speak longer, Senator. But"—I don't even have to think about my next words—"it's a family emergency."

22

I burst through the door, wild and seething, struggling to pull my shit together. Because emotions make you sloppy, careless. And I really need to be on point.

The foyer is empty—I stalk into the living room. There, the first thing I see is Riley, a packed blue canvas duffel bag at her feet, rubbing her little sister's trembling back as she buries her face against Riley's stomach. The fourteen-year-old looks up at me, her eyes filled with tears being kept at bay.

"It's okay." She nods, trying so damn hard to be brave. "I'm okay."

I notice a uniformed police officer in the corner—he looks young, just out of the academy. I wonder if when he signed up he imagined protecting and serving would include sweeping scared kids out of their home. He picks up a framed photograph from a coffee table in the corner.

"Don't touch that," I bite out.

He replaces the frame and raises his hands in surrender. I brush past him to Chelsea, with Regan beside her, oblivious to the turmoil, and Ronan in the baby carrier at her feet, taking it all in. Chelsea's eyes are wide and terrified, her hands twisting together. She sighs with relief when she sees me.

"What the hell is this, Janet?" I bark at the social worker standing beside her.

Janet shakes her head. "It wasn't my call. This came down from the top."

"Who's at the top?" *Whose head do I need to cleave in two?*

"The director of CFSA reviewed the case file and petitioned to have the children removed from the home. Dexter Smeed."

I take the court order from Chelsea's hands. "'*Neglect and child endangerment*'?" I read. "Is this a fucking joke?"

Janet rubs her lips together, looking anything but happy. "I'm really sorry."

I look over the paper again, checking the date, the wording, the signatures. Looking for something. *Fucking anything.*

"You can do something, right?" Chelsea asks, begging me with her eyes. "A response, a postponement? So they can stay?"

There's hope in her voice. Faith. So much trust. And it destroys me.

I grasp her elbow and swear on my soul. "We'll get them back. I promise, Chelsea . . . we'll get them back."

She stares at me for a moment, unblinking. Like she can't comprehend what I'm telling her. Until she does. Her eyes pinch closed and she inhales harshly through her nose. Then she opens her eyes, and I see a wall being erected within them. Brick by brick, she shores it up—so she can take the hit. So she can be strong for the kids, until . . . after.

Chelsea nods and forces a wet-eyed smile. Then she scoops up Regan and moves to Riley and Rosaleen, stroking their hair, telling them they'll be staying with friends of Janet's for just a little while. How wonderful it'll be. How much fun they'll have.

I pray they can't hear the tremble in her voice.

"Where are you taking them?" I ask Janet.

I read an article to the Judge last month about the crowded group homes, the shortage of adequate foster families in DC. And I envision three cars, each with two of them inside, driving away in different directions. Tearing them apart.

"I can't tell you that."

"Then tell me they can stay together, Janet," I growl. But my voice is so strained, it sounds more like pleading.

She takes pity on me. "There's a family I've worked with before. They're good people. The real deal. They've agreed to take all six of the kids . . . for the weekend."

I look up sharply. "The weekend? That's it?"

Janet faces my heated expression head-on. "After that, it'll depend on what's available." Her voice falls back to professionalism. "Everything's in the packet—Chelsea's rights, her options. She can request an emergency hearing."

"God fucking damn it."

Footfalls clunk down the steps. Raymond appears first at the bottom, wearing a stoic mask, but his red-rimmed eyes and sniffling give him away. He lets the bag in his hand go and rushes over to Chelsea, where he's immediately enveloped in her arms.

I try to think of something to say. Words that could make this less of a nightmare for them. Before I can say the first word, Rory comes down the stairs, his blue eyes round and shaken. I expect him to join his brothers and sisters in their close-knit cluster. To run to Chelsea. But he doesn't.

He runs to me.

His warm little body crashes against me, arms wrapping, holding on for dear life. His voice is muffled against my waist, but I hear every word. "I'm sorry. I'm so sorry. I'll be good. I swear I'll be good."

My eyes sting as this poor, lost kid pours out his heart . . . and tears mine to pieces.

I slide to my knees in front of him and pry him back. "This isn't your fault, Rory. Nothing you did made this happen."

"But—"

"It's *not* your fault, kid."

He hiccups. "Don't let . . . them take . . . us."

My voice is low and irrefutable. "I'll bring you home. I'll bring you all home."

His eyes flicker between mine, searching for honesty. "When?"

And I curse the time of day and the court schedule and a thousand other things that force my answer. "Monday. I'll bring you home Monday." I push his hair back and brush his tear-streaked face. "Do you remember what I told you, about a man and his word?"

He nods. "All a man has is his word. That he says what he means and does what he says."

An aching smile tugs at my lips. "That's right. I give you my word, Rory. I'll bring you all home on Monday."

I glance up at Chelsea and at each of the kids around her—all of them watching, listening. Then I look back to Rory. "But between then and now, you've got to hold it together. I need you to be tough, okay? Take care of each other. Don't fight. Help each other."

After a slow moment, Rory clenches his jaw. Then he gives a small nod and wipes his cheeks with the back of his hand. He's ready.

• • •

We load the kids into the van. Chelsea hugs and kisses each one before they climb in, barely able to make herself let go. Rosaleen's face is red and wet with big, streaming tears. "I want to stay here."

"I know, kiddo." I brush her cheek with my knuckles, wiping at her tears as I buckle her in. "It won't be long. It'll go really fast," I lie.

Regan's lip quivers, though I'm not sure she understands why. "No . . . "

And I can't force out any words to answer her. All I can do is kiss her forehead.

We step back as Janet closes the sliding van door. It's loud—echoing—like a jail cell locking. Then she climbs in the driver's seat.

Chelsea waves, and she keeps talking, even after the kids can't hear her anymore. "I love you! Be good, guys. I'll see you really soon. Everything's gonna be all right. Don't worry. I prom—" Her voice falters. "Promise everything will be all right."

Her hand is still raised as the van pulls away, led by a police cruiser, down the curved driveway, through the gate, and out of sight.

As soon as the blue van disappears, Chelsea's face crumbles. A wheezing gasp comes from her throat and she hides her face in her open palms. I put my hands on her shoulders so she's knows I'm right here with her.

And she screams. A horrible, piercing wail that I'll never forget as long as I live. Pain so bare, so raw, that thoughts aren't even possible—just an endless flow of agonized sobs.

Her knees give out, and I catch her.

She twists my shirt in her hands and hides her face against my chest, soaking it with tears by the time we get into the house. Her shoulders shake as she cries her heart out. "They were scared, Jake. Oh god, they were so scared."

It's horrible. Every word lands like the lash of a whip, cutting me, turning my insides into a raw, bloody mess. I take her straight to her room. The kids are everywhere in this house—their toys, their faces smiling back from pictures on the wall—but there it won't be as haunting. I sit on the bed and cradle Chelsea in my arms. Stroking her hair, kissing her forehead, whispering words of reassurance that have no fucking meaning at all.

She sobs, long and loud. And I know this isn't just about the kids—it's the outpouring of everything that's built up inside her these last months. All the grief, pain, loneliness, and fear she never let herself feel.

"My brother was a good brother," she chokes out.

"I know."

"I loved him."

"I know you did," I answer in the softest voice.

"And he's gone. And I miss him . . . so much."

I hold her tighter. "I know."

Her voice scrapes her throat. "I had to do one thing, just one thing for him . . . and I couldn't! I lost them . . ."

"Shh . . . it's okay." I press my lips to her forehead.

"They're gone. Oh god . . . they're gone . . ."

"We'll get them back. Shhh . . . I promise."

Eventually Chelsea wears herself out, crying herself into a deep sleep. I stay awake all night and hold her. I whisper to her when she whimpers, when her brow wrinkles with panic, until she's calm again. And I think about the kids, each one of them—I picture them in my mind. The sound of their voices, their little hands, the way they smell when they come in from outside—like dirt and sunshine and goodness. I try to tell myself they'll be safer somehow—shielded—if I just keep thinking about them.

But imagination can be a fucked-up thing. I think of all the horrors that I've seen, read about, heard about from clients and colleagues. I wonder if the kids are calling for Chelsea, or maybe their parents. If they're hiding under blankets or crying into pillows because they're surrounded by strangers and they have no idea what tomorrow has in store.

It's the longest night of my life.

23

In the morning, I lay Chelsea gently down on the bed, then head into the kitchen. I put a pot of coffee on, let the dog out, and fill his bowl with food. It regards the bowl with sad eyes, then rejects it, curling up in a ball on the recliner with a heavy sigh. I pat his flat ears. "I know just how you feel, buddy."

I bring a cup of coffee up to Chelsea, put it on the nightstand, and sit on the bed. When I lay my hand on her hip, her eyes flare open with a quick intake of breath, like she's been yanked out of a bad dream. She looks around, and her face clouds over when she realizes the bad dream is reality. She lies back on the pillow, watching me.

"Thank you for last night. For staying with me."

"Don't mention it." I push a strand of hair behind her ear. "I have to go into the office, to prepare for the hearing on Monday."

"Okay. Thank you." Her voice is weighed down. And the unnatural silence of the house closes in around us. "Can I come with you?"

"Of course you can."

• • •

While Chelsea gets dressed I call Stanton and Sofia, then Brent. I fill them in on yesterday's events and tell them to meet me at the office. The procedures in family court are slightly different, so I'll have to familiarize myself with them, but essentially, the custody hearing isn't so different from a trial. I'll need evidence and a shitload of case law to back up my argument that the kids belong with Chelsea and that CFSA was way out of line to take them in the first place.

Chelsea comes into the room, sipping her coffee, wearing jeans and a loose red flannel shirt. Her hair shines red-gold in the sunlight from the window, pulled back in a high ponytail.

She looks . . . better, but not good.

The way a china plate that was broken into pieces looks better once it's glued together. But you know the slightest vibration could shatter it all over again.

We stop for bagels on the way to my apartment, where I change my clothes, and then we head to the offices of Adams & Williamson. Working on Saturday is fairly common there, so there are a few attorneys milling about in casual weekend clothes. I lead Chelsea into my office, where Stanton, Sofia, and Brent are already waiting. After a round of sympathetic hugs for Chelsea and a few arm slaps for me, we sit around my desk.

"They fucking have everything." I curse, flipping through the social services report that accompanied the court order. And on paper, it doesn't look good. "Rory's arrest and his broken arm, Riley getting detained after the party, the stuff with Raymond and Jeremy Sheridan. They even mention Rosaleen's disappearing act. Did they bug the goddamn house?"

"Probably interviewed the neighbors," Sofia suggests. "Parents of friends. Chelsea, the report mentions Regan's speech delay, which CFSA claims you haven't adequately addressed?"

Chelsea shakes her head. "She doesn't have a speech delay—all the kids were late talkers. It freaked Rachel out at first, but the pediatrician always said it was totally normal."

I point at Sofia. "We need to get a statement from the pediatrician. And Rory's therapist. And their teachers—they're smart kids, they do well in school; that'll work in our favor."

Stanton nods. "And I'll dig around into Dexter Smeed and CFSA. See what their track record is lately."

We break up to our respective tasks. Before Brent starts helping Sofia with those statements, he gets Chelsea settled comfortably on the leather couch by the window. He hands her a hot cup of tea, then he takes out his monogrammed flask and pours a shot's worth into her cup. "A little nip in the morning is a good thing. Gets the blood going."

"Thank you, Brent."

"Don't worry about a thing. They've awoken a sleeping giant. And Jake is the scariest giant around."

• • •

A few hours later I'm in the firm's library, looking for several volumes among the long, crowded stacks. I feel Stanton watching me as he pulls his own book off the shelf.

"How are you doin', man?"

"How do you think I'm doing?" I reply without looking up.

"I think you're all twisted up inside about his. Can't decide who you want to kill first. That's how I'd be—if it was Presley." He pauses, waiting for my response. I pull a book from the shelf and scan its pages. "I just want you to know I'm here for you, Jake. Whatever you need."

I slam the book closed with a bang, and I glare at him—not because he's done anything, but just because he's there. "A kid's house is like their fortress. It protects them from the boogeyman, or whoever the fuck kids are afraid of nowadays." My teeth grind. "And they came into their house and they took them, Stanton. You know what that does to a kid?"

He nods. "Yeah, I do."

I don't want to talk about this. I just . . . can't . . . go there right now. "You want to make me feel better?" I push the book in my hands against his chest. "Find me something I can use to walk in there on Monday and nail this fucker to the wall."

• • •

A few hours after that, I'm at my desk, working on our response to CFSA's motion for custody. Chelsea's moved a chair closer to me. She sits, curled up like a kitten, watching me.

"What's that?" she asks, pointing to a huge mother of a text open on my desk.

"Those are statutes. The laws about child custody."

She rests her head against her hand. "Why are they written like that?"

"Well, the classic answer is so there's no room for interpretation. So someone can't argue it means anything other than exactly what it says. But I think they're written like that just so lawyers can earn a shitload of money telling everyone else what they mean."

My answer makes her smile softly. "And what's that?" She points to another volume on my desk.

"That's relevant case law. Decisions other judges have made in cases similar to yours. I use that to back up my argument. Judges like to follow the crowd—they're real all-the-cool-kids-are-doing-it kinds of people."

She smiles again, blinking slowly, looking totally worn out. I brush her hair back. "Close your eyes, Chelsea. Get some rest."

And she doesn't even argue with me.

• • •

It's dark by the time Chelsea and I get into my car. I bring some files home with me—stuff I'll work on later—but it seemed like she was done. Couldn't stand being cooped up in the office for another minute. In contrast to her exhausted demeanor earlier, she seems wired now. Practically vibrating with unspent energy. Desperate.

Her foot taps on the floor of the car. "Can we pick up the dog and stay at your place tonight?"

I don't have to ask why she's asking. Without the kids, the house feels like a tomb.

"Sure."

She nods. "Hey—stop here real quick." She points at a liquor store up ahead, its sign glowing green neon against the darkness. I pull up to the curb and Chelsea gets out. She returns a few minutes later, a large brown paper bag in tow. When we get to her house, she stays in the car while I grab Cousin It, then we head to my place.

Chelsea sets the dog on the floor in my living room and walks straight into the kitchen. I stand in the doorway, watching her, as she takes two shot glasses out of the cabinet and fills both from the bottle of vodka she pulled out of the bag. Her movements are sharp, angry. She downs one shot like a pro and goes back for a second. She breathes out hard after the second shot, then fixes her gaze on me.

She picks up one of the glasses and stalks toward me; a little of the clear liquid sloshes onto the floor as she moves. Her face is serious, hard, and those crystal eyes glow with an almost predatory light. And fuck me if my cock doesn't respond to the frantic energy pouring from her. I take the glass from her offered hand, and keeping my eyes trained on hers, I swallow the burning liquid down.

Chelsea licks her lips and backs up a step. Then she unbuttons her shirt slowly . . . like a challenge. The shirt hits the floor and her jeans smoothly follow.

"I can't stop thinking." Her usually sweet voice is lower, rougher—almost a growl. "I can't turn my brain off, you know?" Her eyes fall to the shot glass as she pours herself another, but she doesn't drink it yet. "It's making me fucking crazy. I don't want to think at all—about any of this." Then she looks up at me through long lashes."Think you can help me out with that?"

I move fast, surprising her. My hand lashes out, gripping the back of her neck. It's a harsh grasp, forceful, and I drag her closer until her bare skin is pressed right up against me. I pick up the shot glass.

"Open."

Chelsea's lips part and I raise the glass to them, pouring the liquid down. As soon as she swallows, my mouth is on hers, crashing and clashing, tasting the sting of vodka and her pain.

I pull back and she's panting. My other hand skims up her stomach, covering her breast. Her nipple hardens under my palm and I rasp, "Yeah. I know just how to help you with that."

And neither one of us gets the chance to think the rest of the night.

• • •

Sunday morning, Chelsea wakes up before I do. I feel her move around the room, gathering her clothes, getting dressed, taking care of the dog. She comes back into the room and sits on the edge of the bed, waiting for me to open my eyes. When I do, there's more life to her features. More . . . determination. And the knot that has been my stomach for the last two days loosens just a little.

"I'd like to go to church today." The corner of her mouth inches upward. "Rachel and Robbie used to take the kids to church every week, but I haven't managed it yet. Getting them all dressed and out the door is such a production." She pauses, probably picturing the kids and all their delightful difficulty in her mind. "But I'd like to go today. Do you want to come with me?"

I'm a pure cynic when it comes to religion. Besides funerals, the occasional wedding, or services on the base with my mother when I was a kid, I don't do church. But I hear myself say, "Yeah, I'll go with you."

We leave Cousin It at Chelsea's house, where Chelsea changes into a demure short-sleeved yellow dress with matching high heels. I follow the crowd at Mass, the kneeling and standing, but mostly I just watch her. The way her lips touch her hands when her head is bowed in prayer, the serene expression on her face as the priest gives his final blessing.

We stand outside my car in the parking lot of the church. "I don't know what to do with myself." Chelsea laughs humorlessly. "All these months there never seemed to be enough time, and now that there is . . . I don't want it." She glances my way. "You have that thing you do on Sunday afternoons, right?"

She's noticed I disappear every Sunday—but she's never asked me about it. I wonder if she was waiting for me to tell her about it myself.

"Yeah, I do."

She nods and just as she starts to look resigned to a lonely afternoon, I say, "You want to come with me?"

Her head whips back to me. "Only . . . only if you want me to."

"There's someone I want you to meet."

• • •

I hold Chelsea's hand as we walk down the halls of the Brookside Retirement Home. Marietta is just exiting the Judge's room when we get to his door.

"Hey, Jake." She greets me with a wide smile.

"Hi, Marietta. How's he doing today?"

"Oh, honey, he's having a really good day."

I blow out a relieved fucking breath. The last thing I wanted was to make Chelsea more depressed than she's been—and the Judge on a bad day is not a happy sight.

I nod past her and walk into the room with Chelsea just behind me.

He's reading in his leather chair by the window, dressed in a dark blue sweater and tan slacks, those ugly brown loafers on his feet.

"Hey, old man."

His face is alight, his eyes confident and wonderfully aware. "Jake!" He closes his book and rises, wrapping me in a strong-armed hug. "It's good to see you, son. How are you?"

"I'm doing good, Judge."

His eyes fall to Chelsea and he throws me a wrinkled smirk. "I can see why." He offers her his hand. "Hello, my dear, I'm Atticus Faulkner."

Chelsea shakes his hand with a huge smile. "I'm Chelsea McQuaid . . . it's wonderful to meet you. Jake's told me all about you."

"Salacious lies, I'm sure." He winks. "Sit down, sit down. Let me get you some tea, Marietta just brought me a pot."

Once we're seated, with our cups in front of us, the Judge tells Chelsea, "You are beautiful, my dear."

And cue the blush. "Thank you."

"Now, I must apologize in advance, Chelsea, if I say or do anything that makes you uncomfortable. I . . . forget things . . . very quickly and often lately."

Chelsea smiles—and she's more lovely than any of the saints on her church's stained glass windows. "Don't worry. If you forget, we'll be here to help you remember."

And for the fucking life of me, I don't know how she's gotten by without filing a shitload of restraining orders, or without gifts and cards and flowers clogging up her mailbox every day. Because as I watch her with the Judge, I don't know how anyone could know her and not ridiculously, pitifully love her.

• • •

Later that night, Chelsea and I are back at her house . . . soaking together in the oversized bathtub off of her bedroom. She sits in front of me, her back against my chest, her hair pinned up, a few damp strands hanging down, tickling my face. She's been quiet for a while now—only the sounds of the water rippling against the side of the tub disturb the silence.

"What if we lose tomorrow?"

My lips linger on her shoulder. "We won't."

"But what if we do? Will they"—her voice cracks—"will they let me see them? Have visitation?"

She turns around to face me and I choose my words carefully. "I know people . . . who can find out where the kids are. And I know other people who make IDs—passports and stuff. Good ones." I trace my finger along her jaw. "So . . . if we lose, I'll call those people. You'll take out any money you can . . . and you'll just go."

"Like . . . to Mexico?"

I chuckle. "No. The glowing-white McQuaid skin would burn to a crisp under the Mexican sun. Maybe . . . Canada? I wonder if Regan would pick up French faster."

Chelsea stares at me, and her eyes seem a shade darker. Deeper. "You would do that for us?"

My fingers splay across her soft cheek. "I can't think of anything I *wouldn't* do for you."

And that fact scares the ever-loving shit out of me.

The water tips over the edge of the tub as she rises up on her knees, straddling my hips. We kiss for minutes that feel like hours. Her hand dips below the water, stroking me even though I'm already hard and hot in her palm. And when she lines us up, sinks down, it's slow and gentle. My arms wrap around her, pulling her closer, *closer*, and I kiss her breasts, toying with her nipples with my tongue. Her hips rise and fall; I move within her at a steady, unhurried pace.

And when she spasms around me with a tender whimper, when I

pulse deep inside her with a rough groan, it feels like more. Like everything. Like nothing I've ever had before and something I can't fathom reaching with anyone else.

Chelsea's head still rests on my shoulder long after the water turns cold. Eventually, we climb out of the tub, dry each other off, and fall asleep in her bed wrapped around each other.

24

Ten a.m. the next morning, Chelsea and I walk into courtroom 7-A in the Family Court of the District of Columbia. We take our place at our designated table; Stanton, Sofia, and Brent sit in the front row behind us. Chelsea is nervous but composed. And me? I'm ready and I'm hungry for a win. It's the feeling I always get. No nerves—just eagerness.

The attorney representing the Children and Family Services Agency takes her own place at the table across the main aisle to my left, smoothing down the skirt of her conservative, well-tailored black suit. She's a redhead in her forties who looks almost as confident as I feel.

The bailiff announces that court is in session and we all rise as the judge—a gray-haired, spectacle-wearing woman who, if the lace around her collar is any indication, is a fan of Ruth Bader Ginsburg—enters the room. She goes through the formalities—who's representing who—then she asks me to begin.

"I call the director of CFSA, Dexter Smeed, Your Honor."

Dexter Smeed looks exactly like you'd picture someone named Dexter Smeed to look. Round glasses; thinning hair; pressed, starched white button-down shirt; brown tweed jacket; and light green bowtie. He's sworn in and takes a seat in the witness box.

"Mr. Smeed, have you ever seen Chelsea McQuaid before today?"

"No."

"Ever met her, visited her home?"

"No."

"Sent her an email?"

Smeed clears his throat. "No."

I nod, taking it in. "Have you ever interviewed any of the McQuaid children?"

"No."

I step out from behind the table and lean back against it. "And yet you felt qualified to override the recommendation of the social worker on the case, Janet Morrison—who has seen, visited, and interviewed Miss McQuaid and the children—to order the removal of custody?"

"I did, yes."

"And how did you make that determination, Mr. Smeed?"

"I periodically review the files of all the case workers in my agency. The file contained all the information I needed. It's my job to be critical. To determine who is a fit guardian"—his eyes scan to Chelsea and pause meaningfully—"and who is not."

Toast. This fucker is toast—the burned kind that not even the dog will touch.

I move to the right, blocking Chelsea from his view. "Your wife is a lucky woman." I shake my head. "You have got some set of balls—"

"Your Honor!" The agency attorney jumps to her feet.

The judge lowers her chin, glaring down. "That comment will cost you five hundred dollars, Mr. Becker. You will maintain proper decorum in my courtroom or your client will be looking for new representation. There won't be another warning—do I make myself clear?"

Most judges are really low on sense of humor.

"Crystal clear. My apologies."

Then I set my sights back on Mr. Smeed. "Let's come back to that later. At the moment, can you tell me if the name Carrie Morgan is familiar to you?"

He thinks for a moment, then shakes his head. "No."

I pick up a file from the table and glance at its contents. "Three years ago, Carrie, age seven, was taken into the custody of Children and Family Services after her mother was convicted on federal drug charges. She was placed with a foster family, under the supervision of your agency. Six months later, she was dead, from blunt-force trauma to the head. The autopsy found signs consistent with abuse." I pin him with a stare, my eyes as cold as my voice. "Ring any bells?"

"I'm not familiar with the particulars of that case, no."

"Hmm. Okay." I grab another file from the table. "How about Michael Tillings, age fourteen? Are you familiar with his case?"

Smeed shifts uncomfortably in his seat. "Yes, I am."

"Good. Please tell the court, Mr. Smeed, what happened to Michael Tillings."

"He passed away."

He's hedging, digging his heels into the dirt as he's propelled closer to a cliff he doesn't want anywhere near. And I'm just the guy to push him over.

"Passed away? That's a very delicate way of putting it. He was murdered, isn't that correct? While in a group home, run by CFSA—he was beaten by several other boys at the facility?"

Begrudgingly, he answers. "Yes, we suspect it was gang related."

"Gang related or not—the boy died. While in your agency's custody."

Smeed nods, his eyes flat. "That's correct."

I pick up a third file. "Matilda Weiss, age four."

The opposing attorney pops up like a rodent in Whac-a-Mole. "What does this have to do with Chelsea McQuaid's competency as a guardian?"

"I'm getting there, Your Honor."

"Get there quickly, Mr. Becker," she replies.

"Tell me about the Weiss case, Mr. Smeed—your signature is on her file."

He rubs his hands on his pants, sniffs, and then answers. "There was an allegation of child abuse against the Weiss family."

"And you investigated? Visited the home, conducted interviews?"

"Yes."

"What were your findings?"

He pauses, like he really doesn't want to answer. But he really doesn't have a choice.

"I determined there was not sufficient evidence of abuse to warrant action."

My fingers tingle with unspent energy. "So you closed the case file?"

"Yes."

"And two months later, what happened?"

"A neighbor found Matilda . . . digging through the garbage. Looking for food."

"Because her parents were starving her," I state, my stomach churning.

"Yes."

"Abusing her—even though you had determined that no such abuse was taking place?"

For the first time he looks me in the eyes, his expression not just strained but guilty. Haunted by the ghosts of lost children and faceless names. "What exactly is your point, Mr. Becker?"

I walk closer. "You said it's your job to be critical—to determine who is a fit guardian and who is not. So, my point, *Dexter*, is sometimes you and your agency just flat out get it wrong."

I let the words hang.

Walking back to the table, I add, "Wouldn't you agree?"

"No, I would not."

"Oh, no?" I lift a box from the floor and place it on the table. "I have a box full of tragic examples that say otherwise. We can do this all day long."

He stutters. "Every . . . each case is different. Just because . . . circumstances may have been overlooked in one instance doesn't mean there will be errors in the next one." He takes a breath, composing himself. "You speak of those children, Mr. Becker, rattle off their names and ages—because they're just names to you. To me . . . they matter."

He couldn't be more fucking wrong. They're not just names—they're faces. Riley's, Rory's, Rosaleen's—I saw them all, in every page of those god-awful reports.

"I will do everything in my power not to fail another child under our care." Smeed taps his finger on the ledge of the witness box. "Which is precisely why the McQuaid children should remain in our custody. The red flags—"

I slap my hand on the table. "Red flags—I'm so glad you brought that up. Let's talk about them." My movements are swift and sure as I stalk back and forth in front of him. "You said in your report it was the combination of events that pushed you to remove the McQuaid children from Chelsea's care?"

"That's right."

"One of those events was Riley McQuaid being detained at a party where alcohol was present."

"Yes." He answers and starts to lecture, "Underage drinking is a sign of lack of parental supervision."

I lift my eyebrows. "Are you aware that fifty-one percent of teenagers experiment with alcohol before their fifteenth birthday?"

"I can't say if that's true or not, I don't know the exact statistic."

Again I'm moving forward, closer to him. "But if it was true—fifty-one percent, that would be . . . average, wouldn't it?"

"That doesn't make it permissible—"

"No, Dexter, it doesn't. It just makes it *normal*."

I flip the page of the file with a snap and trail my finger down the center. "Your next issue? Rory breaking his arm?"

"That's right. Grave injuries, fractures, are always cause for concern."

"Even though over seven million people broke a bone in the US last year?" I inform him. "Even though the average adult will have sustained two bone fractures within their lifetime? Rory is a healthy, active nine-year-old, so again, by these statistics it'd be more surprising if he hadn't broken his arm at some point."

He sighs. And rubs his eyes. Because I'm wearing him down. Stressing him out.

Good.

"What else caught your attention on the red-flag parade?" I ask.

"Rory McQuaid's arrest, as well as the physical altercation between one of the other minors and a classmate at school."

"The other minor's name is Raymond. And again, a schoolyard quarrel really isn't atypical for a boy his age."

"No"—Smeed adjusts his glasses—"but when you add it to the other issues, it compounds—"

"You are aware these children lost both their parents—violently? Unexpectedly?"

"Yes, but—"

"Did it occur to you that they were acting out? Struggling to deal with the emotional trauma they had to endure?"

"However—"

I take a step closer, my voice rising with my anger. Because he didn't take the time, didn't bother to see any of them. All because he thought he knew better. "Did it for one second occur to you that the reason the flags were so numerous is because there are so many kids? Perfectly normal children experiencing everyday milestones—they're just doing it all at the same time!"

"No. You don't know—"

"I'll tell you what I *do* know, Dexter," I spit. "I know that you wrenched these kids away from the only family they have left. You took them from the only home they know—where they were wanted, and loved, and most of all, they were safe!"

"They weren't safe!" he shouts back, pointing in Chelsea's direction. "She's not capable—"

"You wouldn't know capable if it came along and bit you on—"

The judge's gavel bangs and she calls for order.

I take a deep breath and reel it in.

I hold up a supplicating hand to the judge. "Just one or two more questions, Your Honor."

She doesn't look happy. "Proceed."

My voice is even as I ask, "If Robert and Rachel McQuaid had survived, and if all the 'red flags' had unfolded the same way—would you have sought to terminate parental custody?"

This is the big one. More important than the stats I've cited or the counterarguments I've given.

"I deal in facts, Mr. Becker. Truths. I'm not going to entertain your hypotheticals," he sneers.

Until the judge speaks up. "Actually, that's an answer I'd like to hear as well, Mr. Smeed. If the children had been in the custody of the biological parents, would the situation have been dire enough—given the information you have—to warrant their removal from the home?"

He blinks and swallows. Stares and shifts. But he's not dumb enough to lie to a judge. "To the extent that I can predict such a thing, Your Honor, if it had been a two-parent household, with the biological parents present . . . no, it is more than likely we would not have sought custody of the children."

"Would they have even been on CFSA's radar?" I ask. "A broken arm, a fight on the playground, a busted-up keg party—would you have ever even heard of the McQuaids?"

He looks down, fidgets again, and then says, "Most likely . . . no."

Swish. Nothing but net.

"I'm done with him, Your Honor."

• • •

After the CFSA questions Smeed—reinforcing his bullshit claims about dire consequences and the potentially unsafe environment Chelsea's guardianship poses—he's excused from the stand. I squeeze Chelsea's knee under the table, then I stand up and call her as a witness. She gets sworn in and sits in the witness box, looking small—timid.

I catch her gaze and give her a smile, then I lean back casually against the table.

"Are you nervous, Chelsea?"

She glances at the judge, then back to me. "A little bit, yeah."

"Don't be. It's just you and me, having a conversation."

She nods her head and I get started.

"Tell me about the kids."

Chelsea practically glows as she talks about the strong-minded woman Riley is growing into, Rory's precocious energy that will one day lead him to do great things. She smiles as she discusses Raymond's kind nature, and how no one can be in a room with Rosaleen and not smile. She gets choked up when she mentions Regan and how she learns from her brothers and sisters, and what a good baby Ronan is, how badly she wants to be there to watch him grow into the amazing kid she knows he'll be.

"You're twenty-six," I say. "You had a whole life in California—friends, an apartment, school. And you put that all aside and came here to be a guardian to your nieces and nephews. Did you ever consider *not* raising them? Letting child services find new homes for them?"

She raises her chin. "Never. Not for a second."

"Why?" I ask softly.

"Because I love them. They're mine. Raising them is the most important thing I'll ever do." Her eyes are wet as she turns to the judge. "And some days it's hard, Your Honor . . . but even on those days, there's so much joy. They're everything to me."

I give Chelsea a nod, letting her know she did great. Then I sit down and the agency's lawyer gets her turn.

She stands. "Miss McQuaid, what is the nature of your relationship with your attorney, Jake Becker?"

And I'm on my feet. "Your Honor, unless opposing counsel is suggesting I pose some type of danger to the McQuaid children, this type of questioning is completely out of line."

"I agree. Move on, Counselor."

She does. Trying to spin the incidences with the kids into some kind of negligence on Chelsea's part. But there's no damage done. When there's no smoke, there's no fire.

After Chelsea is excused, I submit the statements from the pediatrician, which attest to the kids' health and how they're all up to date on their well visits. I also submit statements from Sofia, Stanton, and Brent, corroborating Chelsea's competency as a guardian and to show that she has a support system. CFSA stands by the argument that originally won them custody and we both rest our cases. The judge says she'll deliberate and return with her ruling as soon as possible, then court is adjourned.

After the judge leaves the courtroom, Chelsea turns to me. "What now?"

"Now . . . we wait."

25

We stay close to the courthouse for lunch, and despite Brent's most annoying efforts, Chelsea doesn't touch her food. Two hours later, court is back in session. Chelsea holds my hand in a death grip under the table as the judge clears her throat to render her decision.

"As one of nine children, I feel particularly qualified to rule in this case." She peers down through her glasses at us. "As Miss McQuaid stated, raising children is hard—particularly six children between the ages of six months and fourteen years. Whether there is one child or ten, however, it is still the court's responsibility to ensure these children are raised in the custody of a guardian who will care for them and provide a safe environment that allows them to thrive. After reviewing all of the evidence presented, I believe Chelsea McQuaid is just such a guardian . . ."

Mentally I shout in victory and Chelsea starts to cry.

"And so I am ordering that physical and legal custody of the six minor children be returned to Miss McQuaid, effective immediately." She turns her attention to the Children and Family Services side of the room. "CFSA is charged with not just the task of judging parental performance but assisting them as well. Our job is not to tear families apart and claim they are better for it, but to find a way for families to stay together. Children and Family Services will provide the court with monthly updates on this case, and rest assured, I will be looking for increased involvement by that agency when it comes to providing assistance in all areas." She glances at Chelsea and smiles. "Good luck, Miss McQuaid. Court is adjourned."

Chelsea throws herself into my arms, while Brent, Sofia, and Stanton are all smiles too. She looks up at me. "Can we go get them?"

"Yeah, we can."

"Right now?" She bounces.

"Right now." I laugh.

• • •

We pick up Chelsea's brother's truck, then, with the information Janet provided, we drive about an hour north of the city to get the monsters. Chelsea talks and smiles the whole way there, looking so damn overjoyed. Janet notified the foster family that we were on our way, so they're not surprised when we show up at the front door. It's a nice place—a big house, a quiet street. The pretty blonde who answers the door tells Chelsea the kids are in the back. We open the sliding glass doors and step into the backyard, and you'd think they haven't seen Chelsea in two years instead of two days.

That's how happy they are. How fast they run to her. How loud they scream when they see her. How long they hug her—like they never want to let go.

"You're here!" Rosaleen yells while her aunt tries to hug them all at the same time. "I knew you'd come, I knew it!"

"Can we go home?" Rory asks Chelsea.

"Yes—we're going home."

When Regan loses her footing in the mass of hugging bodies and falls on her ass on the grass, I scoop her up. I hold her high for a minute, then settle her comfortably in my arms. She puts her little hands on my cheeks, looks me in the face, and squeaks her third word.

"Jake!"

And the whole world goes blurry.

"Damn, kiddo, you've got a way with words."

• • •

It's around four o'clock by the time we get back to the house and get the kids unpacked. They're all so hyped up, so excited to be home again, they convince Chelsea to throw a party.

And she agrees.

There's a distinct possibility she's never going to be able to say fucking no to them again.

A few hours later, there's boxes of pizza, soda, streamers, and balloons. Stanton, Sofia, and Brent come, Janet comes, the neighbors come, as well as a bunch of the kids' friends, and their parents. I kind of hang in the background, leaning up against the wall, watching.

Distancing myself. From all of it. Drinking a cup of soda and really wishing I could mix it with that bottle of Southern Comfort that's back to being buried in the freezer.

It's dark by the time I step outside, onto the back patio. Bright purple and white hyacinths bloom all around, their heavy perfume making me feel like I'm gonna puke hard. The noises from inside echo out—shrill, delighted childish screeches, music, Stanton's deep rumbling laugh, the steady drone of adult conversation.

Even though the weather is on the cool side, I start to sweat.

I remember the scripture from yesterday, when I went to church with Chelsea. It was about Jesus, in the Garden of Gethsemane, praying for a pardon that would never come.

Let this cup pass from me . . .

Seems pretty ironic right about now.

"You're gonna dump her, aren't you?"

My head jerks toward the corner of the garden, hidden in shadow from the lights streaming out of the house, where Riley is standing.

And she sounds pissed.

"I see what you're doing—the way you lean away from her. The way you've been avoiding her all night. You're acting like one of the boys in my school, right before he dumps his girlfriend in front of the entire cafeteria." Her anger gives way to confusion and hurt. "How can you *do* that? Aunt Chelsea is the best person ever. And she loves you."

"Riley—"

"She does! It's obvious. She's so happy with you. Why would you take that away from her?"

I rub the back of my neck. I've argued in front of judges with a lifetime of accomplishments behind them. Truly great judiciaries—some of them I studied in goddamn law school. And I was cool as ice.

I can't say the same as I try to explain myself to a fourteen-year-old.

"Riley . . . It's . . . complicated. I'm trying . . . you can't . . ." And I go with the old reliable. The ultimate cop-out. "When you're older, you'll understand."

Fucking pathetic.

She makes a disgusted sound, then slices me to pieces. "That's the first time you've ever talked to me like I'm some dumb kid. And the truth is, *you're* the stupid one!"

Riley shakes her head at my silence. "You don't deserve her. You don't deserve any of us." She stomps past me, a swirl of furious brown hair. "You're an asshole!"

She wrenches open the door and disappears inside.

And I whisper to no one, "Yeah. I know."

Before the door slams shut behind Riley, Chelsea steps out onto the patio.

"There you are. Riley doesn't look happy." She wraps her arms around my neck and leans against me. "Teenage drama already?" Her perfect lips drift closer. "I thought we'd get a few days' reprieve."

I lean back and grip her forearms, slowly sliding them off. My voice is a feeble whisper. "Chelsea . . . we can't do this."

At first she's confused, still smiling. But then the smile fades, and she understands. Her arms fold around her. "I thought we already were. I thought we were doing really well."

We were. But it's too fucking much. Too fast, too intense, too . . . distracting. I meant what I said to her yesterday—I can't think of a single thing I wouldn't do for her. For them.

"I care about you, Chelsea." I gesture toward the house. "I care about you all very much. But a family—that kind of responsibility was never part of the plan for me. My role models were a drunk whose favorite pastime was punching his wife, and a cranky womanizing workaholic who was married to his bench. I don't know how to do this."

I've taken plenty of risks in my career. The bigger the risk, the bigger the reward. But I can't risk . . . them. They're too important, too precious. The risk that I could screw up, harm them because I don't know what the hell I'm doing—even the possibility terrifies me.

I lick my lips, not looking at her. "And now that I know the kids are safe, that you're okay—I need to back this way up."

It was always going to end. Today, or a month, or six months from now—and it was never going to end well for her. I should've pulled away a long time ago.

But she was so . . . her.

And I was a selfish fucking idiot.

She inhales a breath, then lets it out slowly, the way she does when she's trying to calm her heart. I hate that I fucking know that. I hate that I can already imagine what she's thinking, what she'll say.

"Jake, I know it's scary. I'm scared too. But some things are worth being scared for. And together, we could be . . ."

Do it right . . . or don't bother.

So I force myself to look into those heartbreaking blue eyes. And lie through my teeth.

"I don't *want* this, Chelsea."

She gasps, like the wind's been knocked out of her.

"I don't want this life. I can be a friend to you—to them—but this thing between us, whatever it is . . . needs to end now." I scrape a hand through my hair, tugging hard, the pain giving me focus. Resolve. "You're the kind of woman who's gonna want to get married someday. You should be out there looking for that guy. But I'm not him. Any time we spend together will just . . . be a waste."

Her voice is dull. Barely there. "I see."

And I can hear the tears. I won't look—I fucking can't. But I can practically feel them slowly streaking down her face.

She clears her throat. "The boys—they idolize you, Jake. They all do. Please don't—"

"I won't," I promise. "I'm not going to abandon them or you. I still want to help." My voice picks up and I start to talk faster.

"Anything you need. I'll take them to practice, I'll be there at games, babysitting or just being with them. I won't leave you hanging, Chelsea."

I finally get the balls to look at her face.

But I shouldn't have.

She's moonlight pale, her lashes dark with wetness. A tear leaks silently from one corner, leaving a silver trail down her porcelain cheek.

"I'm sorry."

And I am—so goddamn sorry.

Chelsea raises her chin, and her shoulders straighten with that bravery—that quiet, ceaseless strength. Her fingers wipe away tears. "I understand, Jake. Thank you"—she swallows—"for your honesty." Her voice goes even softer. "We care about you too—so much. If friendship is all you want, then we'll make it work just as friends."

Hearing the words from her lips makes me fucking cringe.

But I cover it with a silent nod.

Chelsea steps toward the door, and every cell in my body screams to stop her. Grab her—spin her around and kiss her until she smiles again. To drop to my knees and take it all back. To undo the last five minutes.

But I'm trying to do the right thing. Even though it's harder than I ever could've imagined.

As Chelsea walks away, I squeeze my eyes shut, force my feet and my hands to stay still as stone . . . and let her go.

26

Days go by and bleed into weeks. I keep my commitments to the kids. Sometimes I'm there when they get off the bus from school, nearby during Rosaleen's piano practices. Once in a while I take Regan and Ronan back to fucking Mommy and Me, and I go to Rory's Little League games, cheering louder than any father there. Things between Chelsea and me are . . . civil. Perfectly polite. I almost wish she'd curse at me, yell, tell me I'm a dick. It'd be so much better than the impersonal, tightly measured exchanges we have. She talks to me the same way the Judge does on the days when he has no goddamn idea who I am.

Like I'm a stranger.

Two weeks after the custody hearing, Brent strolls into my office. "Dude, tonight—me, Lucy Patterson, you, and her friend, we're going to grab a bite to eat after work."

"I don't think so," I answer, not bothering to look up from my laptop.

"And therein lies your problem, Jake. Too much thinking. It's time to get back on that horse, little camper. And ride her." He fiddles with a pen on my desk. "I've taken Lucy out a few times already—we're chugging full steam ahead. She says her friend likes you, has been asking about you."

I rub my eyes. "What was her friend's name again?"

He shrugs. "I don't know. But it doesn't matter—you're going. I won't take no for an answer."

When he gets an idea into his head, Brent can be as tenacious as Sofia's Rottweiler's jaws—he just won't let go. So, in an effort to get back to work as quickly as possible, I give in.

"Fine."

"Sweet." He smiles. "We're meeting them at six."

• • •

Dinner with Brent, Lucy, and her friend with the tight ass, whose name I still don't know, is once again casual. Easy. And forgettable. We meet up at a sports bar, have hot sandwiches, then move to the adjoining room to shoot some pool. The friend flirts with me, tries to get me to teach her how to hold the cue. But I'm just not into it. It's an effort not to be rude.

After what seems like forever but is in actuality only two hours, we call it a night. The four of us walk out the door of the bar onto the sidewalk.

I turn to the right, and find myself staring into stunning, crystal-blue eyes.

"Jake!" Chelsea says, as surprised as I am.

"Chelsea . . . hey."

The kids flank her on all sides. Raymond is pushing Ronan in his stroller on her left, Riley holds Rosaleen's hand on her right, Regan is held in Chelsea's arms.

"Jake!" Regan shouts, using her new favorite word.

"Hey, kiddo."

Chelsea's expression goes from surprised to awkward as she takes in Brent, the blond Lucy, and the brunette at my side. She pales slightly, looking . . . wounded.

Not to be outdone, Rosaleen bounces and says, "Hey, Jake!"

I smile at her as the brunette crouches down. "You are sooo cute! My sister is going to have a baby soon and I hope she looks just like you." She taps Rosaleen's nose—which scrunches distastefully.

"Who are *you*?" Rosaleen asks with all kinds of attitude.

"Come on, Rosaleen." Riley tugs at her sister's hand, giving me the cold shoulder and an even colder glare. "Raymond, let's keep walking. Aunt Chelsea, we'll catch up with you down the block."

The three of them walk around us while I'm still staring at Chelsea.

"What . . . what are you doing here?"

"Rory's therapist had to push back his session. He's in there now and I promised the kids ice cream while we wait, so that's what I'm doing. We're heading that way"—she points over my shoulder—"to get ice cream."

As an afterthought, she glances at Brent. "Hi, Brent—it's nice to see you."

"You too, Chelsea," he answers softly.

She hoists Regan higher on her hip and pushes hair behind her ear. "Well . . . I should get going. Have . . . have a good night."

She walks around me. But she only gets a few steps.

"Chelsea!" I call, her name sounding like it's been torn from the deepest part of my lung. I step quickly, moving in front of her. "I can explain. This isn't—"

"Jake, you don't have to explain," she tells me gently, shaking her head. "You don't owe me anything."

And I know that's true—so why does it feel like I've been kicked in the nuts?

We stand that way for a few seconds. Then I reach for Regan. "Let me help you get the kids ice cream."

But Chelsea steps back. Out of my reach. "No. It's okay." Her smile is so soft. So sad. "I can do it on my own."

She walks away. Leaving me standing on the sidewalk. Alone.

• • •

A few days later I'm in the office; Stanton's at his desk. "Are you and Sofia coming over to watch the game tonight?" I ask him.

"Ah . . . no. Change of plans."

"What are you guys doing?"

Sofia brushes into the office, timing as impeccable as ever. "We're watching the kids for Chelsea."

I lean back in my chair, my work totally forgotten.

"Why? I mean . . . why didn't she ask me?"

Sofia hands Stanton a folder. "Probably because she has a date and didn't want things to be uncomfortable."

"A date?"

My first thought is she's doing it to get back at me, because she caught me out on my own stupid double date. But Chelsea's not like that. She's not petty. Which means she's going out on a date because she's moving on. Just like I told her to.

Fuck.

"Do you . . . did she tell you who she's going out with?"

Sofia's hazel gaze regards me with no sympathy whatsoever. "She did actually—Tom Caldwell."

"Tom Caldwell? Get the hell out of here! How did that happen?"

"Apparently, Chelsea ran into Tom at the grocery store. They started talking, he asked if she was available . . . then he asked her out."

Motherfucker.

"And how do you know this?" I ask harshly.

Sofia shrugs. "Chelsea and I talk. We're friends—she doesn't have a lot of friends here, Jake."

I know. With six kids to look after she doesn't have a lot of time for friends. But—bitterness stings sour on my tongue—I guess she's making time for good old fucking Tom.

"I'll watch the kids." I don't leave any room for discussion in my tone.

That doesn't mean Sofia won't try to discuss it. "I don't think that's a good idea."

"Why not?"

She points to my fists, which are clenched tightly on the desk. And she doesn't really have to say anything else.

I force them to loosen, shaking them out. "It'll be fine. I'll be fine. I just want to make sure he knows not to mess with her."

"Stanton and I are fully capable of putting the fear of God into him. Not that he really needs it—Tom is a nice guy."

I scowl at her. "I want to watch the kids."

"I don't—"

Luckily, Stanton has my back. "I think Jake should watch the kids, Soph. If he and Chelsea are going to be strictly friends, he's gonna have to deal with her dating. If he thinks he's up for it, I think we should let him have at it."

And he smirks at her. The smirk gets her every time.

"O-kay." She looks at me hard. "But don't be an asshole, Jake."

I look right back at her. "Who, *me*?"

• • •

That night, I knock on Chelsea's front door. It's locked—and she finally removed the key from under the mat. The door opens, and it feels like déjà vu—like the first time I saw her in this doorway. And just like that time, the breath is knocked out of me.

Her dress is dark green, simple and understated. Utterly stunning. Her long, delicate arms peek out from tiny cap sleeves, a shiny belt shows off her trim waist, and her legs—Jesus—they look fucking endless beneath the short, slightly flaring skirt.

Chelsea's eyes go round with surprise and I'm guessing Sofia didn't give her the heads-up about the babysitting switch.

"Hi."

"Jake—hi. What are you—"

"Something came up with Stanton and Sofia . . ." Which would be me. "So . . . I'm going to watch the kids—if that's okay with you."

She recovers from her shock and opens the door wider. "Of course it's okay. Come on in."

The kids are in the den. "Hey, guys."

"Cool—you're watching us?" Rory exclaims. "You owe me a Halo rematch."

Chelsea says she has to fill Ronan's bottles and heads to the kitchen. After greeting the rest of the rug rats, I follow her. She's at the counter, staring harder than necessary as she fills the bottle in her hands. Silently, I move to stand beside her. Just inches away.

Close enough to touch her.

"You look beautiful."

She glances at me quickly, smiling self-consciously. "Oh . . . thank you." She tightens the cap on the bottle, places it on the counter, and turns to face me. "This is weird, isn't it?"

"No, it's not."

"It's totally weird, Jake. You know what I look like naked—"

Do I ever. The image is seared into my brain. My favorite memory.

"—and now you're here watching the kids while I go out on a date with another man. That's, like, the definition of weirdness."

I chuckle. "It doesn't have to be. We're adults. We're friends. This is what . . . friends do."

She looks up into my eyes, her cheeks flushed, her expression so much more than friendly.

The dog goes nuts barking at a knock from the front door. With another quick smile, Chelsea goes to answer it. I make my way back out to the den just as Chelsea leads Tom Caldwell in, introducing him to the kids, his white teeth gleaming like shiny pearls as he smiles at each one of them.

Then, under his breath, I hear him whisper to Chelsea, "You look ravishing."

Who says that? Who the hell uses the word *ravishing*?

Douchebags—that's who.

"I just have to grab my bag and then we'll go." She blows a kiss at the kids. "Be good, guys. I'll be home in a little while." Then she leaves the room.

And I make my move. "Caldwell."

"Becker." He grins, holding out his hand. "I'm surprised to see you here."

I grip his hand hard when I shake it. "You shouldn't be. I'm here a lot. I'm watching the kids for Chelsea."

"That's nice of you."

Yep—that's me. Fucking nice.

I guide him toward the front door, needing a moment alone. In the foyer, my voice drops low and menacing. "I just want to make a few things clear. If you treat Chelsea with anything less than perfect respect . . . if you ever think about doing something that will in any way hurt these kids . . . when I'm finished with you, there won't be enough left to bury."

My stare is unwavering.

He leans back. "Are you threatening me, Jake?"

"I thought that was pretty fucking obvious."

Then he chuckles, smacking my back like we're old friends. "Message received. You have nothing to worry about with me."

Chelsea comes down the stairs and Caldwell opens the front door for her. He salutes me as he walks out. "Have fun babysitting, Becker."

I stand there for a few moments after they leave, glaring at the closed door. Rory comes up next to me, looking in the same direction.

"He seems like a douchebag."

"You're an excellent judge of character, you know that, kid?"

Rory nods. And I tap his shoulder. "Come on, let's go play Halo. I feel like annihilating something."

• • •

It's about eleven when Chelsea comes home. Blessedly alone. She walks through the front door and into the den—where we're waiting for her.

All of us.

She kicks off her shoes. "Wow, hey—you guys are still up."

I sit in the middle of the couch, Regan on my lap, Rory and Raymond on either side, Riley leaning against the back.

"The kids wanted to talk to you about something," I explain.

Her gaze flickers to each of them. "What's up?

"We don't like him," Rory says.

It takes a moment for Chelsea to understand. "Him?" Her thumb points over her shoulder. "Tom?"

"He's a douche," Rory confirms.

"He doesn't seem very smart," Raymond adds.

"He's booooring," Rosaleen chimes in.

"He's cute," Riley says. "But you could do better."

And Regan ties it all together. "No!"

God, she's eloquent.

Chelsea laughs. "All right. Well, thank you for sharing your thoughts. Your feelings are duly noted. Now"—she sweeps her hand to the stairs—"go to bed."

When the predictable groans and complaints begin, I back her up. "Go on, guys, just make it easy on yourselves. Rory, help Regan brush her teeth."

"I'll be up to tuck you in in a minute," she tells them as they file past her like baby ducks in a row. Then her eyes fall on me, locked and loaded. "Can I speak with you outside? Now."

And her tone means business. Guess her panties are twisted, but that's fine with me—'cause my panties are pretty goddamn twisted at the moment too.

Okay, that didn't come out right . . . but you know what I fucking mean. If she wants a fight, I'm more than happy to give her one. Or more than one.

Multiple.

Long, sweaty, bed-breaking . . . *shit*! What the hell is wrong with me?

Once the kids are upstairs, I follow her out the back door, my stiff strides matching her stomping ones, onto the dark patio. The French door slams with a bang and she doesn't waste any time whirling around to face me.

"This isn't fair! You can't do this!"

"What exactly do you think I'm doing, Chelsea?"

"Turning the kids against any man I go out with. My love life is not up for a vote!"

The only words I process from that statement are *love life*. What the fuck is up with that?

"You have a love life?" I ask, horrified. The popcorn I ate during the movie with the kids turns to lead in my stomach.

She pokes my chest. "I have the right to be happy!"

Poke.

"Believe it or not, Tom actually finds me attractive!"

Poke.

"He likes talking to me, spending time with me!"

Poke.

"He *wants* me . . . even if you don't!"

I catch her hand, spin her around, and press her back against the wall of the house. She glares up at me, chin raised, fearless and daring, her ice-blue eyes cold with fury.

Thinking straight went out the window when she started talking about other men. Weighing the consequences of my actions came to a halt the second she said I didn't want her.

As if that was even fucking possible.

Now it's all just mindless instinct. Pure emotion, fire, need. The need for my touch to be the last one she feels tonight. My lips her good-night kiss. Not. Fucking. Tom's.

"Wanting you was never the issue, Chelsea."

I lean against her, feel her breasts achingly soft against my chest, my knee between her thighs, where she's warm and heavenly. My face so close to hers, we breathe the same air.

She pulls against my grip, bucks. "It is!" she hisses. "That's what you said. This—me—isn't what you wanted."

That awful night is a blur. A vague memory of foreign nervousness, regret, and stumbling words. I don't know what the hell I actually told her.

"Did I?" I press even closer, letting her feel exactly how hard she's wanted. "Then I'm an idiot." My eyes drink her in, every inch—her panting lips, flushed cheeks, the throbbing pulse in her neck that tells me she wants me too. "And even worse—I'm a liar, too."

My mouth covers hers and I taste her moan—it's long and desperately relieved. She whimpers as I release her wrists, just so I can touch her, and she wraps her arms around my neck, pulling me closer. I suck on her bottom lip before delving back into the slick sweetness of her mouth.

It's been so long. Too long.

She arches against me and all I want to do is grab her, lift her, and fuck her against the wall.

It's that thought that brings sanity roaring back.

Shit, what am I doing? I told her this had to stop, and then . . . *Fuck*, I'm a caveman.

Gently, I grip her arms and force myself to step back, separating us. I stare down at the stone patio, so I don't have to look at her. "Chelsea, I'm . . . This was a mistake. It won't happen again. I'm sorry."

She doesn't say anything at first. But I can feel her. Feel the confusion and then the anger—it radiates from her in thick, weighted waves.

When I finally look at her face, her mouth is more of a snarl than a frown. Her brows are drawn together and her eyes shoot blue sparks.

And sick bastard that I am, it turns me on even more.

Until she speaks. "You know, Jake, I always knew you were capable of being an asshole, when you wanted to be. But I never, *ever*, thought you'd be a coward."

And she walks away. Opens the French door and slips back into the house.

And I feel like fucking dirt. Like the kind that gets trapped under Cousin It's claws. That's me—a speck of filth under the tiny nail of a small goddamn dog.

27

The next day, at work, I'm at the very top of Sofia's shit list. This is driven home when she comes barreling into my office and slams the door behind her. Eyes blazing, hair flying, she braces her arms on my desk, leaning over me.

And I have a whole new respect for Stanton. Sofia can be pretty goddamn intimidating when she puts her mind to it.

"What the hell is wrong with you?"

"If you want an actual answer, you'll have to be more specific."

"You're playing games with Chelsea. And it needs to stop."

Obviously, Chelsea filled her in on our interaction in the garden. I wonder what she said, how she described it. And I don't actually mind that Sofia is taking her side—Chelsea deserves to have someone in her corner.

"I didn't mean to." Weak. So fucking weak.

"You're tearing her apart, Jake. She doesn't know which end is up."

I flinch.

"So either shit or get off the pot. Either you're her friend, or you're more than her friend—you can't have it both ways."

"I fucking know that!" I snap. "I'm her friend."

Sofia straightens, folding her arms. "Then I suggest you start *acting* like it."

• • •

Sofia's verbal attack bugs the shit out of me the rest of the day. My focus is crap because of it—so I cut out early and drive straight to Chelsea's house. To talk to her. To make sure we're okay.

'Cause I really fucking need us to be okay.

There's a strange car in the driveway when I pull up—a white Chevy Suburban. The front door is unlocked, so I walk in. The house is quiet, so I make my way into the kitchen and look out the glass of the back door. Chelsea's wearing overalls and a tiny white T-shirt. Her hair is pulled into a shiny bun. Ronan is crawling around on a blanket beside her. She's in the vegetable garden, smacking at the ground with a shovel, maybe a hoe.

And she's not alone.

Beside her, talking easily, swinging his own tool, is Tom Caldwell.

And he . . . fits. Looks like he belongs here—in a house with a garden, a ruglike dog, and a three-car garage. The kind of guy who goes to PTA meetings and Boy Scout jamborees. They match—him and Chelsea—as fucking nauseous as it makes me to admit that. I think of Rachel and Robert McQuaid's wedding portrait in their upstairs bedroom and can so easily imagine Chelsea and Tom's faces in their place.

I drop my hand from the glass and turn around. I make it to the foyer before the five of them converge on me. They seem to come out of nowhere, like brain-sucking zombies in an old-time horror film. Only a lot cuter.

"You're just gonna leave?" Riley asks.

I watch them for a minute, soaking them in. Then I shake my head. "Tom's here."

"We want you," Raymond quietly declares. Without question or doubt.

"Tom's a nice guy, Raymond."

"He's not you," Rory says. "We want you."

They all nod.

Then Rosaleen brings me to my knees.

"Don't you like us anymore, Jake?"

What do you say to that? I mean, really—what are the fucking *words*?

"C'mere," I tell her. And she steps forward into my arms. I clear my throat to dislodge the lump that's suddenly sprung up. "Of course I like you. Out of all the little shits in the world, the six of you are my favorite. But I'm trying to do the right thing here, guys."

"By ditching us?" Rory frowns.

My voice turns sharp. "I'm not ditching you. Ever. Whatever happens . . . between me and your aunt, I'm always going to be your friend. For the rest of your lives—I'm not going anywhere."

Voices come from the kitchen and I hear the sound of the back door closing. I stand up as Chelsea and Tom come into the foyer.

"Jake. I didn't know you were here."

There's an adorable streak of dirt on her cheek that I want to brush away for her. Right before I kiss her.

"Yeah, I just got here. It's a nice day—I thought I'd take the kids to the park. If that's okay with you."

She smiles tightly. "Of course it's okay. I'll just grab Regan's jacket."

• • •

Another week goes by. I don't go on any more stupid double dates with Brent—I don't go out on any dates at all. I even stop jerking off.

Well . . . maybe *stop* is too strong of a word. But there's a drastic decrease.

I'm terrible fucking company—even to my own cock.

Everything just seems to rub me the wrong way. And even worse, the things I used to look forward to, that gave me actual joy—an acquittal, a motion granted, watching a goddamn basketball game—just seem pointless. Hollow.

Empty.

Milton gets arrested again. For vandalism, destruction of property. And I can barely bring myself to yell at him.

He asks me if my dog died.

Then, before he leaves my office, he tells me to keep my chin up. When Milton Bradley has pity for you, that's some rock fucking bottom, right there.

But I don't even care.

I can barely stand myself, and after the second week rolls around, apparently everyone else has had just about enough of me too. Because early one evening, Brent, Sofia, and Stanton charge into my office, and Stanton shuts the door behind them. Brent closes the laptop on my desk and takes it away, like I'm grounded or something.

"What the hell is this?"

"This is an intervention," the bearded bastard says.

"I don't need an intervention."

"Well it's either this or Stanton's gonna take you out back and go Old Yeller on your ass."

I sigh and look at each of them as they sit across from me. "I'm fine."

"Nooo"—Sofia shakes her head—"you're what the opposite of fine looks like."

"You're miserable," Stanton says.

Thanks, buddy.

"Chelsea's kind of miserable too," Sofia adds, but it doesn't make me feel any better.

"And you're both making us miserable," Brent says. "It's like osmosis, it's just spreading out from you. It's messing with my mojo, and it needs to fucking stop."

"Jake"—Stanton stands, his eyes more serious—"it's obvious you want to be with Chelsea. Why the hell don't you just put yourself out of your misery and be with her?"

Finally, a little fire sparks in my voice. "Because I don't want her getting hurt."

"She's hurting now," Sofia argues.

"But this way, I still get to keep her!" My gaze drifts to each of them, daring them to say I'm wrong. "I know how to fight, and how to be a lawyer, how to be a friend." By now I'm breathing hard. "I don't know how to be a family man."

"We thought you might say that." Stanton nods, then gestures to Sofia. "Ladies first."

Sofia rises and paces like she's cross-examining me. "How many ounces of formula does Ronan drink?"

"What does that have to do—"

"Just answer the damn question."

"Six." I sigh. "Except at bedtime—then you gotta top him off with an extra two."

She nods. "And how many words does Regan know?"

"Three. *Hi*, *no* . . . and *Jake*." I can't stop a grin. "She's brilliant."

Sofia sits and Brent stands. "What is Rosaleen's favorite color?" he asks.

"Rainbow. Whatever the hell that means."

He nods. "What is Raymond afraid of?"

I don't even have to think about it. "Space rocks. Meteors. Anything he can't predict or control."

Brent takes his seat. Stanton leans on the back of Sofia's chair, looking me in the eyes. "What does Rory want to be when he grows up?"

"A Supreme Court justice—God help us all."

Stanton smirks. "What is the name of the boy Riley has a crush on these days?"

I frown. "Preston Drabblesmith."

And he's an actual kid—not a character from *Harry Potter*.

Stanton comes around and smacks my arm. "Congratulations, Jake. You already *are* a family man."

I think about his words, their questions, while Brent and Sofia smile like idiots—and I get what he's saying. It's just . . . "I don't know what the hell I'm doing."

Stanton rubs his chin. "I'm gonna let you in on a little secret—none of us know what the hell we're doin'. You think I knew what I was doin' when they put a baby girl in my seventeen-year-old arms? Shit, man, I didn't stop shaking for three days."

"You think Chelsea knew what she was doing when she rushed here from California to raise those kids?" Sofia adds.

"All you really have to do is love them," Stanton says. "That's the biggest thing. After that, the rest . . . just falls into place."

"Besides," Brent says, "do you actually think there's anyone out there who will bust his ass as hard as you will to make them happy?"

And that's the easiest question of all.

Fuck no.

So . . . what the hell am I still doing sitting here?

I stand up. I leave the briefcase, the paperwork. *Screw it all.* "I've gotta go."

But just as they're all smiling, smacking my back, and rushing me toward the door, my boss, Jonas Adams, walks through it.

"Good evening, everyone."

There's greetings all around. And not a little shock—because Jonas Adams, founding partner, doesn't come to his associates' offices. Not ever.

He clears his throat. "There's been an incident, Mr. Becker. Mrs. Holten has, unfortunately, taken a fall down a flight of stairs."

The excitement and anticipation that was bursting out of me just seconds ago shrivels on the vine. My eyes close and I swallow hard, and there's not a sound in the room, except for my question.

"Is she alive?"

Adams takes off his glasses and cleans them with a monogrammed handkerchief. "Oh yes, Sabrina is alive, just a bit bruised. The police have arrested Senator Holten, so I'll need you to head down to the precinct, assist him with any interrogations they may attempt, arrange for bail—"

"No."

The one syllable is so clear and sounds so right on my lips. Almost as right as Chelsea's name. I know the kind of man I am—and I know what I can do. And more important, what I won't fucking do. Ever again.

"I won't do that, Mr. Adams."

His eyes squint, like he can't see me clearly. "May I ask why not?"

"Because he's guilty."

"Has he confessed as much to you?"

"No. But I know he hurts his wife."

Adams's cheeks bloom angry red and his chest puffs out. I've wondered if Jonas is really that blind or just willfully ignorant. Either way, doesn't matter.

"William Holten is a client of this firm, and more than that, he has been my friend for over forty years. He deserves a defense."

"Not from me." I shake my head, staring him down.

Adams's lips tighten into a nasty little bow. "Mr. Becker, you should think very carefully about your next words, because they will determine your fut—"

"I quit."

"Jake." My name rushes from Stanton's mouth in a hushed warning. But I don't need one.

"My resignation will be on your desk in the morning, Mr. Adams. He's your friend—you defend the piece of shit."

Adams lift his nose. "Consider your resignation accepted." He walks out.

And a weight vanishes off my shoulders.

Authority really never was my thing.

"Jake, what did you do?" Sofia asks, her eyes narrowing with concern.

I kiss her cheek. "The right thing."

I smack Brent's arm and shake Stanton's hand, grinning like Ebenezer fucking Scrooge on Christmas morning. "And it was really easy."

I head for the door. "I'll talk to you guys later. Thank you—I don't know how long it would've taken me to pull my head out of my ass without the three of you."

"There's a visual I really didn't need," Sofia says, and I laugh.

Stanton says, "Well, go get her, man."

And that's just what I plan to do.

• • •

Before I drive to Chelsea's, I make a quick stop at the US attorney's office. I take the elevator to Tom Caldwell's office—he's at his desk like I figured he'd be.

I lean against his doorway, scanning the room. "This is a really small office. I knew they were small—but this is like, you'll-get-charged-with-animal-cruelty-if-you-put-a-dog-in-here kind of small."

"Is there a reason you're here, other than to compare office sizes, Becker?"

I nod. "Did you hear about Holten?"

"Course I heard—I'll be the one prosecuting the son of a bitch. Why aren't you down at the police station, protecting his delicate feelings from invasive questions?" I'd have to be deaf not to hear the scathing sarcasm.

"I dropped the case."

His eyes pop wide open. "No kidding? Jonas must've loved that."

"I quit." I shrug.

"Huh." Caldwell looks me over. "Don't suppose you'd be interested in coming over to the light side of the force? We could use you in one of these shit-small offices."

I chuckle. "No . . . locking people up just isn't my style. A beautiful woman once told me I'm more of a . . . defender." I step forward, pulling a business card out of my pocket. "I just wanted to drop this off for Sabrina Holten. My home number and cell are on the back. Tell her I'd like to help."

Caldwell looks at the card. "Help with what?"

I slip my hands into my pockets. "Anything she needs."

I turn to go.

"Jake."

I turn back around. "Yeah?"

Tom looks on the fence about something—but then he decides. "Chelsea had the talk with me the other day. You know, where she tells me she doesn't feel 'that way' about me." He draws a square with his fingers. "I'm in the friend zone." Then he shrugs. "I figured you'd probably be interested in knowing that."

And my mood just got even better.

"I am. Thanks, Tom."

"See you around, Jake."

Look at that—Caldwell's not such a douchebag after all.

28

The kids are on the front lawn when I pull up. Riley's close to Regan, Rory is chasing a screaming Rosaleen around, and Raymond is working on flipping his skateboard.

"Get your goddamn helmet on, Raymond!" He rolls his eyes but puts it on.

"Jaaaake!" Rosaleen screeches, and my ears bleed. "Help!" She throws herself at me, with Rory hot on her heels, dangling a caterpillar from his fingers. "Rory said he's gonna put the caterpillar in my ear, and it'll eat my brain and lay eggs, and when all the baby caterpillars hatch my skull will burst!"

I pin the kid with a hard look. "What's the matter with you?"

Rory shrugs, petting the bug. "She has to learn not to believe everything she's told."

Before I say another word, Riley shouts from the side of the house, "I'll save you, Rosaleen!" Then she fires two automatic water guns high in the air.

"Yes—water guns!" Rosaleen and Rory yell, at almost the same time, before they all take off, screaming, in Riley's direction.

I cup my hands around my mouth and remind them, "Stay away from the pool!"

I watch them for a minute, enjoying the smile that tugs so easily at my lips. And then I march inside the house. Chelsea's in the kitchen, wiping down the counter—her hair is down in soft, silky waves, and she makes jeans and a T-shirt look more alluring than any cocktail dress.

She looks up when I walk in the room. "Hey. I didn't know you were stopping by today."

I don't waste a second, don't stop to overthink jack shit. And honestly, I've waited as long as humanly possible.

I walk up to her, take her face in my hands, and kiss her. I kiss her soft and sweet, hard and demanding. I kiss her until she moans and she has to grip my arms because her knees are weak.

Then I brush my fingers across her cheeks and look into those spectacular blue eyes. My voice comes out strangled and raw. "I love you."

Chelsea gazes back at me, her smile pink and hopeful.

At first.

But then she remembers, and the smile fades. She pulls away from me, stepping back. Her arms fold, a mask of indifference covering her face.

"When did you decide that?"

But she can doubt me all she wants—I'm not going anywhere.

"I've known for a while. I just . . . decided to stop being an idiot about it. To stop fighting it." I tilt my head toward the window, where five screaming voices come through. "I love them, too, in case that wasn't clear. They're awful and perfect . . . and I love them like they're mine. Like they're ours."

She bites her lip and her eyes go wet and shiny. I step closer. "Please don't cry. I love—" I choke on the words, throat burning, eyes stinging. "I love you."

Chelsea sniffles and recrosses her arms, trying so hard to be tough. "Am I just supposed to forget the last few weeks? The things you said—how cold you've been?"

I rub the back of my neck. "I was kind of hoping you would . . . yeah."

She looks down at the floor.

I step in closer, lift her chin with my fingers. "I was trying to protect you. I wanted better for you, Chelsea. For them. A good man. I didn't think I was capable. I didn't think I could be what you needed."

She searches my eyes. "And now?"

"Now I know I can. Because . . . because no one could love you—need you—as much as I do. You're everything to me—the only thing that matters."

A tear streaks down her cheek. She drifts closer. "Don't hurt me again."

"I won't."

"Don't pull away from me again."

"I can't."

She leaps into my arms, squeezing so hard the breath rushes out of me. It's the best fucking feeling in the whole world. Second only to the feel of her lips against mine. Her legs wrap around my waist, like she can't get close enough. Her head angles, moves with mine, like she can't taste deep enough. My fingers dig into her back and our hearts pound.

I set her on the counter, pressing against her, pushing her T-shirt up—needing to feel her skin to skin.

"The kids," she gasps.

I kiss her neck, her ear, her beautiful face. "We'll hear them. As long as they're screaming we'll know they're okay."

And we do hear them, loud and clear, through the window. Still yelling and playing—the good kind of screams.

Her tongue slides against mine and I groan. Then Chelsea pants, "But they could come in any minute. They might see us."

She's right. *Damn it.*

I look around the room, eyes frantic and searching. The pantry!

I carry her in, slam the door behind me with my foot, and reach around with my hand to lock it.

Chelsea nips at my lips, sucks on my earlobe. "I always wondered why the pantry had a lock."

All I'm able to say is, "Locks are awesome."

She laughs against my mouth. Her feet touch the floor just long enough to peel our clothes off. Then I pick her up, legs around me, back against the wall.

I take my cock in hand and test the waters—they're slick and wonderfully hot. I push in slow, gentle, 'cause it's been awhile. When I'm fully seated, when there's not a breath of space between us, Chelsea whispers, "I missed you so much."

I start to move, sliding in and out in a smooth rhythm. And it's so fucking perfect and real. And right. Nothing has ever felt this right in my life.

Her head tilts back and my eyes roll closed. I worship her neck with my mouth. I promise and whisper how beautiful she is. All the things I want to do to her. All the things she means to me.

She squeezes me harder, pulls me closer with her legs, fingers buried in my hair.

Chelsea's breath hitches. "I . . . love you. Oh god, Jake . . . so much. I love you so much."

And it's too much. Overwhelming. And yet, not nearly enough.

The pressure builds, tight and low and fantastic. The purest of pleasure unfurls in my stomach, making my thrusts quicken, chasing that edge with Chelsea. We find it together, pulsing and writhing, clasping hands and moaning voices.

I pant against her cheek, my heart not getting the message yet that it's time to slow. I brush her hair back from her forehead and gaze into her angel face.

"So . . . you love me, huh?"

Chelsea smiles, even as tears rise in her eyes. "Yes. I've loved you since you carried me to bed, sick as a dog, and told me everything was gonna be okay. I love every part of you, even the parts you were afraid to show me. And even though you're kind of an idiot sometimes, I'm going to love you forever."

I laugh and kiss her sweetly. "Good to know."

• • •

I spend that night at Chelsea's. We make sure all the kids take baths and get to bed. Then we spend half the night talking. Planning. The other half is spent . . . *not* talking. Nothing coherent anyway.

I hand in my resignation letter the next day, begin to make the necessary arrangements for my departure from Adams & Williamson. And not a thing about it feels wrong.

Chelsea and I are both waiting when the kids get home from school. We gather them in the den, to talk about what we've planned.

"I know it seems fast," Chelsea tells them while I bounce the hell out of Ronan on my leg. "But there was this movie in the eighties—your parents loved it—called *When Harry Met Sally*—"

"Sounds lame," Rory interrupts.

"It was kind of lame," I tell him out the side of my mouth.

But Chelsea hears me. "It was not lame! It was perfect. Anyway, there's a line from it that says how when you find the person you want to spend the rest of your life with, you want the rest of your life to start right away." She glances at me. "That's how Jake and I feel about each other."

I jump in. "But if you guys aren't good with this, I want you to tell us. It's okay to say no—you won't hurt my feelings. I only want to move in here if you all really want me to."

They look at each other. And think. It's a little fucking weird, how quiet they are.

"Would you move into Mom and Dad's room?" Riley asks.

I wink at Chelsea, 'cause we already talked about this.

"Actually," Chelsea tells them, "we were thinking we'd do some construction on my room down here. Make it big enough for two people, make the bathroom and the closets larger. And your parents' room . . . Jake and I thought it'd be pretty neat if we made it an upstairs family room. Somewhere we can all hang out together. We could get a pool table, a big couch, a new television . . ."

"And an arcade game!"

Rory's obviously on board.

Chelsea nods. "And I could draw whatever you want on the walls. And we could paint it together."

"Oooh, ooh—I want butterflies!" Rosaleen yells. "And unicorns and rainbows."

"And monster trucks," Rory says.

"And skateboards," Raymond adds, tapping his brother's fist.

"And," Riley finishes, "a whole wall with One Direction and 5 Seconds of Summer Fatheads."

"Yeah, we can do all that," Chelsea tells them.

"It's gonna look like a schizophrenic's room," I murmur, and she laughs.

"So about Jake moving in here with us, what do you say, guys?"

"Can I move in with my boyfriend one day?" Riley asks, because she's smart.

"Sure," I answer. "When you're twenty-six and raising six children, you can absolutely move in with your boyfriend, and I won't say shit about it. Until then, no way." Because I'm smarter.

She rolls her eyes. "Whatever—I vote yes, Jake should move in."

"Definitely," Rory agrees.

Rosaleen's smile is huge as she runs up and hugs me. "Yes, yes, yes!"

"Sure," Raymond says.

We all turn to Regan, who grins her tiny baby grin and seals the deal—with word number four.

"Yes."

• • •

That night, after the kids' homework is finished and everyone is in their pajamas, we lie around in the den, watching TV. My cell phone rings on the table—it's Brent.

"Hey."

"Hey, how's it going?"

My eyes land on Chelsea. "Pretty incredible, if you want the truth."

He chuckles. "Good to hear. Listen, are you free for lunch tomorrow? There's something I want to talk to you about. Stanton and Sofia too."

"Yeah, I'm free. What's up?"

"Well, the thing is, I own this building . . ."

"You own a building?"

"Yeah. It's a nice building . . ."

Epilogue

One year later

The office I've worked in for the last six months is bigger than my old one—top floor with a corner window view. And I don't share it with anyone. Legal volumes fill the bookshelves on one wall, and a bunch of family pictures sit proudly on my desk. And Brent, Sofia, and Stanton each have their own corner office on the top floor.

Being a founding partner has its perks.

That building Brent mentioned, the one he owned downtown? It's been extensively renovated and now has a name stenciled in black above the front door.

The Law Offices of Becker, Mason, Santos & Shaw.

Has a nice ring to it, doesn't it?

When I kicked Adams & Williamson to the curb, Brent, Stanton, and Sofia started thinking about branching out on their own too. Calling our own shots, picking our own cases. It was a risk, but for the four of us, it was a risk worth taking.

Mrs. Higgens pulled a Renée Zellweger from *Jerry Maguire* when I left and came over here with me. She pops her head through the office door right now, pearls hanging off her ears, accenting the formal dress she's wearing. "Jake—you're going to be late!"

"I'm not going to be late. I'm never late."

Then I check my watch. "Shit, I'm gonna be late!"

My leather desk chair rolls back as I stand. I check the pockets of my sharp black suit—keys, wallet, phone; I'm good.

"Go, go." Mrs. Higgens waves. "I'll shut everything down and lock up."

"Okay, thank you. I'll see you there, Mrs. Higgens."

I jog the four blocks to the day-care center where Regan and Ronan spend part of their day. I greet the teacher through the Plexiglas window and sign the clipboard next to the kids' names. The cheerfully decorated door opens a few minutes later, and the sound of Barney's "Clean Up Song" echoes through it.

The hairs on the back of my neck stand up—I have nightmares about that song.

A teacher's assistant brings out the troublemakers, holding their hands. Ronan is about a year and a half now—a full head of blond hair, freckles on his nose, and a devilish look in his eye that reminds me of his brother. He's walking, slowly and unsure still—which is why I scoop him up with one arm and Regan with the other. They wave good-bye to the teacher as we haul ass out the door.

"Today, we made paper flowers for the room, and mine was the biggest. Then Mrs. Davis brought a stuffed bear in for story time and I got to hold him. He was gray. And he had two black eyes, and two arms and two legs and a bow tie that was red and—" Regan grips my cheeks in her tiny hands and gives me the bitch brow. "Are you listening to me?"

"Yes, yes." I jog across the street. "Two arms, two legs, red bow tie—I'm riveted."

Eight months ago, Regan started talking more . . . and she hasn't stopped since.

"And then we read *Stone Soup* and in the book, someone brought carrots, and someone brought cabbage, and someone . . ."

Ronan laughs as I run, jostling him around. A few minutes later we reach the church without a minute to spare. I set the kids down, straighten Ronan's shirt, and retie the yellow silk bow on the back of Regan's dress.

"You made it. I was afraid you'd be late." Chelsea comes walking down the church steps—and she looks mind-blowingly fantastic. Her dress is a dark blue satin that looks amazing with her creamy skin. It's snug in all the right places and falls just below the knee, with a deep V neckline that literally has my mouth watering. Her hair is down and curled and shimmers in the sun.

I run a hand through it as I pull her closer. "I'm never late. And you look amazing. That dress is hot."

She reaches up to my ear. "You should see what I have on underneath it."

"Oh, I plan to. Top of the to-do list."

I lean down and kiss her deeply for several long moments.

"Cha-ching, cha-ching," a smartass voice rings out. "All this kissing, I can just hear the therapy bills adding up."

I frown at Rory, who just smirks back.

Chelsea rubs her lipstick off my lips with her thumb, and her engagement ring sparkles in the sun. A two-carat cushion-cut diamond, surrounded by baguettes, in a platinum setting with an antique feel. I gave it to her a few months ago, even got down on one knee. She was really enthusiastic with her yes.

These days Chelsea is finishing up her graduate degree in art history; she went back to taking classes this year. She even has a part-time job lined up when she's done, at a small gallery, a branch of the Smithsonian.

She slides her hand into mine and nods her head toward Riley, who stands on the sidewalk with a tall, skinny, dark-haired kid in a clip-on tie. "Riley would like to introduce you to her date." She drags me over.

"Jake," Riley says with a smile. "This is Parker Elliot."

The kid holds out his hand. "It's an honor to meet you, sir."

I stare at his hand, then his eyes, my face hard and unforgiving. My gaze travels over him down to his shoes. I look back to his face—and shake my head with a disgusted sound.

Then I walk away.

"Don't pay any attention to him, he's like that with everyone," I hear Riley say comfortingly.

Chelsea giggles beside me. "That wasn't very nice."

"Good. The last thing I want the little prick thinking is that I'm nice." Then I lean down and kiss her again—because she's so goddamn pretty. And just because I can.

We walk midway up the stairs and I hold out my arms, gesturing for my party of seven—eight if you count fucking Parker—to gather around. "Let's go, team—huddle up." Their heads turn my way, their little faces attentive. I clear my throat. "This is a very special day for Stanton and Sofia and we want everything to go perfectly for them. So for the next forty-five minutes, I expect you to behave like ladies and gentlemen. That means no whispering, no pinching, no hair pulling, no teasing, no fighting, no giggling, no nose picking, no name calling, no crying . . ." I whisper to Chelsea, "Did I miss anything?"

"No looking at each other," she whispers back.

"That's right," I say louder, "no looking at each other."

That's kind of a big one.

"Consequences will be swift and severe."

"Severe" to them is a weekend without TV or Wi-Fi.

"Do we all understand?"

They nod. I smack my hands together. "All right, let's head inside."

Chelsea carries Ronan and leads the pack into the church, while I hang back and make sure no one gets left behind. Raymond brings up the rear. He's staring at the bride's limousine, which just pulled up, at the gorgeous bridesmaids who climb out.

One junior bridesmaid in particular.

"Presley looks great, doesn't she?" he asks in a sighing voice while he watches the blond-haired, sunshiny thirteen-year-old hold up the back of Sofia's dress as she gets out of the limo.

I'll be damned.

"You know she's older than you?" I ask him.

"Yeah, I know. That's why I'm gonna bide my time. Then, when I own my own multibillion-dollar software company, I'll make my move."

I smack him on the back and his glasses go crooked. "Sounds like a plan, Raymond."

• • •

Stanton and Sofia's wedding goes off without a hitch. Her dress is the perfect blend of sexy and stunning: ivory, beaded, and clinging with a teasing dip of cleavage that made Stanton stare. They both got choked up during the vows, and it was just damn good to see them both so happy.

The reception is an elegant, white-glove affair at the DC Ritz-Carlton. Stanton practically flew the entire town of Sunshine, Mississippi, in, and in addition to Sofia's brothers and their families, she has a couple dozen relatives visiting from Brazil. Needless to say, it's good food, good drinks, and really good people.

Rosaleen finds me by the bar, her hair curled into Shirley Temple ringlets, her blue eyes wide with excitement. "Jake! You didn't say anything about my lip gloss! Riley let me use hers—isn't it pretty?"

"You're gorgeous, Gorgeous. As beautiful as your aunt."

She grins even wider, and I laugh as she grabs Rory by the arm and pulls him onto the dance floor to dance with her.

Momma Shaw, Stanton's mother, regards me with an appraising eye. "You know, Jake, I've seen you smile more in the last thirty minutes than you have the entire time I've known you."

"Well, I have seven pretty amazing reasons to smile now."

She pats my arm as I walk over to Chelsea. On the way, I pass Brent talking to Stanton's sister Mary—channeling Pee-wee Herman.

"You don't want to get involved with a guy like me, Mary. I'm a loner, a rebel . . ."

Chelsea's arms wrap around my neck and we sway on the dance floor to some slow song.

"Guess what?" she asks.

I brush my nose against hers. "What?"

"I was just talking to your mother. She and Owen offered to take the kids back to the house tonight and stay over. Soooo . . . I booked a room here, for you and me."

"Fuck, you're brilliant," I murmur. "Have I ever told you how much I love your mind?"

"I thought you loved my body," she says teasingly, pressing it against me up-close and personal.

"Oh, I do, believe me. I'll give you a thorough demonstration of how much I love it tonight—and tomorrow."

"And we're sleeping in tomorrow—Mr. Five A.M.," she says insistently.

I smirk. "Well, we'll be in bed . . . but there won't be much sleeping going on."

Chelsea rests her head against my chest. "Sounds perfect."

It does, doesn't it?

I don't mean to brag, but like everything else in my life these days, it sounds perfect because . . . it really. Fucking. Is.

Keep reading for a sneak peek at Brent's story in

APPEALED

The third book in *New York Times* bestselling author Emma Chase's sexy Legal Briefs series

Coming Fall 2015 from Gallery Books!

Prologue

Once upon a time, in a land not so far away . . .

"Kennedy?" Brent Mason's voice whispered. "Are you awake?"

She wasn't supposed to be; her mother had tucked her into bed long ago. A wonderful bed, fit for a princess. Hand-carved mahogany columns at each corner, with an arched satin canopy that hovered above her like a puffy cloud, draped with white sheer curtains on the sides. Her head rested on the fluffiest down pillow, and cashmere blankets kept her snug and warm. It was one of the many beds, in one of the many rooms, at Mason Castle. No one else called it a castle, but that's how she always thought of it, with its winding gardens, grand double staircase, the two-story library, the endless hallways, and especially, the ballroom.

"Kennedy!" The whisper was louder now, bouncing with impatience.

"Shhh! Yes, I'm awake!"

Kennedy slid from the bed and donned her slippers and tied her pink robe, all without turning on the bedside lamp, which might give them away.

Her eyes had adjusted to the darkness enough to make out his robe-clad form just inside the room, beckoning her with his hand.

"Did it start yet?" she whispered, reaching him.

The dark, wavy hair that hung over his forehead swayed as he shook his head. "But before we go, you have to swear on your eyeballs you won't tell anyone about the new spot. I'm the only one who knows about it—and now you'll know."

"My eyeballs?"

Brent's blue eyes were solemn as he explained, "That means if you break your promise, your eyeballs will explode."

Kennedy's hands reflexively rose to her temples. She didn't want them to explode. She also liked the spot they had used for the last four years: the velvet-cushioned window seat in the red bedroom at the end of the east wing, which allowed them to see everything.

But Brent had told her yesterday that he'd found a new secret place—the very best. He'd been so excited, and now she was excited, too. "I swear on my eyeballs, I'll never tell."

Brent nodded, then he cracked the door open to look and listen. Everyone—guests and servants alike—was downstairs, making their way from the ballroom to the rear veranda for the big show.

The Mason's New Year's Eve party at their estate on the Potomac River was a legendary affair. It was also tradition—their families, and close friends like Kennedy's family, were invited to spend the night and the days that followed. Unlike Kennedy's older sister or Brent's numerous cousins, the two of them were considered too young to stay up for the midnight festivities.

But they had a secret tradition of their own.

With Brent leading the way, they padded quickly to the east wing of the house, through the little door at the end of the hall—the entrance to the third-floor crawl space. On her hands and knees behind him, Kennedy felt just like Alice from Alice in Wonderland*, and her heart thrummed with anticipation. They arrived in a small, dark, windowless room. They stood up and Brent switched on his flashlight. There was a staircase in front of them, steep and dusty.*

"Be careful," Brent warned. "Some of the steps are uneven."

They climbed the steps single file and Kennedy gasped when they arrived at the top. Alice may have crawled into a beautiful garden—but this was so much better than a garden. It was an attic. There were boxes and trunks, paintings and mirrors, furniture and books, and more dresses sheathed in protective plastic than she could count.

It was magical.

Kennedy wanted to touch everything, explore every corner. Maybe there was a treasure map up here. Or, even better, ghosts! Maybe they could have a séance and speak to them.

Brent watched Kennedy's mouth go round in wonder. He'd known she'd love it. She wasn't like any other girl he knew. She didn't burst into tears if her shoes got muddy, like his cousin Charlotte did. She didn't scream if she saw a spider, like her sister, Claire, did. She hated her daily violin lessons, and never worried about tearing her dress while climbing a tree. Kennedy was an adventurer. She wanted to run and go, to see and do.

And like him, she was fearless.

He glanced at the ladder that led up to the loft. "Come on, it's going to start soon. We'll come back here tomorrow."

She was still gazing around the massive attic as she nodded. "All right."

Kennedy went up the ladder first. She was small for her age and Brent was big, so he could catch her if her foot slipped. In the ceiling of the loft there was an access door, and Brent pushed it open and hoisted himself through, then reached down his hand to Kennedy. Up she went, and the two nine-year-olds found themselves on the flat peak of the roof of Mason Castle.

The sky was a black blanket above them, filled with infinite stars, so big and bright, Kennedy felt like she could reach out and pluck one from the night. She turned in a circle, her blond hair fanning out as she gazed toward the heavens. "You were right—this is the best!"

Brent grinned, then grabbed Kennedy's hand when she got too close to the edge, where the roof sloped steeply, with nothing to stop her from sliding right off. "Watch out!"

He led her to the end, near one of the five chimneys, and they sat down close to each other; it was very cold. When Kennedy's teeth started to chatter, Brent put his arm around her, and she snuggled into his warmth. They could hear the tinkling of champagne flutes, the hum of conversation and laughter from the guests far below them. As they waited, they talked.

". . . so they let me quit fencing and start lacrosse instead. It's awesome."

"You're so lucky!" Kennedy cried. "Mother said I couldn't stop ballet even if my leg was broken. She said I'm going to marry a prince, and no prince wants a princess who doesn't know how to dance."

Music floated up from the band downstairs, and Kennedy wondered if her sister was dancing. "Claire likes your cousin Louis. She said she's going to kiss him at midnight."

Brent's nose wrinkled. "Why?"

That's what Kennedy had asked, interrupting her sister's conversation with Brent's sixteen-year-old cousin, Katherine.

"She said that's what you do at midnight. Kiss the boy you like."

Claire had also confessed her hope that Louis would be her escort to the debutante ball in Paris in the spring. She'd said a kiss at midnight on New Year's Eve was something special—something a boy wouldn't forget.

Then a chorus of voices surged from the veranda below. "10, 9, 8 . . ."

Kennedy stared up at Brent's profile. He was as handsome as any hero in a storybook. And he was brave and kind and noble, as any prince should be.

". . . 4, 3, 2, 1 . . ."

The band began "Auld Lang Syne" as the sky exploded in color above their heads. Bursts of reds and blues, slashes of silvery purples, and swaths of sparkling greens lit up the night and reflected on the river's surface. Kennedy and Brent's upturned faces glowed with the changing colors in the sky, and then Kennedy turned her head, leaned up, and kissed his cheek.

He looked at her with surprise.

"Happy New Year, Brent."

He smiled.

"Happy New Year, Kennedy."

• • •

There was no New Year's Eve party at Mason Castle the following year, or the year after that. Tragedy came to visit to the nine-year-old-boy that summer. Though their family homes bordered each other's, Kennedy and Brent didn't really see each other again for three long years.

And when they did, everything was different.

Chapter 1

23 years later

"You rotten bastard!"

She sits up and stares at me like she doesn't recognize me. No—like she's never met me at all. Which is pretty weird, considering we're both bare-ass naked in my bed. Every inch of us is intimately acquainted.

But it's the tone of her voice that bothers me most—flat with tightly controlled anger and breathy with pain. Like I stole the air from her lungs—like I punched her in the stomach.

The words don't worry me. Insults are our flirting. Arguing is our foreplay. One time, she was so worked up, she hauled off and took a swing at me, and my reaction was a boner that wouldn't be denied.

It's not as twisted as it sounds. It works for us.

At least it did up until ten seconds ago.

"Wait. What?" I ask, genuinely surprised.

I thought she'd be grateful. Happy. Maybe offer me a blow job to demonstrate her supreme appreciation.

Her eyes glitter dangerously, and thoughts of letting her anywhere near my dick flee, like tiny fish in a big aquarium. Because she's not the type of woman to be taken lightly—not anymore. She's a force to be reckoned with. A breaker of hearts and a buster of balls.

"You planned this all along, didn't you? Screwing me silly, lulling me into a false sense of security so I'll drop my guard and you can win the case," she hisses.

She moves to hop off the bed, but I grab her arm. "You think my cock is powerful enough to turn you stupid? Aw, precious, that's really flattering, but I don't need to whore myself out to win my cases. You're freaking out over nothing."

"Fuck off!"

I used to have a way with women.

If the word *fuck* came out to play, it was always followed by *me* and then words like *harder, please,* and *my friend, more.*

Those were the days . . .

She jerks out of my grasp and scrambles off the bed, furiously gathering clothes that are strewn across the hardwood floor. And because she's doing it naked, bending down, jiggling in all the best places, I have to watch. There are teeth marks on her ass—*my* teeth marks. No broken skin, just dark-pink indentations. It's possible I got a little carried away last night, but her ass is just so damn sweet and round and biteable.

I grab the sleeve from the bedside table and slide it onto the stump on my left leg. Yes, part of my leg was amputated when I was a kid. I'll get into that later, because she isn't waiting. I actually like that about her—she doesn't give an inch. Doesn't even think about making special concessions or treating me any differently than the fully capable man I am.

Or more accurately . . . like the prick she apparently thinks I am at the moment.

I snap the pin of the sleeve into my prosthesis and stand up, just as she finds her shoe in the corner, adding it to the pile in her arms.

"Calm down, kitten," I try, my voice level.

"Don't call me that!" she snaps. "We said we wouldn't discuss the case—that was our agreement."

I move in closer, palms out, the universal sign of *I come in peace.* "We agreed to a lot of things that no longer apply, sweet cheeks."

Her nostrils flare at the trial nickname. Guess I can add "sweet cheeks" to the *no* column, which is a damn shame. It suits her.

"I only brought it up because I'm trying to help you."

It's official: I'm a fucking idiot. Of all the wrong things I could've said, that's the wrongest of them all.

"You think I need your *help*? Condescending cocksucker!"

She turns for the door, but I grab her arm again.

"Let go. I'm leaving."

I want to respond with a good old *Like hell you are* or the more direct *You're not going anywhere.* But they both have a psychotic kind of vibe, and that's not what I'm going for.

Instead, I snatch the clothes from her arms and head to the window.

"What are you—? Don't!"

Too late.

Her designer skirt, sleeveless silk blouse, and beige lacy underthings float on the air for a fraction of a second, then fall to the sidewalk and street below us. Her bra gets snagged on the antenna of a passing car and waves majestically down the street, like the flag on a diplomat's vehicle from some awesome country named Titsland.

Feels like I should salute it.

I close the window, cross my arms, and smile. "If you try to leave now, poor Harrison may be scarred for life." Harrison is my butler.

"You son of a bitch!"

And her fists come flying at my face. All those years of ballet classes have made her quick, gracefully agile. But as fast as she is, and as mighty as her disposition is, she's only five foot one at best. So before she can land a punch, or thinks to knee me in the balls, I toss her on the bed. Then I straddle her waist, leaning over to press her wrists into the mattress above her head. My cock brushes hot and hard against the smooth skin just below her breasts, which gives it some fabulous ideas, but that's gonna have to wait until later, too.

Pity.

I gaze down at her. "Now, peaches, we'll continue our conversation."

That nickname fits her. Her silken skin is all peaches and cream. And the way she smells, *Jesus;* the way she tastes on my tongue is sweeter and softer than a ripe peach on a summer day.

Strands of blond hair dance across her collarbone as she bucks beneath me, giving my dick even more fabulous ideas. "Fuck you! I'm done talking."

"Good. Then how about you shut that beautiful mouth and listen? Or I could always gag you."

I may gag her anyway, just for the fun of it. Probably should've held on to her panties.

"I hate you!"

I chuckle. "No, you don't."

Her brown eyes burn into me, the same way they branded me decades ago. "I never should have trusted you again."

Keeping her wrists pinned above her, I lean back a little to enjoy the view. "Bullshit. Best decision you ever made. Now listen up, buttercup . . ."

And I start to tell her all the things I should've said weeks ago. No, *years* ago . . .

• • •

4 weeks earlier

I slide my arms into the custom-tailored navy suit jacket Harrison selected for me today. The guy's got good taste, and he's an expert at which cut of an Italian three-piece suit is stylish and which is just vulgar. I wasn't aware that a lapel could be "vulgar," but apparently it's possible.

After adjusting my burgundy silk tie, I step out of the dressing room into the bedroom just as Harrison enters from the hallway carrying a tray with freshly pressed coffee and all the trimmings. He places the tray on the desk, without rattling the delicate china, and pours me a cup.

"Your coffee," he whispers so as not to disturb my guests, who are still asleep in my bed.

"Thank you, Harrison," I whisper back.

Tatianna—the one with the long, black hair and even longer legs—is an honest-to-goodness princess. She's a couple dozen relatives away from the throne, but her blood is as blue as it gets. Which, as I see it, is the best of both worlds—all the perks, only a few of the responsibilities.

And if there's one thing royals know how to do, it's party.

As demonstrated by the equally tall and lithe blonde asleep beside her. Marie is her lady-in-waiting. Her assistant. And her *very* close friend, going by last night's festivities.

I'm not an asshole. I've had girlfriends, and when I do, I'm faithful. I've also had lovers, one-night stands, and mutually satisfying arrangements with beautiful female acquaintances. Tatianna falls into the last category; we get together whenever she's in town.

Despite Harrison and my quietest efforts, Tatianna rolls over with a groan. "It's too early. Why are you up?"

I sip my coffee. "I have to go to work."

She sits up, putting her full, bronzed breasts on display. Not a single tan line to be found. Europeans are a lot better with nudity than Americans, *praise the Lord*.

She pouts. "I know your family, and the only work you have to do is paying someone to manage your assets." She waves her hand dismissively. "Why do you do this? Nine to five is not for people like us, Brent."

Coming into more money than one could spend in three lifetimes, at eighteen years old like I did, has its own set of dangers. Go ahead—roll your eyeballs—but I'm serious. See, most people work because they have to, for things like food, a house, clothes, a car. The result of having to work for those necessities is ambition. Drive.

Work gives purpose to your life.

Boredom has killed more in my social class than cancer and heart disease combined. Because when your necessities are covered, what the hell do you do with yourself?

I'll tell you what: you search for ways to stay occupied. To not be bored out of your fucking mind. You can buy your own plane? How about learning to fly one. You were taught to ski at four years old by an Olympian? How about playing football on the ski slopes. Got too much free time on your hands? How about going on safari to pit yourself against a man-eating tiger, or seek out an isolated tribe that still practices cannibalism.

Boredom is a disease, and the cure is a career that gives you a reason to drag your ass out of bed in the morning.

But I have a meeting in forty-five minutes, so I just tell her, "I do it because they need me. The firm would fall apart without me."

She gazes up at me and her smile turns devilish. She runs her hand up Marie's smooth calf, pushing the sheet away as she gets to her shapely thigh and the delectable swell of her ass. "I return home tonight. I was hoping we could enjoy my last day here together. I guess Marie and I will have to play without you."

I give serious consideration to blowing off the meeting. "You're diabolical."

And she looks like such a sweet girl.

"Or maybe your young man can join us?" Her eyes alight on Harrison. "Do you want to play, houseboy?"

I catch Harrison's eye and rapidly reddening face, and tilt my head Tatianna's way with a go-for-it grin.

"Is that the telephone?" he squeaks. "If you'll excuse me." He gives a short bow, and practically runs out the door.

Tatianna removes her hand from the sleeping beauty and giggles. "He's too young to be so serious."

"Yeah, I'm working on that." I shrug. "And you're welcome to spend the day here. Enjoy the hot tub, enjoy . . . Harrison. Playing's probably not in the cards, but he makes a killer omelet." I step closer and gently run my fingers through the endless strands of her dark hair. "When's your next trip back to the States?"

"I don't know. But most likely, it will be after the wedding." She gives me a farewell smile. "The next time you see me, I'll be a duchess."

My eyes skip to the obscene jewel on her hand, given to her by a duke from a small but wealthy constitutional monarchy. It's not an old-fashioned arranged marriage, but it was orchestrated. Have to make sure those genes get mixed with the right pool, because the last real duty of today's nobility is to make sure the wealth stays in the family, by producing offspring to inherit it.

My finger trails along her jaw to her chin. "Do you think he'll make you happy?"

She considers it. "We understand each other. It could be worse."

After a moment, I lean down and kiss her forehead. "Bye, princess."

"Good-bye, Brent."

• • •

Harrison waits for me at the front door, his complexion back to his everyday pallor, with a hearty dose of freckles scattered across his cheeks. They make him look younger than his twenty-two years, which I can relate to. It's why I decided to grow the beard I keep neatly trimmed. And women definitely approve—these bristles have all kinds of creative uses.

I take the offered briefcase and inform him, "I'll walk to the office today. I'm feeling surprisingly energetic this morning."

Harrison nods and steps away from the door. "Very good, sir."

I raise an eyebrow reproachfully.

Harrison's brown eyes pinch closed, then he forces out, "I mean, very good . . . Brent."

The butler school he went to in England must have drilled shit into them *Full Metal Jacket* boot-camp style, because those habits are hard to break. But even though I was raised in a house full of servants and I'm used to the relationship between employer and personal employee, "sir" isn't my style.

I tap his shoulder. "Take good care of our guests. And don't be scared of Tatianna—she only bites if you ask very nicely."

With a wink, I'm out the door.

• • •

I step up to our building at 9:00 a.m. on the dot, to the law firm of Becker, Mason, Santos and Shaw. I've seen my last name etched on buildings before—on libraries and hospital wings—but there's a special thrill in seeing it stenciled on these doors. Because it's *mine*, something I did on my own.

"Good morning, Mr. Mason."

"Hi, Jessica."

Gotta love interns. Hungry, idealistic, so eager to make a good impression, and so willing to please. They take care of the grunt work, the boring research necessary to bring home a win. And when the minion looks like Jessica—cute face, great rack, fiery red hair—that's a special kind of awesome. A few years ago, I would've been all over that.

I don't remember exactly when twenty-four became too young; I just know it is. At thirty-two, the age difference isn't extreme, not like my Uncle Randall and his blushing bride. He's older than dirt, and she couldn't legally drink at her own wedding. I have no idea what they even talk about, though I suspect her oral skills are more important to him than her verbal ones. But to me, the Jessicas of the world are girls. They have the experiences of a girl, see the world through a girl's eyes. And these days, whether it's a casual hookup or more, I want a woman.

She hands me a stack of messages and gestures to the closed door beside her. "They're in the conference room."

"They" are my partners. The best criminal defense attorneys in the city, and my best friends. Starting up your own firm isn't easy, despite the plethora of criminal activity in this area. You have to build up a client list; earn a reputation for being winners and hard-ass negotiators. And that's what we've done. We're the little firm that could—and business is booming.

I walk into the conference room for our biweekly meeting. The hulk of a guy at the head of the table with the dark hair and sharp gray eyes is Jake Becker. Jake's the straight man in our little troupe—the Abbott to my Costello. He can be a scary motherfucker when he chooses to be, which makes it all the more entertaining when the soft spot he tries so hard to pretend he doesn't have gets revealed.

"Does it matter?" he says into the phone, looking bewildered. "I don't know. Whatever you want, I'm good with. Okay, I gotta go. Brent just got here. I love you, too."

That would be Chelsea McQuaid on the other end of that phone, the owner of the finger Jake is completely wrapped around. They're getting married in two months. For a long time, Jake was a hard-core bachelor—a Dark Knight in a lonely Batcave without a Vicki Vale. Then Chelsea and her six orphaned nieces and nephews came along and adopted him, kind of against his will. It was the best thing that ever happened to the grumpy son of a bitch. When he's with Chelsea and the kids, there are moments that he's so happy, it almost hurts to look at him.

Jake sets his phone on the table. "Jesus Christ, why am I doing this again?"

He doesn't sound it, but he's happy. Trust me.

"Because you're totally whipped, and you want your girl to have the wedding of her dreams," Stanton says with his trademark smirk.

"I thought getting a wedding planner would make things easier," Jake says. "I mean, really, who gives a fuck what color the roses are in the table centerpieces."

"That's what weddings are all about," Sofia offers. "Stressing about details you won't notice on the day you actually get married. Just go with it."

They should know; Stanton and Sofia got married nine months ago. And they didn't waste any time in the baby-making department. Sofia's always been a curvaceous Brazilian bombshell, but now she's got an extra curve to her—the seven-month baby bump across her middle.

"How's the little guy treating you today?" I ask.

Her hazel eyes sparkle as she caresses the bump beneath her dark blue maternity dress. "Good. With the amount of kicking he's doing, he's going to be one hell of a soccer player."

Stanton's thick blond hair falls over his forehead as he looks down, covering her hand with his own. "Nah, he's gonna be a football player. I've been telling him the finer points of the game after you pass out at six o'clock."

Sofia and Stanton are both sharks in the courtroom. And despite his best efforts, she hasn't let a little thing like growing a new person inside her slow her down. She pushes herself hard, maybe too hard, judging by the dark circles under her eyes.

I shake my head. "You're both wrong—football and soccer are for pansies. Lacrosse is a real man's game. The Native Americans invented it. I'm gonna buy Becker Mason Santos Shaw his very first stick."

Sofia rolls her eyes. "We're not naming the baby after the firm, Brent."

This is an ongoing debate, and I'm determined to win it.

"You have to! It's a kick-ass name—and he's our first baby."

"No, he's *our* first baby," Sofia argues, gesturing to her husband. "Anyway, let's get started. I have a phone conference at ten."

We dive into upcoming court dates, motions, new clients, and schedule conflicts.

"Justin Longhorn's case has been assigned to a new prosecutor," I tell them a while later. "K. S. Randolph. Any of you heard of him?"

Justin Longhorn is a seventeen-year-old hacker accused of wire fraud, theft, and a whole host of federal crimes, for allegedly tapping into a major bank's computer system and siphoning money from various retirement accounts. But he's not a bad kid, he sort of reminds me of Matthew Broderick in *WarGames*—he didn't realize he was in deep shit until he was already at Defcon 1.

When they shake their heads, I say, "Well, I'm going to reach out to KS and plead it down. It's the kid's first offense and he didn't spend a dime of the money. Shouldn't see the inside of a courtroom with this one."

Then Sofia tells us, "I have a consultation with a new client on Monday."

Stanton's green eyes cloud over. "That the aggravated assault?"

"Yep, the guy who went after his sister's boyfriend with a hammer."

"I don't think so, Soph."

She holds up her hand. "Don't start."

But start he does. "You're seven months pregnant! I don't want you anywhere near violent scumbags like that."

Can't say I blame him there.

Sofia doesn't see it that way. "It's my job to be around them. You're being ridiculous."

In a mix of begging and commanding, he comes back with, "Take the deadbeat dad cases. Take all the tax evasion, money laundering, and federal corruption. Hell, I'll even be generous and throw in a drug addict or two, as long as they—"

Sofia stands. "*Generous*? No. You don't get to—"

She stops suddenly. Her caramel skin goes pale and her hand rises to her lips. But she tries again. "You can't—"

And then she's running for the bathroom. Thankfully it's close, connected to the conference room, and before she can get the door fully closed the sounds of wretched puking fill the room.

We listen in silence, flinching with every scraping heave and landing splash.

Wow. Pregnancy sucks.

Brows furrowed, Jake asks, "I thought the morning sickness was supposed to stop after the first trimester?"

Stanton's mouth twists. "Apparently the baby's unaware of that fact."

A few minutes later—after the toilet flushes and the sink runs—Sofia emerges, looking unsteady and ashen. But her eyes still breathe fire.

"Not a word," she warns Stanton. "Not a single word."

The southern boy lets it go for now. He brushes her hair back tenderly. "Even if the words are *crackers* and *ginger ale*? There's some in the break room. You want me to get them for you?"

She smiles, soft and loving. "Yes, please. Thank you."

With a nod, he leaves the room. Sofia doesn't sit down, holding the back of her chair for support.

"Okay, I'm just gonna say it," Jake tells her. "You look like shit, Sofia."

She snorts. "I can always count on you to be sensitive, Jake."

"Screw sensitivity—you need to take it easier. You're not doing yourself or the baby any favors here."

I stand and move closer to her. "He's right, sweetheart. Get some rest, recharge. What good is having awesome partners if you don't let us pick up the slack once in a while? You'd do it for us."

Before she can argue, I sweep her up into my arms.

Upper-body strength is important, particularly for someone like me, and I use hand grips, even do chin-ups on the bar in my office to keep my muscles in prime condition. There are days when I can't use my prosthesis, and the wheelchair hits the pavement. Times when I have to lift myself in and out of the chair, or my bed—and I'll be damned if my arms can't handle the load.

"I can walk, Brent," she only half argues as Jake opens the door.

"Of course you can. But why should you, when you've got manly men like us to walk for you."

Despite the prime male specimen that I am, I have to say—Sofia's not light. A grunt escapes as I adjust her in my arms and head for her office.

And of course, she notices.

"If you say anything about my weight, I'll rip your beard hairs out."

I chuckle. "I would never comment on a woman's weight—especially a pregnant woman's."

Then, because Sofia is like a sister to me, I add, "But I think my titanium leg just bent under the strain."

She pinches me. My neck, my arms—it's merciless.

"Ow! Jesus! No pinching! Pinching is *not* cool."

By the time I get her to her office and set her on the couch, she's smiling—so, mission accomplished.

Stanton comes in behind us with crackers and a glass of soda . . . and a cell phone. He holds it out to his wife. "There's a call for you."

Suspicion fills her features as she takes the phone. When she looks at the number, she hisses like a wet cat. "You called my *mother*?"

Stanton is unrepentant. "You didn't leave me much choice."

"I will never forgive you for this."

Stanton winks. "Never is a long time, baby. I'm willing to take my chances."

Hesitantly, Sofia brings the phone to her ear. "Mamãe?" And she must be getting an earful. "No, no, I'm fine. He's crazy. But . . ."

With our meeting adjourned, I head for my office to get to work.